Sistah Knit

R. L. CHISOLM

Sistah Knit

Editing by Ange Z

Book cover art by Jamal Tate, of Tate Design Group

ISBN: 9798668944293

Dedication

Thanks to my family and friends who supported me on this journey. I could not have done this work without you all cheering me forward. To my amazing editor Ange Z and book cover artist Jamal Tate, of Tate Design Group. Your amazingly gifted skills and talents together made this work complete. I am grateful to everyone.

Acknowledgments

Yarn Lovers, Knit One, Purl Two

We are a beautiful group of people who love crafting and creating. We knit, crochet, spin, felt, and loom. We dye wool into endless hues of color that can make a rainbow in the sky take notice. We create with love, passion and inspiration. Hand making items for ourselves, family and friends. Cozy wraps, sweaters, socks, gloves, mittens, dolls, and cute knitted animals. We have donated to hospitals, nursing homes, orphanages, shelters, schools, firehouses, and prisons. We make dolls that look like us so our daughters can see themselves. We gather in groups at libraries, restaurants, coffee shops, and all throughout social media to share and admire our beautifully crafted works.

We talk about events like Vogue Knitting East and West, Rhinebeck, Knitting in The City, Yarn Crawls and yarn shops, magazines, and so much more. We're like a musical group of crafters on a beach, and the ocean is a wave of colorful yarn rolling onto shore. Our time together is as priceless as the garments we make. We share our thoughts, dreams, hopes, and wishes. We share and teach what we know to anyone willing to learn. Knitting relaxes and strengthens us in many ways. I am thankful to knitters who have become social media influencers and are shaping and molding the industry into what is today.

Thank you to those who work in and behind the scenes of knitting and crocheting. From books, magazines, and fashion shows to fact checking of articles and patterns. Thank you to all the people who have created places and spaces that welcome everyone into this industry by organizing knitting meetups: The Harlem Knitting Circle, knitting in the City Pitch, Knit and Sip, Knit One, Knit All,

United we Knit, Blessed to Stitch, and Stitch and Pitch ... and the list goes on. A special thank you to Gigi of GGMadeit.com for being her wonderful self and stepping into the world of knitting with bold beautiful expressions of Orange LOVE and heartfelt hugs. Her truth and natural authenticity made this community a better place. Many of us cannot imagine this community without you. We are grateful to you. Thank you to everyone who loves knitting and crocheting. Let's pick up our needles and craft on!

Shante Jackson, age 20. Yonkers, New York

Shante was the oldest of eight children in the Jackson family. Dante, her twin brother, came into the world eleven minutes after she did. There was Denise, 18, Michael 17, Tracy 16, Chris 15, Dewayne 14, and Cherise 13, the baby. Their mother Debra, only forty-two years old, stood five feet, five inches, with a small-framed body of a hundred and twenty pounds. The nine of them all lived in a small three-bedroom apartment in the Gordon housing projects on the south side of Yonkers, New York. Here, patchy areas of grass were trashed with beer and wine bottles, cigarette butts, dirty diapers, spoiled food, and other unsightly discards. Cats, mice, and rats crawled around in search of food. Broken elevators and mailboxes forced tenants to stand in the lobbies and wait for the mailman to deliver their welfare checks and food stamps, in fear that the neighborhood thugs would steal their only means of survival. Kids ran wild up and down the halls and stairwells. Drug dealers pushed crack and weed. This was not the life Shante wanted for her baby boy, Phillip.

If Shante were the star of a reality show, it would be titled "Your Worst Nightmare Come True," and she truly believed she was living it. Phillip's father Phil-Quan was one of the drug dealers around the Gordon projects, and although Shante loved him, she knew they could never have a meaningful life together given his chosen lifestyle.

Shante hit the snooze button on her alarm clock for the fourth time and pulled her floral print comforter over her head. She was comfortable tucked tightly between the warmth of the blankets and her soft worn out mattress. The cold December air slipped through the nooks and crannies of her small room. Her two-year-old slept soundly at her side holding his favorite cuddly teddy bear that he called Sam.

1

"Get up Shante! It's 7 AM!" shouted a voice from the hall. "Shante!"

Shante clung tighter to her pillow as she tried to drown out her mother's agonizing voice. "SHANTE! GIT UP GURL! YOU SAID YOU HAVE CLASSES TODAY!"

Frustrated, Shante quickly got out of bed. She rubbed her arms together to knock off the chill. Her long braids brought her some warmth as they rested on her shoulders.

She headed toward the bathroom. Cherise, her youngest sister, ran down the hall past Shante and slammed the bathroom door shut, only to open it again and stick her tongue out, teasingly.

"Shante, did you hear me, girl? I said get up!" Debra shouted.

"Yes, Mama, I hear you!" Shante replied.

"Stop yelling at me, Shante!" Debra's voice grew louder.

"Mama, will *you* please stop shouting?" Shante banged on the bathroom door. "Cherise get out of the bathroom now!" Cherise darted out of the bathroom and poked her tongue out at Shante. Shante raised her hand as if to hit her little sister. "Cherise, girl, I'm going to beat your behind!"

"Mama! Shante said she going to beat my behind!" Shante closed the bathroom door to her mother's screaming voice,

"Shante isn't going to beat anybody's behind in this house!"

As she splashed warm water on her face, Shante thought, "Why did God put me in this crazy family?" Shante's mother had lived off welfare for years, and it seemed as though she wanted nothing in life besides that bi-weekly check and an EBT card. Shante wanted to be nothing like her mother. She thought about how her whole big family was living in a small three-bedroom apartment in the projects with a bunch of other neighborhood kids. Shante finished brushing her teeth and went back to her room. Phillip had woken up and started to cry after noticing his mother was no longer next to him.

"Don't cry little man. Mommy is right here," Shante picked him up and gave him a good morning kiss on the nose.

Cherise entered the room with a bowl of warm oatmeal for Phillip; she adored her little nephew. She took him from Shante's arms, "Don't cry Philly, I have some oatmeal for you."

She began to feed him. Shante thanked Cherise for getting Phillip's breakfast; she was relieved she was able to get just a few more moments of quiet time.

"You're welcome, Shante. Sorry I stuck my tongue out at you."

Shante smiled, "Girl, I don't pay you no mind."

Shante got dressed while Cherise fed Phillip. She thought about how her day was to start with school. Cherise interrupted the silence. "Shante ... when you going to marry Philly's daddy?"

Shante sighed, "It's too early for that kind of talk Cherise."

"When I asked you last night you said it was too late for that kind of talk. When should I ask you, Shante?"

"When *you* get married," replied Shante.

Cherise frowned and shook her head in disagreement. "What kind of answer is that Shante? *I* ain't gonna marry nobody."

"Well, that's what you say now because you're still very young."

"Is you old Shante?" Cherise asked. Shante corrected her sister,

"Are you, not is you."

"How old are you Shante?"

"None of your beeswax business, girl."

Cherise laughed, then asked again, "So when you gonna marry Philly's daddy?"

"I don't know, Cherise, okay?"

"Why don't you know?" Cherise asked as she continued to feed Phillip.

"Because I just don't know, that's why. Please stop asking me questions. I have to get Phillip washed up and dressed." She paused. "Thanks for feeding him ... besides, don't you have to get ready for school?"

"Yeah, we have a spelling test today." Cherise sighed. She disliked spelling tests.

"Good, I hope you get all the words correct."

"I'll try; bye Shante. See you later Philly," she waved goodbye.

Shante finished dressing Phillip, grabbed her backpack, and headed out the door.

She quickly returned after she realized she had forgotten her knitting bag while trying to balance Phillip on her hip.

As she left the house for the second time, she glanced at her mother, who was fast asleep on the sofa. Her twin brother Dante was asleep on the floor. She heard the sounds of her other siblings meddling around in the other rooms as she locked the apartment door behind her. She was surprised when the elevator arrived promptly. She had anticipated the usual ten or fifteen-minute wait like most mornings. She carefully avoided a small puddle of urine in the middle of the elevator car as she entered. Shante looked at the Obama campaign flyer posted on the elevator wall and glanced down at her baby boy. "Mommy would love to see a black man as president. Would you like to see Obama become President, Phillip?" He looked at her and smiled. "We are going to vote for Barack Obama. What do think about that little man?" She kissed Phillip on his forehead. After she exited the elevator on the twelfth floor, Shante rang the doorbell for apartment 12A.

Mrs. Brown, a small elderly lady, opened the door. A bright warm smile grew on her face as she quickly reached for Phillip. Mrs. Brown was born and raised on a farm in Montgomery, Alabama, and was one of twelve children. She had witnessed many protests and marches during the civil rights era, and she and her family had even attended the Dexter Avenue Baptist Church when Dr. Martin Luther King Jr. was a pastor. For some reason, she had taken a special interest in Shante and always tried to help her when she could.

"Thank you, Mrs. Brown." Shante kissed Phillip. "Love you, little man, see you later." Shante figured she wouldn't get the same luck with the elevator as she had before, so she ran down the remaining twelve flights of steps and made it to the bus stop just in time as the next-to-last passenger entered in front of her.

Within twenty minutes, Shante was sat inside the well-heated waiting room of the Yonkers Rail Station as she waited for her train into Manhattan. Out of a canvas bag, she pulled a baby blanket she had begun to knit weeks earlier; she enjoyed the feather and fan pattern needle work. She rubbed the extra soft Red Heart brand yarn between her hands.

There was a volunteer knitting teacher at the Yonkers Library named Mrs. Smith, who had become very fond of Shante. She was a retired English professor who taught knitting on the weekends, and she also taught Shante how to pronounce words correctly. Shante would teach Phillip everything she had learned. Mrs. Smith was a beautiful woman with flawless, mocha colored skin. She exercised and ate a healthy diet. She wore clothing that flattered her curvy size eight figure. Shante often wished that Mrs. Smith was her mother. "Knitting is a lost art," Mrs. Smith would often say. "It takes my mind to a place of peace and relaxation." Shante would smile in agreement. Shante remembered an argument she had with her mother after returning home from a recent knitting class.

"Who the hell do you think you are Shante? Trying to correct the way I talk? I know how to speak. You so damn uppity, knitting and shit, talking like you a fancy rich woman. I'm your mama and I will talk to you and anybody else the way *I want*. Nobody told me they don't understand what the hell I'm saying."

"Mama ... ," Shante had replied cautiously, "that's because your friends speak just as badly as you do."

"Listen Shante, you betta show me some damn respect! You think you're betta than us, girl? Trying to be something you not!"

"Well, you're right about one thing Mama ... I *am* trying to become something that I'm not, because I don't ever want to become like you."

Justine Whitaker, age 35. Tarrytown, New York

JW Records would be the name of Justine's new record label. She had just purchased and registered the domain name with pride. She was only days away from her dream becoming a reality. Her parents, Mr. and Mrs. Whitaker, wished their daughter would put the thought of a career in music completely out of her mind and pursue a more stable career path, as they had done.

Mrs. Whitaker was a history professor at Spelman College for more than thirty years, and Mr. Whitaker was a business and legal professor at Morehouse. They'd met when Justine's mother was a freshman and her father was in his sophomore year. He had asked her to dance at a Spelman Homecoming party. Soon, they began dating, and their relationship flourished throughout their college years and long after.

"Justine, what about a career in finance?" her mother asked as she handed Justine a copy of *Fortune* magazine. They sat at the dinner table eating a delicious meal of fried chicken, collard greens, and potato salad.

"Your brother is doing well at the investment firm in Atlanta." She looked at her husband. "William, what is the name of the firm Stanley works at?" She put another scoop of potato salad on his plate.

"Martha, I told you yesterday," he said without taking his eyes off his plate, "Omni Core Investments." Mr. Whitaker was eager to skip the career talk and get straight to dinner.

"Mom, I don't *want* to go into finance. It's boring. I like music," Justine reached for the bowl of potato salad from her mother. She put two scoops on her plate. "Music is my life. You and Daddy know that. I don't want to be like Stanley, practicing law and business at a firm that will never pay him what he's worth, no matter how hard he works."

"Justine, your father and I worked hard all our lives to give you and Stanley the best of everything. A beautiful home in a great neighborhood ... private schooling. We want our children to do well in life."

"I realize how hard you and Daddy have worked ... and I'm doing okay right now. I plan to do extremely well by owning and running my record company. Stay Paid records is a place for me to learn and grow. I've had two promotions in just three years!" Her father cleared his throat while dusting the chicken crumbs from around his mouth. "Justine, you have an MBA from Harvard. You can have *any* stable career."

"Daddy, I want a career in the music industry. I will own my record label. I remember you and Mom always had music playing in the house. Stanley and I loved singing those old Motown songs. I knew back then I wanted a career in music."

Justine's knitting bag was hanging on the back of the dining room chair. She pulled out a sweater and started to knit and purl at the sleeve while she talked. Her mother frowned. "Justine please, sweetheart, no knitting at the dinner table. Let's enjoy our meal."

"Sorry, Mom." She stuffed the sweater back into her bag and placed it on the floor beside her chair and continued eating. After a moment of silence, she continued, "I want to do what I truly love, and that's music." Her parents listened with frustration. "There is a lot of talent in the world!" Justine spoke with excitement in her eyes.

"When do you plan to begin a married life with Ronald?" Her mother asked. Her father grunted in agreement.

"Oh, Mom ... Ronald and I will get married soon." Justine twirled her locks around her fingers. She often did this when she felt nervous.

"What do you call soon?" her father asked. "You've been engaged for three or more years now?"

"Daddy please!"

"Justine, your father is right. You never talk about wedding plans."

"Mom, Dad ... Ronald is very understanding of me wanting to put my career first."

"His understanding may not last forever," said her father as he put another piece of chicken on his plate.

"Daddy, you and Mom don't understand younger people these days." Justine rolled her eyes.

Her father's voice was hard and stern. "Justine. You are thirty-five years old. You have to think about building a life with Ronald before some other woman comes along and does it with him instead. You will end up with *just* a record company and no family."

"What about children, Justine?" Mrs. Whitaker admired Justine's strong will and believed her daughter was smart enough to manage a company, but she worried for her daughter's chances of marriage and lasting love. Justine smiled.

"I'll get married, Daddy, and I'll make you and Mom grandparents."

Her mother spoke with softness in her voice. "We hope you do Justine. We really hope you do."

Michele Nelson, age 42. Harlem, New York

Michele was warm and comfortable, snuggled into her thick terrycloth robe and soft fuzzy wool socks. She held her "I Heart NY" coffee mug in between the palms of her hands as she sipped peppermint tea. Pushing her thick sandy brown hair out of her face and tucking it behind her left ear, she looked out her window at the people going about their morning, braving the cold gusty winds of winter. She was glad she was indoors.

The shiny faces of some of the black kids reminded Michele of when her mother used to rub her and her siblings' faces with Vaseline every day before they left for school. She would say, "This will protect your beautiful skin from the cold." Kids called Michele "greasy girl." She remembered going to the school bathroom to wipe it off so she could avoid a day filled with cruel comments.

Michele noticed a handwritten note taped to the TV remote. She smiled as she read it:

"Good Morning Sweetheart, I will pick up Ashley from tennis practice, be home by 6:00 PM. Love you very much."

Michele and her husband Charles would soon be celebrating eighteen years of marriage. He was a good man and her soulmate. Michele grinned every time she thought about how she had married her college sweetheart. In her eyes, he was the best-looking guy on campus. She felt butterflies and melted like ice cream on a hot summer day whenever she saw him. Ashley, their only child, now twelve years old, was their pride and joy.

She pressed the buttons on the remote, flipping through the TV channels until she reached GMN, Good Morning News. The morning news story was about Barack Obama possibly becoming the first black president in American history.

The doorbell rang twice. "Just a minute!" Michele tightened the belt around her bathrobe before opening the door.

"Good Morning," a FedEx delivery man handed her a large blue and white box. "Sign here, please." Michele scribbled her name quickly. "Thank you, Ma'am, and have a good day." He was admiring her beauty, but Michele was oblivious to his gaze.

Michele opened the box to find a dozen skeins of multi-colored yarns made from silk, cotton, cashmere, and wool. It was from her friends Terri and Sherri. She read out loud the card they'd written.

> *A new yarn and knitting shop opening in Harlem. The First Ever, in the history of Harlem. Please join us at our Grand Opening celebration on Saturday, November 1st at 12 noon.*
>
> *Love, Terri and Sherri*

Michele smiled, delighted at the invitation, and thought, "Harlem's first yarn shop. I wouldn't miss this for anything." She put the skeins in a white wicker basket next to her grandmother's old rocking chair. She rocked back and forth, remembering her grandmother. Nana Bea is what the family called her. Nana Bea would sit in her rocking chair knitting socks, sweaters, baby blankets, or booties and mittens for her children and her grandchildren. Michele learned to knit at eight years old; when she was thirteen, she could knit socks, sweaters, and hats almost as well as her grandmother.

Nana Bea had left the Harlem brownstone home to Michele twenty years ago. "One day, granddaughter, when you are grown up, and Nana Bea is long gone to Heaven to meet the Lord, and you have a family of your own, this will be your house."

As Michele rocked back in her chair she thought, "Nana Bea was right." Michele and her family enjoyed living in the six-bedroom, four-bathroom brownstone on Strivers Row. Michele and Charles would one day pass the property on to their daughter. Michele took her red afghan off the arm of the rocking chair and settled it around her shoulders, snuggling it close to her face. It was the last thing Nana Bea had knitted before she died. "I miss you so much, Nana Bea. You were everything to me."

Rhonda James, age 50. Bronx, New York.

"What the hell?" Rhonda could feel her blood pressure rise as she read the test results. Positive. "Oh my gosh, a baby!" She looked at herself in the mirror in disbelief. "Oh, Lord! What am I going to do?" She thought of her two children in college. What would they think if they knew their mother was pregnant? They had no idea she was dating. She was deeply in love with her boyfriend Joe. It did not bother her that he was ten years younger. At his late age in life, Joe had dreams of becoming a music producer. He liked R&B and hip-hop music and going to the hottest clubs around the city.

Rhonda had one day reached for one of the promotional flyers Joe was handing out while walking through Times Square. She thought he was good looking, and minutes later, after a brief conversation and exchange of phone numbers, she was planning to attend a record release party he was promoting at the Gold Floor Night Club. She wanted a chance to see him again; for Rhonda, it was love at first sight.

She'd divorced her children's father, George, after years of physical and mental abuse. He was an alcoholic for the majority of their twelve-year marriage. He could never hold down a job. Rhonda worked and paid all of the bills and took care of the kids. George drank himself to death five years ago. Rhonda had a two hundred-thousand-dollar life insurance policy on him. As her mother often told her, "George will be worth more dead than alive."

She had tried online dating and blind dates but nothing good had come of it. Rhonda saw something different in Joe. He was charming and always quiet and reserved. She never went for younger men, and was surprised by her forward flirtatious actions. She had thought, "Hey, what is it going to hurt? I'm just having a little fun." But now she felt like the fun was over.

"Pregnant at fifty?" She looked at herself in the mirror. Abortion was not something she favored. Rhonda needed to get her thoughts together and figure out what she was going to do.

She made herself a cup of ginger tea as she wiped tears from her eyes. She felt alone and confused. She sat at the kitchen table slowly sipping the tea as she stared at a pile of beige yarn that sat on the kitchen table. It had her green metal knitting needles sticking through it. She was going to start knitting scarves for her daughter Twinkle and her son Tyree. She reached for the yarn and squeezed it tightly between both hands. "Oh Lord, what am I going to do?"

Monday October 27th, 2008

8:01 A.M.

Shante walked quickly as she entered the Metro North train, glad to be out of the freezing cold air. She spotted an empty seat near the window. "Mind if I sit here?" she asked at the young woman sitting in the aisle seat. The woman parted her thin bob-style dreadlocks from over her smiling face.

"No, I don't mind at all." Shante returned a smile and sat down. She pulled out her knitting project from her backpack and began knitting.

"What are you making?" the woman asked.

"It's a sweater for my son Phillip," Shante replied.

"That's a beautiful blue yarn. My name is Justine, by the way," the woman extended her right hand out to Shante.

"Nice to meet you, I'm Shante."

As they shook hands, Justine continued, "I'm a knitter also; I'm making a scarf for my mother. Her birthday is coming up in a few months." She pulled her project out of a large black leather bag.

"Nice cable pattern. Is your mother a knitter?" Shante asked as she touched the scarf gently.

"No, but my grandma Ella was the knitter of the family. She was a knitter of perfection." Justine paused as she reminisced about her grandmother. "Who taught you to knit, Shante?"

"Mrs. Smith. She teaches knitting classes every other Saturday at the Yonkers Library."

"How long have you been taking classes?"

"A year ... and I learn something new all the time."

"Tell me about it," chuckled Justine.

"Knitting relaxes me. Mrs. Smith warned me that knitting could become addictive."

"I think Mrs. Smith is right, because I knit every day and it sure does relax me." The women smiled in agreement.

The smell of French vanilla coffee filled the air as a gray-haired man sitting across the aisle working on his laptop took a sip from his cup. Justine sniffed the air.

"That coffee smells good. I wish these trains had car attendants like airlines do. Like a tall, dark, handsome man, asking 'what can I get you this morning, ladies? Tea, orange juice, or a French vanilla latte?'"

They laughed and the man glanced at them; he seemed annoyed at their mildly loud chatter.

Their laughter was interrupted by the conductor's announcement, "125th Street, watch your step exiting and entering the train." Justine looked through the scratched glass window and then asked Shante, "Did you know a new yarn shop is opening in Harlem soon, on Saturday, November 1st?"

Shante, suddenly excited, replied, "No, I didn't know. A yarn shop in Harlem?"

"A co-worker gave me a flyer last week." Justine searched through her bag. "The yarn shop will be the first ever in the history of Harlem."

Shante continued her knitting; "I've never been to a yarn shop before. Mrs. Smith always brings bundles of different yarns to class. She just lets us take whatever we want. She always manages to give me one or two extras."

"She sounds like a very nice lady," Justine said, still looking for the flyer.

"Mrs. Smith is the best."

"Grand Central Station, last stop!" The conductor announced, "We are arriving at Grand Central Station. Have a good day and watch your step exiting the train. Remember, if you see something, say something. Grand Central Station. Last stop." Passengers gathered their belongings and hurriedly walked toward the doors to exit the train.

"Will you be on this train tomorrow?" Justine asked.

"Yes, I will."

"Great. I'll bring the flyer about that yarn shop."

"Okay. Thanks, Justine. It was nice meeting you."

"Yes, nice meeting you as well Shante. See you tomorrow."

Terri and Sherri Constable, Age 28. Harlem, New York

Michele had the day off. The cold air and falling snowflakes did not stop her from going out for an afternoon walk. She wrapped a bulky red knit scarf around her neck and pulled a matching hat tightly over her ears. She had knit both herself.

The snowflakes tickled her nose as she turned the corner off Saint Nichols Avenue and onto 125th street toward Fifth Avenue. A strong gust of wind pushed her backward. Michele tightened her body and pushed forward. Managing to keep her balance, she continued on, only stopping at a peanut vendor to purchase a bag of roasted walnuts.

Lots of other vendors lined the streets of 125th Street selling all types of merchandise plastered with Barack Obama's name. Posters, t-shirts, hats, caps, buttons, canvas bags, mugs, anything. Michele bought an Obama button and pinned it on her scarf. Other vendors tried to get her attention, shouting things like, "Organic African butter soaps! Exotic skin oils. Gospel tapes! Movies! Books! Incense! Jewelry! Perfume! We got it!" An old gray-haired man stopped her. "How about some Barack Obama bath soap, my beautiful sister?" He was holding a bar of soap in each hand, soap with Obama's picture on it. Michele laughed.

"No thank you, my brother, not today." She continued on and walked past the open door of Manna's Soul Food Place. The fresh aroma of collard greens and candied yams smelled so good to her. Tempted to go in for some of her Southern favorites, she thought, "Maybe one day black people will own Manna's. Koreans are selling us bags of fake hair and wigs, fruits and veggies – and now they are selling us our own soul food. Damn!"

She crossed the corner of Fifth Avenue and walked up to the windows of Sistah Knit. Her friends Terri and Sherri were too busy putting skeins of yarn neatly on the wooden shelves to notice her. Michele tapped on the window to get their attention. Sherri rushed quickly to the front door and unlocked it.

"Hey girl, come on in!" Sherri and Michele embraced with a warm and friendly hug.

"How are you, Michele?"

"I'm doing well, Sherri." Terri came over and gave Michele a hug.

"Nice to see you, Michele. How about some tea to knock off that winter chill?"

"Yes, please. I need something to warm me up and wash down these roasted walnuts." Sherri hung Michele's hat and coat on the hooks near the door.

"Make yourself at home, Michele," said Terri. "I'll be right back with the tea." Michele looked around at the beauty of the yarn shop and said, "This place is beautiful."

"You like?" Sherri asked, smiling.

"Yes, looks like you ladies are fully ready for the opening next week. This place is lovely."

"Terri and I are very pleased."

"Yes, we are very pleased," said Terri as she returned with a tray of tea. She was smiling from ear to ear. "Michele, you know how long Sherri and I have wanted to do this." She placed the tray on an oak table and began to pour into the small tea cups.

"Your grandmother would be proud," said Michele.

"I know she would," said Sherri. "This is a dream come true."

"Chamomile tea, your favorite, right?" Terri asked.

"Yes, it is," Michele replied. Michele could not stop looking around, noticing every detail of the shop. "I can't believe it. This place is just breathtaking." Colorful skeins of yarn arranged beautifully in baskets and wooden bowls sat on the shelves and tables. There was a buttery soft leather sofa in a dark plum color, and on the walls hung oil paintings of African history and original photos of Malcolm X, Dr. Martin Luther King Jr., Rosa Parks, Marcus Garvey, Medgar Evers and other legends, including black musicians, artists, actors, and sports heroes. There were African figurines and wooden drum sets. The wood floors shone like sparkling mirrors. African jewelry made of ivory beads hung from elephant tusks on the walls. Even a private wine cellar had been built behind one of the walls. Michele walked around in amazement.

"No way!" she exclaimed. "A full-sized kitchen, two baths, and a room with two queen beds? Is this your new home?" Terri and Sherri laughed. "Everything is beautiful, tastefully decorated," Michele continued, "but I wouldn't expect anything less coming from the two of you. I feel like I'm in the warmest and safest place in the world right now."

"We put our hearts into every detail," said Sherri, looking at her sister.

"Well, I can feel it," said Michele. "This is definitely not your average yarn shop." Michele looked across the room at the wall, "Oh my God! Is that the blanket your grandmother knitted for you girls twenty-five years ago?"

Terri and Sherri answered simultaneously, "Yes, it is." The twins were giggling as they looked at each other. Sherri walked over to the blanket. "We thought it would look great on this wall."

"What a great idea to have it framed," said Michele.

Michele got a closer look. She ran her fingers on the oak wood frame. "The community needs this. I am so happy for you ladies. I know the opening will be great."

"We are proud of Sistah Knit," said Terri. Sherri looked on smiling in agreement as she sipped her tea.

"So, Michele, what's going on with you these days?" Sherri asked, "Everything all right in the world of news media and reporting?"

"Yes, all is good," Michele sighed, "I'm glad I don't have fly out of the country to cover tragic stories anymore."

"I know ... flying around to unknown, dangerous territory was never pleasant," said Sherri.

"I don't like leaving Charles and Ashly for extended periods of time."

Terri jumped in, "Michele, I love when you report on the Obama Campaign. Heck girl, I love when any reporter has news on Barack Obama." They all laughed.

"I do enjoy my career. I might have a one-on-one interview coming up with him!"

"What! Are you serious?" asked Sherri.

"Yes. I am."

Terri giggled, "Hey, Michelle Obama, I think Michele Nelson from Harlem wants your man!"

"Now you two know I love Charles, so don't start any mess," laughed Michele.

"Yes, we know you love your husband ... but every sister I know loves Obama," replied Terri.

"You see the walk on that brother? Obama and Denzel both have that *sexy walk*," said Sherri.

"Now, you guys stop it! It's just an interview, and I don't even know if I got the assignment yet."

"Okay," sighed Terri, "we understand, but when you get that interview, and you will get it, you better call us right away. We have some Marilyn Monroe-looking dresses and, girl, you know we will sing happy birthday to Barack Obama!" And together the twins started singing, "Happy birthday to you. Happy birthday Mr. President, happy birthday to you."

"You guys are too crazy," said Michele. Sherri was laughing.

"Yeah, we crazy for Barack Obama. We got Bill Clinton up the street in the Harlem State Office Building on 125th Street, and that's cool. Lord have mercy, if Obama came to Harlem and set up an office, the party will be on and popping all night long!" Sherri was swaying her hips from side to side and snapping her fingers. Terri and Sherri started dancing and chanting, "Obama, Obama, Obama!"

"Stop! I can't take it anymore," laughed Michele. "You two are just too much!" She was laughing and holding her stomach. The twins sat down, and after a while the laughter dwindled down to calm, smiling faces. Michele looked at her two friends. "It's always good to see you guys. You always keep me in stitches. But I have to get going now. Charles and Ashley will be home soon." She got up and walked toward the coat rack.

"Thanks for stopping by," said Terri.

"Yes, this was fun," said Michele. "Thank you so much for that beautiful basket of yarn you sent. I'll make something for Ashley." Sherri and Terri hugged her.

"Our pleasure! We love you, Michele. See you next Saturday?" Terri asked.

"Yes, and Ashley is coming with me."

"Wonderful! It's been a while since we've seen her," Sherri smiled. "Ashley is growing up so fast. She's a great girl and smart just like her mama!"

"We know that's right," said Terri. They hugged, exchanged kisses, and waved goodbye as Michele stepped out the door. She blew them a goodbye kiss through the big glass window.

"I am really looking forward to the opening," said Sherri to her sister as she re-arranged skeins of yarns and other knitting items around the shop.

"Yeah me too," said Terri. She was putting the tea cups back on the tray. "Mom said she and Dad will be in New York the night before the opening."

"Is Mom sure that Daddy will come?" asked Sherri. "You know how much of a workaholic he is."

"Mom said Dad is ready and plans to be here for our opening. Daddy has put his top man in charge to watch over things at the office while he is away."

Sherri was skeptical. "Terri, you know Dad is always finding a reason why he can't leave his precious office work to just anyone. He believes that no one can run the business as well as he can."

"I know Sherri, but Mom said Dad would be here on Saturday. He won't let us down."

"How are you so sure?" asked Sherri.

"I can't explain it, Sis ... it's just a feeling I have that he won't let us down this time."

"Well, I wouldn't bet my last dollar on Dad's word," replied Sherri.

"Well, Mom always said there comes a time in life when some things simply *have* to change."

Michele rode comfortably in the taxi, relaxing in the back seat as she thought over the pleasant visit she'd had earlier with her friends. Her Nana Bea would have loved to have seen the Sistah Knit yarn shop, God rest her soul.

"Seven dollars, fifty cents please," the driver turned to face the back seat. Michele snapped out of her deep thoughts of her grandmother. She reached into her purse and handed the driver a ten-dollar bill.

"Keep the change." She climbed out of the taxi. She hurried to her door so she could escape the cold. She preferred warm weather, never really caring how hot the temperature climbed during the summer. She often talked with Charles about retiring to a tropical island, but he actually enjoyed the winter season. He would sit for hours in freezing temperatures at football games. Michele did enjoy those things back when she and Charles were dating back in college.

As she walked inside the house, her cell phone rang. Pulling off her Prada red leather gloves, she reached deep into her purse searching for the phone. The caller ID displayed the number from her workplace at GMN.

"Hello, this is Michele."

"Hello, Michele. It's Christine Blue."

It was Michele's new assignment producer. Michele could hear her own heart pounding through her chest. She tossed her coat on the sofa and sat down in her grandmother's rocking chair. She knew this call would let her know if she would be assigned to interview Barack Obama. She tried to hide her excitement.

"Hello Christine, how are you?"

"I am well, Michele. Thank you for asking," Christine continued, "Michele, the assignments and questions for the Obama interviews have been carefully reviewed by the station managers and directors. We have decided to assign other reporters to cover the local areas regarding the Obama campaign and his supporters." Michele's heart sank. "There will be several interviews scheduled for the duration of the elections campaigns."

"Thank you for calling me, Christine. I do appreciate your filling me in." Michele was ready to end the call. "Is there anything else?"

"Michele," Christine interrupted, "Although we have assigned other reporters to cover the campaign trail, we've decided to have *you* do all the lead stories and one-on-one interviews with Senator Barack Obama."

Michele leaped from the rocking chair with joy. "Really?"

"Yes," replied Christine, "Michele, you are the best reporter to take charge of the interviews, and we are proud to have you take on this assignment, as well as all the upcoming elections."

"Thank you, Christine!" Michele's heart was racing. "I am very excited. Thank you *very* much."

"You're welcome, Michele. There is a meeting tomorrow morning at ten, and we will discuss the details then."

"I will be there. Thank you, Christine."

"It's my pleasure. See you tomorrow."

Wednesday October 29th, 2008

3:30 P.M.

Shante had just passed her PowerPoint presentation with an A-plus.

"Great job!" said her professor, Mrs. Flowers.

"Thank you, Mrs. Flowers, I worked very hard."

"Don't thank me, Shante. You did study and put in extra work."

"I know," said Shante. "You're a great teacher."

"Thanks, Shante, and you are an excellent student. One of the best students I've had in a long time. Make sure you stop by the employment center by the end of this marking period. I heard they have some great entry-level positions."

"Thanks, Mrs. Flowers. I will." Shante packed her books and left the classroom. She felt her cell phone vibrate and reached for it in her jacket pocket. She read a text message from her mother: "Bring me a pack of Newports on your way home." Shante rolled her eyes and under her breath said, "Buy your own damn cigarettes." She pressed the down button for the elevator. She heard a voice from behind her,

"Hey, Shante! A-plus on that PowerPoint project! You go girl." Shante turned to see Yolanda, an overweight, loud-mouthed, bubblegum chewing classmate who wanted everyone else to do her classwork for her. She was chewing on a Hershey's bar as she stood waiting for the elevator. Shante politely smiled, saying nothing. "So," Yolanda continued, "How you get an A-plus? I can't get that PowerPoint thing to save my life."

26

"I just studied and practiced, that's all," replied Shante, stepping into the elevator and pressing the lobby button. Yolanda followed behind her.

"Girl, I'm studying too, but I ain't got no A-plus. I got a D for dumb!"

Shante sighed, "Yolanda, you have to get a tutor to help you." Both girls stepped out of the elevator.

"Yeah, Shante. I'm going to do that," Yolanda said with a mouth full of chocolate.

"Good luck!" said Shante as she walked away from her classmate as quickly as possible. Yolanda called after her.

"Maybe you could tutor me sometime, Shante? What you think about that?" She pushed the last piece of chocolate into her mouth and looked anxiously at Shante, who was still walking away. Shante pretended to not hear Yolanda and hurried out of the building. She glanced over her shoulder and was relieved to see that Yolanda stayed behind. She was unwrapping a second candy bar.

5:30 P.M.

Shante could hear the echoing of Phil-Quan's laughter as she entered the lobby of her apartment complex. He and the other drug dealers were congregated inside the cement hallways of the project building. She frowned when she saw them. Phil-Quan approached her smiling. Shante could see he had been smoking weed. His eyes were red, and he was sucking on a cherry lollipop like it was his last meal.

"Hey Baby!" He leaned forward to kiss her on the lips. She turned her head and leaned back.

"Hi Phil-Quan," she said, unpleasantly.

Phil-Quan raised his voice, "Girl, what is up with you and the attitude? Why are you acting like you don't know me?" Shante didn't make eye contact with him at all. She just punched the elevator button.

"Sometimes I wish I didn't know you." She finally turned to look him in the eye. His home boys were watching them closely. "Look at you, high as a damn kite flying on a windy day ... and your breath stinks worse than a dead skunk." His friends started laughing. She pressed for the elevator again, impatient that it was taking so long.

"Aww damn, Shante. Why you always have to be like that? You know I love you, girl."

He leaned in again trying for a kiss. She pushed him back.

"Get away from me, Phil-Quan." Frustrated, she pressed several times for the elevator door to open. "Did you go see your son today, Phil-Quan? Did you see him?" He didn't answer; he was still trying to get a kiss. "Do you even know where your son is Phil-Quan?"

"Of course I know where he is. Up at that old lady's house. What's her name again?"

His crowd of boys were still laughing at him. The elevator door finally opened. Shante stepped inside and Phil-Quan followed her inside. She quickly pressed the button for the twelfth floor. "I'll come and see him now," Phil-Quan said, "I know you're going to pick him up."

"Phillip needs a good father," Shante replied sternly. "You haven't seen your son all week."

"Yes, I have seen him this week!" Phil-Quan pulled out a picture of Phillip from the back pocket of his sagging blue jeans. "See here, my son Phillip."

"Oh, you got jokes Phil-Quan?" Shante stepped off the elevator. He followed closely behind her, smiling. She continued, "If you tried to pull your life together, you could be a good father."

"I am getting myself together, Shante. Give me a chance."

"How are you getting your life together? By selling drugs?" She knocked on the door. "It's me, Mrs. Brown, Shante."

"Girl my life is fine," Phil-Quan scoffed. "I just gave you twenty dollars last week for Phillip."

Shante raised her voice, "Are you serious Phil-Quan? What the hell is twenty dollars?"

"It's money. That's what it is. You know I love my boy!"

"Well if you love him, get your sorry-ass life together." Mrs. Brown opened the door,

"Hello, Shante. Come on in."

"Hello Mrs. Brown," said Phil-Quan. He pushed his way through the door behind Shante. Mrs. Brown looked him over through her cat-shaped eyeglasses.

"Oh," she frowned, "it's you, Phil-Quan." She was unimpressed. "Young man, take off your hat when entering my house."

"Yes Ma'am." Phil-Quan quickly removed his backward-facing baseball cap and made a silly face at Mrs. Brown when she turned her back to pick up Phillip from the playpen. Using her elbow, Shante nudged Phil-Quan, indicating for him to stop being disrespectful.

"Here's your baby boy," said Mrs. Brown. Phil-Quan reached his arms out to take his son, and Mrs. Brown handed the child directly to Shante. Shante held him tight, kissing him on his forehead.

"How is my baby doing today? Mommy missed you," she smiled.

"Hey, little man. How daddy's boy?" Phil-Quan rubbed his son's head. Mrs. Brown sucked her teeth in disgust of Phil-Quan. He

29

gave Mrs. Brown a dirty look and made sure she saw it. Shante, stilling cuddling Phillip, didn't notice the tension growing between the two of them.

"He was a good boy today, just like he is every day. You got a fine boy, Shante."

"That's *my* little man. Right Phillip?" Phil-Quan interjected. Mrs. Brown rolled her eyes and shook her head.

"Thank you, Mrs. Brown," Shante said. "We'll see you in the morning."

"Okay sweetheart, see you tomorrow." Shante picked up her baby bag, but Mrs. Brown took it out of her hands and handed it to Phil-Quan for him to carry. He shot another look at her. Mrs. Brown, ignoring him, kissed little Phillip on the cheek.

"See you tomorrow, precious baby. I hope you grow up to be like Barack Obama and run for president of the United States one day. Now that's a *positive* black man doing great things for the people." She stared at Phil-Quan. Shante smiled at her baby boy. Mrs. Brown opened the door and Shante exited as Phil-Quan followed behind, struggling with the overstuffed baby bag and a handful of Phillip's toys. They waited for the elevator. Shante looked at her son's father. She broke the silence.

"Phil-Quan ... I cannot be with you if you don't change your life. This is not the life I want for me and Phillip."

Phil-Quan got defensive, "Oh, now you tripping off what that old lady said to our son? Saying he gonna grow up and be like Barack Obama. Shante, you always rambling about something."

"No Phil-Quan. I am always rambling about the *same thing* I rambled about last week and the week before that, and the week before that. As a matter of fact, Phil-Quan, the same shit I been rambling about all year long and the year before that. Get your shitty life together! Get a job, go to school. Stop selling drugs.

Think about your future. Be a damn man and take care of your son!"

"Why you coming down on me like this Shante!" She stepped off the elevator, taking the bag and toys from Phil-Quan.

"Because I don't plan to be with a boy who thinks he's a man!" Phil-Quan was holding the elevator door open. He stuck his head out as he watched her walk down the hall toward her mother's apartment.

"You'll see Shante. I am gonna get my life together. You got to be patient with a brother."

"No Phil-Quan!" Shante turned to face him. "*You* will see! You think I'm playing around with you? I have plans for me and Phillip." She turned back around.

Phil-Quan called out to her, "I love you boo!"

"Yeah right," she kept walking.

"I love you, Shante ... Love you, Phillip," and he let the elevator door close. Shante unlocked the apartment door and stepped inside; she was shocked at what she saw.

5:45 P.M.

Justine rushed out of the meeting and headed back to her office. She quickly locked the door behind her to make sure no one could walk in without knocking first. She checked her phone, scrolling through the list of recent text messages. Mom, Stanley, Ronald, and ... yes! Mr. Goldstein. She smiled at his message: *"Justine, call me. Good news."* Her office phone rang, breaking her excitement. She looked at the caller ID and saw that it was her fiancé Ronald.

She wanted to call Mr. Goldstein that very minute, but answered the phone instead.

"Hello. Justine Whitaker speaking."

"Hello Justine baby, this is your loving man."

"Hey, Ronald. How are you?" She put on her soft sweet office voice.

"I am fine darling, but I will be better when I see you tonight." She blushed. "I want to see my best girl. I'm missing you, Justine. Dinner tonight at seven, our usual place?"

"Ronald ..." Justine sighed. "I'm really busy and have a lot of work on my desk." She did *not* want to see Ronald tonight. She was not completely sure about taking their relationship to the next level. He, on the other hand, was willing to jump the broom tomorrow if she would agree.

"Oh, come on sweetheart, don't you want to see me?"

"Yes, Ronald but work is piling up and I – "

"Justine, I want to see you." She picked up her scarf project from her bag and starting knitting. Ronald continued, "We haven't been out to dinner all month because you've been busy with work. You know I'm very understanding about your career but – "

"Yes, Ronald, you are," Justine cut him off, "Thank you for that. I'll see you later. We'll talk then, okay?"

"Sure, Justine. I'll see you this evening, I love you."

"See you later Ronald." She hung up and quickly set her knitting on top of the desk. She dialed Mr. Goldstein's number. His office phone rang twice before the secretary's voice answered.

"Hello. Mr. Goldstein's office."

"Good afternoon. May I speak to Mr. Goldstein? This is Justine Whitaker, returning his call ... . Yes, I will hold. Thank you." She tapped her French-manicured nails on the mahogany desk. Her heart was beating fast. She was anxious to get her record company going. She heard a man answer the phone.

"Hello, Mr. Goldstein. How are you?"

"I am well, Miss Whitaker, and you?"

"I'm doing well ... Thank you for asking."

He got straight to the point. "Miss Whitaker, I have great news. All of your legal paperwork and licenses have been filed and approved."

Justine was thrilled. "Thank you, Mr. Goldstein!"

"You just need to come to my office this evening and sign a few more documents, and then you're all set. Can you come in at seven?" Justine paused before answering, remembering she had agreed to meet Ronald at that time.

"Mr. Goldstein, how about seven-thirty?"

"I am sorry, Miss Whitaker. I have a conference call at that time."

"I see. Okay. Then seven tonight it is. I will be there."

"See you then, Miss Whitaker."

Justine thought about texting Ronald to tell him she would stay late for dinner, but instead she sat dwelling on her thoughts of owning a record company. She leaned back in her high back leather chair and smiled; she spoke out loud to herself.

"Goodbye Stay Paid Records. Hello JW Records!" She sighed in relief. The joy of the moment was interrupted by a sudden loud knock at her office door.

"Justine! It's me, Brian!"

"What does he want now?" Justine mumbled under her breath. Brian was the irritating boss that Justine and her coworkers loved to hate. He yelled louder.

"Justine!" She put on her fake *"happy to work for you"* smile and opened the door. "Brian, hello, can I help you with something?"

6:00 P.M.

Shante stepped inside her apartment, shocked to see at least fifteen boys and young men rolling dice and shooting craps in the middle of the living room floor. She recognized many of them from the neighborhood. The smell of booze and weed was heavy in the air. A man was making out with a topless woman in the corner of the room near the window. Cigarette smoke was hanging at eye level. Shante found the noise of the gambling unbearable. She looked around the living room and saw her mother drunk on the sofa.

She cuddled Phillip closer to her chest and moved quickly through the living room calling for little sister Cherise. None of her siblings seemed to be at home. Shante ran to her room and grabbed some clothes out of her drawers and closet. She threw them into a gym bag and dashed out the door. She took the stairs back down to Mrs. Brown's apartment. She had knocked a few times before Mrs. Brown answered the door.

"Come on in here Shante, Cherise is here." It seemed as if she was expecting her. "She knocked on my door about five minutes after you left." Mrs. Brown reached out her arms. "Give me the baby. I'll put him in the playpen in the back room. He didn't have a nap today; I can see he's sleepy." Shante handed Phillip to Mrs. Brown, who said, "Go talk with your sister, Shante. Phillip will be fine." Shante crossed the room and sat next to Cherise on the sofa.

"Are you okay little sis?"

"I'm all right." Shante could see Cherise had been crying. Her cheeks were wet with tears. "I was scared, Shante ... all those men in our house." Shante got worried.

"Did anybody hurt you, Cherise?"

"No," Cherise replied. "I stayed in the back room hiding under the bed. I was calling for Mama, but she never heard me."

"Don't worry, Cherise ... I'll figure something out for us. We can't live in that crazy house much longer. If I had a job, I would rent a place for us to live. Me, Phillip, and you." Shante hugged her sister tightly. She noticed Cherise had a plastic grocery bag with some clothes inside. "You did the right thing by coming to Mrs. Brown's house. It's safe here."

Mrs. Brown came quietly back into the living room. "Phillip is fast asleep," she said. "You two come sit at the table. It's time for dinner. I have a pot of chicken gumbo on the stove."

"Thank you, Mrs. Brown. We appreciate it," Shante followed Mrs. Brown into the kitchen, holding her sister's hand. "I don't know what we are going to do about my mother."

Mrs. Brown tied a Mount Zion AME Church apron around her chubby waist and then set a steaming pot in the center of the dinner table. She stood next to Shante.

"Well, we can start with saying grace for this meal and a prayer for your mother."

"What do you mean, Mrs. Brown?" Shante asked.

"I have known your mother since she was a teenager. When your grandma Becky died, your mother just went down the devil's path and never turned around. The Church reached out to get your mother some help but she always refused," she sighed and shook her head. "Debra is on our daily prayer list, and I believe God will save her. In the meantime, you, Cherise, and Phillip are welcome to stay with me. I have the extra bedroom so don't worry. Things will work out."

She set bowls and silverware on the table. "Go wash your hands before we eat." The girls vanished and Mrs. Brown ladled gumbo from the pot into the bowls, then set a small platter of freshly baked cornbread on the table with a pitcher of iced tea. Shante and Cherise rushed back to the table; they were both very hungry.

"Bow your heads, girls." They bowed, and Mrs. Brown began her prayer. "Dear Lord, bless these children and their mother. We ask you to bless this food you have graciously provided for us today. In Jesus' name, we pray. Amen."

"Amen," Shante and Cherise replied. They looked at the food in their bowls and smiled.

"Enjoy your dinner, girls."

"Thank you, Mrs. Brown," said Cherise.

"You're welcome child, now eat up. God is Good."

"Mrs. Brown, Cherise and I won't take advantage of your kindness," Shante said. "I might be able to find a part-time job to pay you for our stay."

"No Shante. That's not necessary. I watch Phillip because I know you are trying to make something of yourself. I can see you don't want to be like most of the girls around here. Heck, I can see you want to be much different from your mother." Mrs. Brown looked into Shante's eyes. "It's not about money for me, Shante. It's about being able to help somebody while I am still alive on this earth. You just keep your head in those school books, and you will be okay."

She shook her head. "Now your baby daddy Phil-Quan is a story for another time." She glanced at Cherise and added, "We can talk about that when it's just the two of us."

Cherise looked at Mrs. Brown and asked, "Why not Mrs. Brown? I like Phil-Quan. He's going to marry Shante one day." She waited for her sister to agree.

Mrs. Brown cut in before Shante could respond, "Do you like the gumbo, Shante? It's an old family recipe."

"Yes, it's very good, Mrs. Brown."

After they finished dinner, the rest of the evening was quiet. Shante and Cherise washed the dishes and cleaned up the kitchen. Mrs. Brown had fallen asleep on the sofa in front of the television. The evening news reported about the Obama and McCain campaigns.

"Cherise," Shante whispered as to not wake Mrs. Brown up, "you keep an eye on Phillip. I'm going upstairs to see if Mama is all right."

"Shante, I want to go with you."

"No Cherise, you stay here. I'll only be gone a few minutes."

"Okay ... but hurry up." Shante kissed Cherise on the forehead, then went into Mrs. Brown's room and kissed Phillip, who was sound asleep.

"Boy, you must have been tired." She rubbed his back gently and pulled the covers over him. She walked past the kitchen and through the living room. She unlocked the door very quietly. She jumped when she heard Mrs. Brown's voice.

"Be careful Shante."

"Yes, Mrs. Brown, I will." Shante took the elevator back upstairs to the eighteenth floor. She could hear music and voices coming from the apartment. Getting closer, she could see the door was slightly ajar. She peeked through the small opening and saw her mother on the couch kissing a man.

Suddenly, the apartment door behind Shante opened, apartment 18H. A woman named Miss Odessa stuck her head out the door. Her thick coke-bottle glasses and missing teeth always gave Shante the creeps.

"Hey! Gal! Shante!" she said. "Your mama been keeping bad company all day every day. I was just about ready to call the police. I'm an old woman, and I need my rest."

"Yes, Miss Odessa, I understand."

"I know you a good girl, going to school and all. But your mama is going to meet her death soon if she keeps this mess up! I swear I am going call the police one day. You better talk to her, Shante."

"Thank you, Miss Odessa, for not calling the police." Miss Odessa was about to speak again, but Shante cut her off before she could say a word, "Good night Miss Odessa. I will see after my mother right now." Shante walked in slowly. Miss Odessa was trying to sneak a peek inside. People were still gambling in the living room while others danced around them. There were people in the kitchen eating and drinking. There was a woman lying drunk on the kitchen floor with an empty wine bottle on the floor next to her. Shante walked over to her mother, who was still locked in some man's arms.

"Mama," said Shante in a low voice. Debra did not hear her. "Mama," she tried again. Still no response. She moved in closer and shouted, "Mama!" Her mother and the man stopped kissing. Shante stared at her mother with a hardened face.

"Hi, Shante." Her mother's hair was wild – greasy and messy. She had no bra on under her ripped T-shirt.

"What do you mean 'Hi Shante'? Who the hell are these people, Mama?"

The man looked Shante up and down. "Hi Shante, my name is Harry."

"I ain't talking to you, *Harry*. I am talking to my mother." She looked at him with disgust.

"Shante, don't be rude to my guests! This here is my house. I pay the rent, not you!"

"No Mama, you don't pay nothing up in here. The welfare pays the rent and your kids pitch in to pay everything else. Do you know Miss Odessa was going to call the police today?" Her mother reached for the red cup of wine sitting on the coffee table,

"That old nosy bitch is not gonna call no damn police. She's just talking, that's all."

"Well Mama, if she or anybody calls the police, you could get kicked out of this apartment." Her mother seemed unbothered. "Where are we going to live if you get kicked out?" Shante's twin brother Dante came out from the back room with his girlfriend, Cathy. Cathy was only eighteen and already had two kids. One of them looked just like Dante; the older child was fathered by someone else. "Dante, how long you been here?"

"I been here for an hour, why?"

Shante grew furious, "You see all this mess going on in this house? Mama is going to get us all kicked out."

"Who said Mama's going to get kicked out?" Dante was growing tired of his sister's talk. Debra chimed in.

"That old witch Miss Odessa across the hall told Shante she gonna call the police on me."

"Miss Odessa is a nice lady," offered Cathy.

"Nobody is talking to you, Cathy, so just mind your damn business okay?" Shante seemed to be the only one concerned by her mother's behavior. Cathy rolled her eyes.

"Hey, don't you talk to Cathy like that!" Dante shouted.

"The hell with you Dante! This is about Mama and these damn critters in the house!"

"Shante, my friends have names, they ain't critters. You always thinking you better than everybody else!" As if no one else was standing there, Harry again started kissing Debra on the lips.

"Mama, why do you insist on being a bitch all the time?" Shante yelled.

"You stop talking to Mama like that," said Dante. Cathy stood looking on. Harry, fed up by the arguing, excused himself and walked toward the front door.

"Sit down Harry!" Debra called after him, "Where are you going? Harry! You don't have to leave! This is *my* house! Come back!" Harry left without so much as a nod of acknowledgment. Embarrassed, Debra continued to shout, "Okay, Harry keep going! Don't bring your black ass back here no more!" Dante lit a cigarette, looking at Shante.

"Sis, what is your problem?"

"What is *my* problem? Look around, Dante. Half the fucking neighborhood is in here. Who are those people in the kitchen?"

"I don't know, Shante."

"Mama, do you know who they are?"

"That's *family* in the kitchen," said Debra, lighting a cigarette of her own as she leaned back on the sofa.

"Mama, they ain't no damn family of ours. You don't know who they are, do you?" Debra didn't respond. Shante raised her voice, "Look at the drunken woman on the floor. Who is she?"

Cathy spoke up. "That's my Auntie Louise."

"Why don't you get her out of here?" Cathy turned on Shante.

"Because I didn't bring her here, that's why."

Shante turned her attention back to her mother. "Mama. Where's Tracy and Chris?"

"I don't know where Chris is. Tracy is at a friend's house." Debra threw her hands up, "Are you the police, Shante? Asking me all these damn questions!"

"No Mama, I'm not the police. I just want to know where my family is."

"They just hanging out with friends," said Dante, blowing smoke rings into the air.

"I can only imagine what kind of friends they're hanging out with." Shante felt hopeless. "Mama I think Tracy and Chris are selling drugs."

Dante looked at his mother. "Mama did you hear what Shante said?"

"Yeah, I heard her. She doesn't know what the hell she talking about."

"Mama, do you know something that I don't know?" asked Shante. "Maybe you know something Dante?" Dante shook his head. "Well, then why do they have more sneakers than Foot Locker or Modell's? Somebody answer that for me!"

"Maybe they have jobs," said Cathy.

"*Nobody's talking to you Cathy*," scowled Shante. "By the way, Dante, your sneakers look brand new. Where you'd get them?"

"Don't answer her, Dante," said Debra, mashing her cigarette in the ashtray. The drunk woman on the floor began to wake up.

"Hey, people, let's party!" She looked around. "Somebody give me a drink."

Shante was adamant. "So they are selling drugs Mama, is that it?" Her mother would not answer and neither would Dante. "Okay Mama, you don't have to say anything. I know they're selling drugs," she paused. "Just one more question, Mama. Where is Cherise?" Debra suddenly looked stunned. Her eyes were darting around the room. She sat up straight on the sofa. "Where is she, Mama?" Dante and Cathy glanced around the room.

"She's at her friend's house," said Debra.

"What friend Mama?" Shante stood with her arms folded, waiting.

"She must be at one of her classmates' houses," said Dante.

"I'm not talking to you Dante, so shut up."

"Yeah, she is at her classmate's house," said Debra, convincing herself. "She's staying the night. I saw her with a bag of clothes earlier. She was going to her friend's house up the street."

"You know Mama, it's a damn shame you don't know where Cherise is." Shante replied, "You don't know where any of your kids are, do you, Mama?"

"Well, you and Dante are right here," Debra drank some wine from her red cup.

"All Dante does is make babies in the back room with Cathy," Shante scoffed. Cathy spoke up,

"What I do with Dante is my business, Shante. Not yours."

"You're right, it is your business Cathy. You keep doing your business with Dante and you'll have enough babies to keep you on welfare for the rest of your life." She looked Cathy over. "Looks like you're about four or five months' pregnant now. Am I right?" Cathy turned away. Dante tried not to look at Cathy.

"The hell with you, Shante! What does Phil-Quan do for you?" said Cathy.

"He doesn't do a damn thing for me, and I am not afraid to say it."

"Both of you shut up!" yelled Debra. She glared at Dante. "Dante, you and Cathy go on about your business and get out of here."

"Why you are telling them to get out, Mama?" Shante asked. "They're just gonna come back later and lay up in the back room like they always do."

"Mind your business, Shante." Dante was angry with his twin sister. He took Cathy's hand and led her out the door.

"Mama, this house is insane. I can't live like this."

"So, then *don't* live like this," said Debra, lighting another cigarette.

"I won't," replied Shante. She turned around and stepped over the drunken Auntie Louise who was now sitting up on the floor. Shante left the apartment, tears running down her face. She made her way back to Mrs. Brown's apartment. Once back safely inside, she stood at the bedroom door looking at Cherise, who was lying on the bed asleep with Phillip in her arms. Shante kissed them both on the forehead and whispered goodnight. Gathering a few toiletries, she went into the bathroom and started the water for a shower. She giggled at Mrs. Brown's loud snoring that could be heard even over the faucet. The hot water felt good running down her lean body. She relaxed her muscles, trying to free her mind of the events that had happened earlier at her mother's place. And she began to cry. "God, help me," she whispered. "How am I going to survive?" The problems she faced felt like an iron ball and chain.

Thursday, October 30th, 2008

7:00 P.M.

Rhonda sat on the edge of her bed thinking about her situation. She stood up and began to pace back and forth in her bedroom. "Maybe the test was wrong," she said aloud. "I should take it again ... Oh my gosh! What is my mother going to think?" She paused, imagining her mother's voice. "*Having a baby is always a blessing ...* that's what Mom would say."

She picked up her new bamboo knitting needles and a skein of yarn from her nightstand and started casting onto one needle. She completely forgot that she had already begun knitting a scarf the day before; she had left it sitting on the dining room table next to an empty tea cup. Her hands moving fast, she thought, "I'll knit a baby blanket, maybe some booties too. Oh Lord Jesus!"

Her cell phone rang. She dropped the needles and yarn. Her racing thoughts made her jumpy. It was Joe calling. She could hear her heart pounding, and resumed her pacing. After a few rings, she answered the phone. "Hi, Joe."

"Hey, baby, how are you?" Rhonda could hear loud music in the background, a familiar sound which let her know Joe was at a club.

"I need to talk to you, Joe." There was a long pause.

"I can't hear you Rhonda, speak louder."

"Joe, I need to talk to you!"

"I'm listening baby, what's up?"

"Joe, I ... I need to talk to you face to face. When can we meet?" Joe was shouting now. "Why don't you come down to the club and we can talk!"

"No, Joe, I need to speak with you alone, in a quiet place. Come to my house."

"Damn Rhonda, baby – tonight? You miss your man baby? You want me?" Rhonda rolled her eyes.

"Joe, we need to talk. It's important."

"Okay chill, Rhonda. I'll come by around nine."

"All right Joe, I'll see you at nine o'clock." After she hung up, she spent the rest of the evening thinking about how she was going to tell him the news. She decided it would go like this:

"I will just come out and say it, Joe, you're going to be a father." She went to the kitchen cabinet and took out a small bottle of red wine. "Oh, darn, I can't have wine, I'm pregnant." Feeling frustrated, she picked up the knitting she had left on the table and began to knit.

Before she could finish a row, her house phone rang. Rhonda picked up, thinking it might be Joe calling back. But it was her mother, Barbara.

"Hello Rhonda, it's your mama. How are you doing? Did you get the flyer I mailed to you about the new yarn shop opening this weekend in Harlem?"

"Hello Mama. Yes, I did get the flyer, thank you." She paused. She didn't want her mother to start asking questions that could lead to the baby news slipping out, "I'm actually knitting a scarf right now. How are you doing, Mama?"

"I'm doing well; Rhonda, you sound like you have a cold." Rhonda was trying to keep her stitch pattern count in her head. Purl one, knit one, purl one, knit one ...

"No Mama. Just a little sniffle. Mama, I'm kind of busy right now. Can I call you tomorrow?"

"You said you're knitting a scarf. Is that what you call busy?"

"I, uh, I have a vegetable stew cooking on the stove." Rhonda did not like lying to her mother. "I should probably get off the phone now, Mama. Don't want it to burn or something."

"Oh, all right Rhonda. I just called to let you know I picked up that cranberry-colored alpaca yarn you asked for."

"Thanks, Mama, I will see you soon."

"Rhonda, girl. Sweetie, are you all right?"

"Yes, mama, just busy right now. Call you tomorrow, Mama. Good night." Rhonda hung up the phone. She closed her eyes and took a deep breath. After some time, she returned to her bedroom and picked up the yarn and knitting needles that had fallen to the floor earlier. She wasn't in the mood to knit a baby blanket. She tossed the project onto her bed and picked up her *Knitting Today* magazine from the night table and flipped through a few pages, then tossed the magazine onto the bed, too. "Maybe I should take a nap before Joe gets here," she thought. Rhonda stretched herself out across her king-sized bed, lying on her back. She then nestled herself into a handmade quilt her great Aunt Peggy had made for her when she graduated from Spelman College with honors. The comfort of that quilt always seemed to take Rhonda's mind off her problems. She moved her hands back and forth across the different textures of patchwork. Cotton, fleece, corduroy, wool, and kente cloth. "Life is full of surprises" is what her Aunt Peggy used to always say. "Auntie was right," Rhonda said out loud. Ten minutes later she was asleep.

The phone rang, waking her. "Hello," she answered.

"Hey Rhonda. I'm looking for a parking space, be at your door in a few minutes." Rhonda's heart began to beat fast.

"Okay Joe, see you in a minute." She hung up and ran into the bathroom to get ready. She applied a thick layer of ruby red lipstick, sprayed a veil of perfume across her body, and fluffed her kinky Afro with her fingers. Looking at her reflection, she ran her hands down her dress and over her curvy hips to smooth out any wrinkles. The doorbell rang, and Rhonda felt her heart skip a beat. "Lord Jesus, help me," she said as she took one last look in the mirror before walking to the door.

She took a deep breath and tried to relax. She waited a few seconds before she opened the door. Seeing Joe standing there looking as handsome as ever brought some ease to her mind. He was six feet four inches and fit, with dark chocolate velvet skin. His hazel eyes mesmerized Rhonda every time she looked at him. She felt a sudden sensual warmth come over her entire body.

"Hey Joe," she smiled, "Come on in."

"Hey Rhonda baby," Joe stepped inside and kissed her on the forehead. She could smell he was wearing the *Blue Night* cologne she had given him for his birthday a year earlier; it mixed perfectly with his body's chemistry. He took off his Italian leather jacket and tossed it across the loveseat.

"Want a drink, Joe?" Rhonda asked. She figured some alcohol would make him better suited to receive the news.

"Sure. How about some Scotch on the rocks?" Rhonda smiled and headed over to the kitchen to prepare his drink. Joe looked

Rhonda over as she did so; something seemed off to him. "How are things baby, you got something on your mind?" Rhonda handed him the Scotch.

"Yeah Joe ... I need to talk with you." Suddenly Joe's hands were caressing Rhonda's hips. He kissed her on the neck. Rhonda had to control herself. For the first time, she did not want to end up in bed with him.

"You smell amazing, Rhonda." He started to rub her breasts.

"Joe, come on now, relax."

"I *am* trying to relax, Rhonda. Work with me, girl."

"Joe, we really need to talk," Rhonda pulled herself from the hold of his strong arms. He finally let up.

"Okay baby, let's talk." He took her by the hand and led her to the sofa. They sat, and he took a sip of Scotch. He noticed she did not have a glass for herself.

"Hey, baby, where's your drink? You know I hate to drink alone." Rhonda thought of an excuse,

"Oh ... no, I can't Joe. I just got over an awful migraine." Joe was staring into her eyes. "Rhonda you are beautiful." He tried to give her a sip of his drink.

"No Joe, didn't you hear me?"

"Yes girl, I heard you. A headache." He kissed her on the forehead again, and then on her nose and lips. He slipped his tongue into her mouth and gave her a long, passionate kiss. He put his drink down on the coffee table and pulled her closer to him. They were wrapped in each other's arms, and Joe's hand was slowly sliding up her dress. Rhonda wanted Joe badly, and it was clear he wanted her. She pulled away.

"Joe, I need to talk to you."

"Can't we talk later, Rhonda?" He was kissing her on the neck again. She wanted to give in to him and make love. She pulled away again.

"I wish we could Joe, but this is important." He picked up his drink and took another sip.

"Okay Rhonda, I'm sorry. You did say you needed to talk to me. I'm all ears for you, baby. Tell me what's on your mind." He was looking directly at her again with those beautiful eyes of his. She had to look away.

"Joe, you're not making this easy for me."

"What girl? I'm just admiring you."

"No Joe ... it's the way you're staring at me."

"I can't help it, Rhonda, you are absolutely beautiful." She blushed.

"Joe, you always make me feel special."

"Rhonda baby, you *are* very special to me. You're my lady." He played gently with the kinks and coils of her hair. "What do you need to talk about?" Rhonda, nervous, rubbed her hands together. "Are you all right Rhonda?"

She turned to face him and realized there was no other way to do this than to come out and say it.

"Joe, I'm pregnant."

Joe stared at her as if he had seen a ghost. There was a piercing silence in the air. Rhonda's heart raced. "Joe. Did you hear me?" He swallowed the rest of his Scotch and asked for another. "Joe, I am pregnant."

"I need another drink, Rhonda." She took his glass and quickly refilled it. He gulped down the second drink. "Rhonda ... are you sure?"

49

"Yes, Joe. I am sure." Joe was silent. He was clearly unhappy at the news. His voice became stern and rough.

"Rhonda, I thought you were protecting yourself. The pill, a diaphragm, the patch, something?" He paused, staring at his empty glass, "You're kidding me, right?" Rhonda folded her arms across her chest,

"Kidding about what, Joe? Protecting myself, or being pregnant?" Joe covered his face with his hands.

"This *cannot* be happening to me."

"What do you mean not happening to *you*? What about me, Joe?" He looked up at her.

"I'm sorry baby, I didn't mean it like that." Rhonda was offended. He continued, "Baby, I'm not ready to be a father, and you already have two kids in college. I mean, you're fifty years old." Rhonda stood up and looked Joe directly in his eyes. She was angry and hurt. Her age had never seemed to bother him before.

"Yes. I have two kids in college. Yes I am fifty years old. And yes, I was protecting myself Joe. But sometimes ... *shit happens.*"

"What are you going to do, Rhonda?" She was stung by his use of the word *you.*

"Joe, you're acting like this is not your problem."

"Well Rhonda, it doesn't have to be a problem for either of us." Rhonda's eyes widened.

"You mean I should have an abortion?"

"Do you really want to become a mother all over again? Do you?"

"I wouldn't mind. I love you, Joe." He looked away.

"Rhonda, I don't want to have a baby with you." Rhonda felt her heart sink.

"But Joe ... I thought you loved me?"

"I do love you, Rhonda but ..."

"But what Joe? You won't love me if I have this baby?"

Joe raised his voice, "What the hell are you gonna do with a baby at fifty years old?" Rhonda felt tears building up in the corners of her eyes.

"How could you say that to me?"

"Don't sound surprised, Rhonda," he sighed, "I am who I am, and a baby with you does *not* fit into my life right now. I just want to be with you and enjoy what we have together. What's wrong with that?"

"There is nothing wrong with that, Joe. I just thought you would be happy about the baby. I mean, we've been together so many times and ... and never once did you use a condom. What did you think ..."

"And *you* never stopped me for not wearing a condom." He raised his voice again.

"Oh, so this pregnancy is my fault, Joe?"

"I'm not saying it's anybody's fault. We're both adults. I enjoy my life just the way it is. No strings attached."

"You don't have to remind me, Joe. I remember you saying that when we first got together. You enjoy your life just the way it is. No ties to anything or anyone."

"Rhonda ..." he sighed. "You know we were just kicking it, having fun with each other." She tried to hold back tears.

"You made me feel like I was the only woman you loved or cared about."

"I do love you, and I do care about you, and that's the way I'd like it to stay. Kids would change what we have together. Do you understand what I am saying to you?"

"Yeah Joe," she looked away. "I hear you loud and clear."

"Rhonda baby, you know me. I'm a freestyling, easygoing man. I don't hate kids, I just don't need this right now. If you decide to keep this baby it's your business."

Rhonda was still standing. She finally sat next to him on the sofa. The only thing she could manage to say was, "How could you be so cold? "

"Baby, I'm not being cold. I'm being truthful." After a few minutes of silence, Joe picked up his jacket and left. Rhonda had tears rolling down her face. Her heart was crushed.

Friday, October 31st, 2008

3:00 P.M.

The sun shone bright on the corner of 125th Street and Fifth Avenue. Terri swept in front of the shop and paused to lift her face up toward the sun, feeling its warmth. Sherri tapped on the glass display window, signaling for Terri to come inside.

"Terri, we still have a lot to do before the grand opening tomorrow."

"Calm down sis, everything is going to be great for the opening." Terri reached for a small notepad that was in her back pocket. She flipped through it, "All right, the flowers are scheduled to be delivered by 9:00 A.M., and the caterers should be here by 10:00 A.M." She looked up at her sister, who was frowning. Terri glanced at her notepad again, "Oh," she said, "and the chilled wine will be here exactly one hour before we open the doors." Sherri shook her head,

"Well Terri, I think you forgot one thing."

"Really, what?"

"Who is picking up Mom and Dad at the airport this evening?"

"Oh Lord, Sherri! I almost forgot about Mom and Dad! I can call car service to – " and Sherri shut her right up.

"No worries, Terri. Auntie Louise and Uncle Willie will meet them at the airport."

Terri smiled. "You see! I told you Dad wouldn't let us down. Mother said Daddy really wants to be here for us tomorrow. She said they're really proud of us. You remember how much she enjoyed teaching us to knit when we were kids? Even then you and I would pretend we had our very own yarn shop."

"Yes, I do remember," said Sherri. "It was such fun when we were little." She paused. "I also remember how Daddy wanted us to go into the family construction business with him. I think he really wanted to have two sons. Remember when he tried to sign us up for softball? He was upset when Mom told him she had signed us up for ballet classes instead." They both laughed. Terri looked at her sister with a warm, loving smile.

"You know Sherri, Dad worked really hard to give us and Mom a good life."

"You're right, he did work hard, but he was never really there for us as kids. We both missed him at class plays and dance recitals. I think that's why he wants to be here now for us."

Terri sighed, "Sherri, let the past go. Dad did the best he knew how for us, we never wanted for anything."

"I think you're wrong on that one. Mom was lonely for her husband most of the time."

Terri was taken aback. "Mom always seemed so happy."

"I'm sure she was happy sometimes, but not all the time. Dad built his business up over the years. I admire him for that, but sometimes I feel like we just never really knew him. I mean honestly, how much do we know about Dad?"

"Sherri, we know that he loved us then and he loves us now. His hard work was for us."

"Okay, he loves us and he provided for us. But what kind of person is he, really? We know he's a good businessman, but is he the man that Mom dreamed of having a life together with?"

Terri was growing impatient with her sister's questions. "What do you mean exactly?" she asked. "Mom and Dad love each other, Sherri."

"I never said they didn't love each other. Mom is a beautiful woman. She gives so much of herself. She put her dreams of becoming an actress on hold for a lifetime in order to raise us. She cooked, cleaned, sewed ... and she came to every school event we ever had. She was always so involved with the community and school just for us. She helped us and the other kids with homework every day. She gave them milk and cookies ... she treated them just like one of her own children. She was and still is so active in church. She goes to the nursing homes twice a week to visit the sick. She knits hats and scarves and donates them to homeless shelters, hospitals, and senior centers. And that's just a *few* of the things our mother does."

Terri wasn't sure where her sister was going with this. "Wow, go mom!" she replied.

"My point is," Sherri continued, "with everything that Mom has done and is still doing, I just can't help but wonder if she ever felt loved by Dad, I mean truly loved. She told me that when they were young, Dad swept her off her feet the first time she saw him on the basketball court at college. She knew he was the man she would one day marry."

"Yeah, I remember Mom telling that story."

"What I am saying now, Terri, is I wonder if he is still that special man she adored years ago. She said he would always take her to dinner and for long romantic walks in the park. He'd buy her ice cream cones on Sundays, after church on warm summer days. He would take her to school dances and homecoming parades. He baked her a cake once – for her nineteenth birthday."

"They were two young beautiful people," said Terri, "madly in love with each other. Sherri, I'm sure they're still madly in love."

Sherri frowned. "Tell me how you know that, Terri."

"Well Sis, they're still married, and Mom is happy."

"Okay. When's the last time Dad took Mom out?"

"Well, they go out to dinner every year for their anniversary."

55

Sherri's eyes lit up. "Hey! You're right!" Terri could tell a million thoughts were racing through Sherri's mind. "Terri, do you remember how we could never really plan a surprise anniversary party for them because we never knew what time Dad would be home from the office?

"Yeah, I remember," answered Terri, cautiously.

"Well, next June will be their thirty-fifth wedding anniversary, and Dad is planning an early retirement next year ... I think we should do something special for them!"

They were both smiling now. "You're right, Sherri. Mom did say that Dad cut back on working late nights at the office." She glanced around the shop. "Well, I know one thing for sure. It will be really great to see them tomorrow. We can talk about planning something special for them *after* the opening." Sherri agreed. "Come on, let's finish up here, we've got a big day tomorrow."

4:00 P.M.

Shante had not spoken to her mother all week. She had told Cherise to not go not up to the apartment without her. Their mother had not even come looking for them. Mrs. Brown had been kind enough to let the girls stay with her, but Shante did not want to trouble her much longer. She thought of going to stay with relatives. Maybe her Auntie Diane, but she had two of her own sons living with her, and they were wild. They did have their cousin Anna in the Bronx, but she was almost eighty years old and practically blind. Shante could already imagine her and Cherise doing everything for her. They would become live-in slaves.

Shante heard the sound of keys jingling outside the door. Mrs. Brown had returned from doing the laundry. Mrs. Brown smiled, glad to have Shante there to help out a little. Shante helped her pull the shopping cart filled with clean clothes inside.

"Thank you, Shante," Mrs. Brown scanned the room, "Where is Cherise? "

"She's in the back room watching cartoons."

"I'll get dinner started in a few minutes for you girls." Mrs. Brown sank down on the sofa. "Oh Lord! I am tired."

"Why don't you just relax tonight," Shante offered, "and I'll make dinner." She wanted to help Mrs. Brown with anything she could to repay her for her kindness.

Mrs. Brown sighed, "You know I don't mind doing the cooking, chile." She looked Shante over. "Besides, what can you cook? You just as skinny as six o'clock." Shante laughed.

"I can cook, Mrs. Brown. I have to do *something* to help out around here."

"I told you that you and your sister are welcome to stay. You girls are not a problem." She paused. "And there is no way I can stand by and watch you girls go back your mother's crazy house." She stood. "Now, I'm going to take a nice warm bath and put on my fuzzy slippers and robe." She smiled.

"So yes, I will take you up on your offer to cook dinner." She did a little curtsey and said, "Miss Shante, the kitchen is all yours." Shante laughed and kissed Mrs. Brown on the cheek. The thought of going to live with anyone else never crossed her mind again. Before Mrs. Brown could disappear into her bedroom, though, Shante spoke to her.

"Mrs. Brown, tomorrow is the grand opening of the new yarn shop in Harlem. I was wondering, would you like to go with me?"

"Oh, I heard about that. My sister Ruby gave me a flyer. She said they was handing them out at the senior center last month."

"Well, would you like to go, Mrs. Brown?"

"Sure, Shante, I would love to go." Shante tried not to look too excited.

"Great Mrs. Brown! I wanted to take Cherise and Phillip too."

"Good. It will be a ladies' day for the three of us then. Plus, I can look after Phillip if he gets fussy." She rubbed her belly, "Now gal, *please* go get some food cooking on that stove, Mrs. Brown is getting hungry!" They both laughed.

"Right away!" Shante felt so happy for the love and care Mrs. Brown had shown her that it brought her to tears.

5:00 P.M.

Rhonda must have called Joe's cell phone a hundred times during the night. She had stayed home from work and spent the day lying in bed, replaying the events of the night before over and over in her head. "What kind of man is he? This is his baby and he just walked out like it's nothing?" The phone rang. She grabbed it on the first ring.

"Hello!" she was hoping to hear Joe's voice on the other end.

"Rhonda, it's your mother. Are you going to the opening of that new yarn shop tomorrow?" Rhonda sighed with disappointment.

"Mama, I thought I told you last night that I was planning on going."

"Yes you did Rhonda, but you always say you're going somewhere and then you don't. Especially since you met what's his name, Joe? You don't have time for anybody."

"Mama please, stop it! This is not the time. I said I would be at the opening tomorrow."

"All right Rhonda. I was just checking to make sure. You know I got the yarn you asked me to pick up for you."

"Yes, I know you got the yarn. You told me that last night as well."

58

"Okay Rhonda. I can see that you don't want to talk right now. See you tomorrow."

"All right Mama, enjoy your evening. See you tomorrow." Rhonda hung up the phone. It rang again. She picked it up immediately.

"Yes mother? What is it now?"

"Hey Rhonda, it's Joe." Rhonda sat up.

"Joe! Where have you been? I was calling you all night." There was a pause.

"I needed to get my thoughts together, Rhonda."

"What do you mean get your thoughts together?"

"Rhonda, I told you that I am not ready to be a father."

"You're not a daddy yet, Joe. Just a sperm donor at the moment." Rhonda was angry but trying to keep her cool. She continued, "Look, I know this is a shock, and I'm not trying to pressure you. We are not going to get anywhere like this. We need to talk seriously about this." She heard Joe sigh.

"What is there left to talk about? You already know how I feel." Rhonda felt her heart sink.

"So, it's really like that Joe? This is the way you treat the woman you say you love?"

"What do you want me to do? I can't handle all this!" He raised his voice.

"Joe. It's just a baby, what do you mean all this? It's not like I am asking you to marry me. I was informing you about our current situation is all. I was hoping you would tell me that you'd be there for me through this pregnancy. And maybe we could be a family?"

"Rhonda, there is no other way to say this ... You are just too damn old to have a baby, least of all *my baby*!" That was the dagger in Rhonda's heart.

"How *dare* you say such an awful thing to me!"

"Rhonda, do the damn math! If you have this baby, in ten years you will be sixty and the kid will be ten. Your other two children will probably have kids of their own. Is that what you really want?"

"I ... I wanted a life with the man I fell in love with. That's what I want, Joe." He said nothing. She had tears streaming down her cheeks. "You know what Joe? I think I am beginning to hate you." She hung up the phone. She was devastated. But this was just the beginning of her nightmare.

6:00 P.M.

For the past couple of days, Michele had worked sixteen to eighteen hours a day at the office. She had been researching and compiling questions for her upcoming interviews with Presidential Candidate Barack Obama. It felt great to finally be home at a decent hour. Charles and Ashley were in the kitchen together preparing dinner.

"Hi Mom," Ashley met her at the door to give her a hug. "Dinner will be ready in five minutes."

"Hello sweetheart," Michele kissed Ashley on the forehead.

"Hey honey!" called Charles from the kitchen. He tossed a spinach salad around in a wooden bowl. He planted a short but passionate kiss on Michele's lips and nestled his nose briefly in her coconut scented hair.

"Mm, dinner smells good!" Michelle looked everything over.

"It's turkey meatloaf, Mom. Your favorite!"

"Well thank you, Ashley." Charles handed Michele a glass of white wine. Michele took a sip then set the glass on the table so she could grab an apron.

"No, no, no," said Charles, taking the apron from her. "Baby, have a seat at the table, take your shoes off. We got this."

"Yes Mommy, we got this," said Ashley, who was smiling ear to ear. Michelle tried not to get emotional as she looked at her beautiful family.

"All right!" she threw her hands up. "I'll admit it does feel good to relax and enjoy a meal with my wonderful husband and lovely daughter." Charles kissed her again, this time more passionately, on the lips.

"Hey, hey! Cut it out, you two," Ashley covered her eyes. "We're about to eat dinner." Charles and Michele laughed.

"Okay sweetheart. Let's set the table." Charles said as he finished preparing the salad. They sat down at the table.

"Ashley would you say grace, please." Michele asked. They joined hands and bowed their heads.

"Dear Lord, we thank you for this day and all the blessings you have afforded us. Thank you for this meal that we take as nourishment for our bodies. And Lord thank you that my parents love each other so much, Amen."

"Thank you, sweetheart," said Charles, "that was beautiful." Ashley smiled at her father. They began to eat.

"Mom, I'm glad you're home early today."

"Me too, sweetheart. It's been so hectic at the office lately." Charles wiped some gravy from the corner of his mouth.

"Well honey, it's not every day that a member of this family gets to interview the first black man to run for president!"

"Yeah, Mom. I've been telling all my friends at school about it. My history teacher, Miss Johnson, is really excited. She said she wants to call you so you can come speak to the class about Mr. Obama."

"Really?" Michelle was surprised.

"Yes. She said that it's important for us to have discussions about Mr. Obama."

"Your teacher might be onto something, Ashley. I'd love to come speak to the class. Tell Miss Johnson it would be my pleasure."

Charles spoke up. "I told a few of my clients that my beautiful wife is going to be interviewing our next president." Michele was beaming.

"You two are just too much. I love all the support, but I haven't even met the man yet!"

"But you will, right?" asked Ashley.

"Yes, I'm going to do several interviews with Mr. and Mrs. Obama."

"Wow," Ashley sighed, "Mom, you're a celebrity and you don't even know it!" Michele laughed.

"I am *not* a celebrity."

"You are to us," said Charles. Michele sighed.

"I just love you both so much. The support of a loving family is all I need to keep me going." She stared at her husband and daughter for a moment and thought about how thankful she was for them. "Enough about me. How was your day Ashley?"

"Well, I got an A on both my English and chemistry exams. My friend Brenda and I are teaming up to work on an idea for the science fair coming up in April next year. We *really* want to win first prize. It's a thousand dollars!"

"Wow, that's a very generous first prize, baby girl," said Charles.

"Yes, it is," added Michele. "You can put that money toward your college fund."

"Oh Mom, Brenda and I want to go on a shopping spree with our prize money." Charles frowned at Ashley.

"Your mother is right, sweetheart."

"But Daddy, you and Mom have been saving for my college since before I was born. There should be plenty of money by now." Charles laughed.

"And now *you* can start saving and contribute your half of the prize money – that is, *if* you win." He sipped his wine.

"Well, we're going to do our best to win."

"Just do your best," Michele smiled. "Daddy and I are here to help if you need us."

"Thanks guys. Right now, I just need you both to agree to let me go shopping." They all laughed.

"Well, we can discuss a shopping spree at another time," said Michele. "Now let's finish enjoying this delicious meal."

7:00 PM

"Justine. I just need to know why you kept me waiting at the restaurant for over an hour, just to get a simple text saying you can't make it." Ronald set his fork on the table and stared at her, waiting for a reply. "You know," he continued, "you could have at least called me. I felt like a fool just sitting there drinking water. Waiting around for you." Justine sighed.

"Ronald, that was two days ago. Why can't you let it go? Besides, we're having a nice dinner now."

"No, Justine. I can't let it go. You're acting like this isn't a big deal."

"That's because it isn't. I told you, I got stuck at work and had to finish some reports for my boss, and then I had to rush over to my lawyer's office to sign some documents for my record label." Justine was becoming annoyed. "I explained this to you already. I'm sorry." Ronald shook his head. "How many times do you want me to apologize?"

"Please lower your voice, Justine. People are staring at us."

"You lower your voice, Ronald. I'm so tired of you nitpicking at everything I do all the time." She knew Ronald was right. She should have called, but there was a part of her that didn't feel sorry for what she had done. She took a deep breath and sipped some wine. Ronald lowered his voice to just above a whisper.

"All right Justine, I don't want you to apologize for it ever again."

"Thank you. Now can we just enjoy our dinner?"

"Sure, we can enjoy our dinner ... just tell me one thing." Justine rolled her eyes.

"And what's that?"

"Why do you always put me on the back burner in your life?" Once again, she knew he was right, but she needed to create a distraction.

"What are you talking about, Ronald?" She started to play around with the food on her plate. She didn't want to look at him.

"Justine, honey, look at me?" She took another bite and sipped her wine before looking at Ronald. He reached across the table and took her left hand in his. "Baby I love you, and I've loved you for the past three years. And I have tolerated a lot in that time."

Justine quickly interrupted him, "Tolerated?" She pulled her hand back slightly but he held on tighter.

"Please hear me out, Justine," he said softly, "I know you're very ambitious and I love that about you. You're smart *and* beautiful.

You go after everything that means something to you Justine, but you never seem to go after me."

She became defensive. "I don't do that to you, Ronald! I – "

"Yes you do," he was still calm. "I'm never first in your life. I'm never second in your life. I'm not even third in your life. I'm always put on the back burner. I wait there only because I love you ... because I believe, deep in my heart, that you will come back for me. But you never really do." He took a deep breath. "You know I want to get married and start a family with you, but I don't think that's what you want." Justine could feel the sadness and hurt coming from Ronald. It was radiating from him, as it had been for the last leg of their relationship. She felt tears building up behind her eyes. She hated to hurt him, but she also knew he was speaking the truth. "Justine, you have left me on the back burner so long ... that now I feel completely burnt out. I don't think you love me half as much as I love you." Justine's chest felt heavy. "You're my world." He squeezed her hand tighter. "I know you say you love me, but your actions say the opposite. I've tolerated it for so long only because I love you so much. You missed my mother's birthday party because you were tied up at work. You missed my company picnic last summer because you had to fly to California with a new artist. You missed my father's funeral because you were working on an image contract with a new recording artist." He took a deep breath again. "My *father's funeral*, Justine."

"Ronald, I really – "

"Please, let me finish." Justine's eyes widened as he said, "I put this engagement ring on your finger because I love you and wanted you to be my wife." Justine hung on the word *wanted*. He continued, "I don't believe this relationship is what you want. Is it?"

"I do want a relationship, Ronald."

"That's not what I asked you." Justine looked puzzled. "I asked you if you want *this* relationship Justine. You and me."

"Yes, of course. I do want this relationship. I want us."

"Well sweetheart, it's been very hard to tell. You say you want us but you don't fight for us."

"Ronald, I love you."

"And I love you Justine, but I can't go on like this. I've have taken a back seat to your career goals for too long. It's been like this ever since we first got together. Don't get me wrong, I love how ambitious you are. I am so proud of how you go after your dreams. I just feel like ... I feel I'm not a part of your dreams anymore."

"Ronald, of course you are. You're a part of my life."

"I know that. But which part am I?" Justine's eyes darted away from him once more.

"How could you ask such a thing?"

"It's true." He released her hand and took a big swallow of wine. He looked at her a few moments before speaking again. "Justine, let's take some time."

"Yes Ronald, let's take some time and go away somewhere. A nice trip."

"No Justine, I mean let's take some time apart from each other."

"What? What are you saying? Are you breaking up with me?"

"No, I'm not breaking up with you. I know what I want. But I want you to think and really figure out what you want."

"But Ronald I know what – "

"Justine, I think it's best that we take some time apart for a while." She was suddenly overcome with sadness.

"How long are you talking about, Ronald?"

66

"Baby, I want you to take as much time as you need to figure things out."

"Ronald ... I don't know about this."

"What are you unsure about? The possibility of my finding someone else? That's not what this is about and you know it. I love you. Like I said, I know what I want. I want marriage and a family. This is not about me. I have no doubts. It's about you, and you knowing for sure that I am the man you want to marry and spend the rest of your life with. All I ask is that you take some time and think about us." Justine could not believe what she was hearing. She loved Ronald. She believed that they had a good understanding about her desire to wait a while before getting married.

"Ronald, I do love you," she paused. "I suppose ... I haven't been fair to you."

"Justine, you need to – "

"No Ronald, now *you* need hear me out. Please." He sat up in his seat. "I can't turn back the hands of time and correct the wrongs I've done. I am so sorry that I put you on the *back burner*. You know that owning my own record business is important to me. I'm not saying you are not important. You don't understand how this business works. It's not easy to build a business from the ground up; it takes time. It takes a lot of time. I thought you really understood that. I know I want to get married and have a family ... one day. And when I do, I want to be able to provide for my family just like you want to be able to provide. I am ambitious, and that won't ever go away because I like to make things happen. I want a bright future with all that God has planned for me."

Ronald looked unconvinced. After staring at each other in silence for some time, Justine finally said, "Okay. I'll take some time and think about us. Maybe it's what I really need to do." Ronald glanced at the engagement ring on Justine's hand and then up at her. "Take all the time you need, Justine."

Saturday, November 1st, 2008

11:00 A.M.

Grand Opening Day

A van pulled up in front of the yarn shop. Terri was looking out the window, "Sherri, I think the flowers are here!"

"Okay!" Sherri replied, "I'll be right out. I'm on the phone with the caterers." Terri walked out to greet the driver.

"Good morning! Thank you for coming on time." An older gray-haired man stepped out of the van along with two teenage boys.

"Good morning," the man said, extending his hand to greet Terri. "I'm Mr. Wilson, owner of Wilson's flowers, and these two young men are my grandsons, Eric and Michael." Terri smiled.

"Hello Mr. Wilson, very pleased to meet you." She turned to the boys. "Hello Eric, Michael. I'm Terri." The boys were too stunned by Terri's beauty to respond. They simply smiled and nodded. "Please come with me," she continued, "I'll show you where to put the flowers."

They followed her into the shop. Sherri was still on the phone when they walked in; she gave a friendly wave to Mr. Wilson and went back to her conversation. "You can place the flower arrangements along this countertop," said Terri. "The orchids, you can set here on this coffee table." Terri pointed to spots as she spoke. "The Birds of Paradise can go here, and the roses on the other table on the left, and the African violets go right here." She pointed to a mahogany credenza against the back wall. "You can leave the rest of the flowers at the front counter by the register and I'll place them around." Terri smiled with pride.

"Okay Miss Terri," said Mr. Wilson, "We got it." Sherri was finally off the phone.

"Hey Terri, everything good?"

"Yes, Mr. Wilson and his grandsons are getting the rest of the flowers now. Is everything okay with the caterers?"

"Yes. They will be here at nine with a staff of ten. Eight of them are waiters to serve."

"Great," said Terri. She paused to look around the shop. It was all coming together. "Can you believe this is the day of our *grand opening*?" Sherri smiled back at her.

"A dream finally comes true. I am so happy for us!" The sisters hugged. Mr. Wilson came in with flowers. Eric and Michael stumbled over each other as they stared at Terri and Sherri.

"Boys, pay attention! Get over here with those flowers!"

"Yes Granddad," they said, still staring at the twin sisters. Terri and Sherri giggled as Mr. Wilson scolded the boys. Sherri's cell phone rang and she hurried to the counter to pick it up.

"Hello?"

"Hey Sherri, it's Michele. You ladies ready for the big opening?"

"Yes, girlfriend! Terri and I are ready."

"That must be Michele," said Terri as she placed the flowers around the shop. Sherri gave Terri a thumbs-up indicating that she was correct, and she continued, "Thanks for offering your help Michele, but we're fine. Everything is going smoothly. The caterers will be here soon, Mom and Dad will be here ..." she laughed, "There's a few people peeking through the window right now! Okay, I'll see you and Ashley later. Bye now." There was a deliveryman from *House of Darion* dresses ringing the doorbell of the shop. Sherri exclaimed, "Oh Terri! Our dresses are here!" Sherri ran to the door and signed for the package.

"Great," said Terri, "I'll get changed in a minute." The yarn shop had a full living space in the back: a bedroom with two queen sized beds, a large walk-in closet space, two full bathrooms with vanities, two stoves, and two refrigerators. Sherri hung the garment bags on the coat rack in the back of the shop. The window cleaner came by early, as promised, to remove any dirt and smudges from the glass.

"How do you think the arrangement of flowers looks?" asked Terri.

"Beautiful! Flowers always make a colorful difference. Mr. Wilson did a nice job."

"Oh my!" Terri said as she glanced at the clock, "It's eight-forty. We had better get changed." As former models, the two sisters specialized in changing in and out of clothes quickly. Within fifteen minutes they looked like they were ready for the catwalk. Terri wore a cranberry colored hand-beaded dress of fine China silk. It was a flawless fit on her slender size two figure. The boat-neck cut of the dress brought attention to the lovely bone structure of her neck and shoulders. It fell just above her knees. Her hair was up in a French twist, and she wore light makeup with a touch of lip gloss for a natural look. Her four-inch heels felt like flats compared with the seven-inch stilettos she and Sherri had frequently worn during their modeling career.

Sherri wore a hand-beaded royal blue dress with a deep V-neck line. Her dress length was also just above the knee and the sleeves fell to right above her elbows. She wore large solid gold bangles with diamond rings on each pinky finger. Her long silky hair hung past her shoulders and lay gently against her slender back. She liked her Chinese-cut bangs and hoop diamond earrings. Unlike her sister, she loved wearing her seven-inch stilettos.

It was 9:05 A.M., and the caterers rang the bell. Terri opened the door for them. Behind them was their Public Relations specialist, Willa.

"A little less than two hours before opening. Is everything all right with our guest list, Willa?" asked Terri.

"Oh yes, and I have *good news* for you. I didn't want to call you because I wanted to see the look on your faces." Sherri's and Terri's eyes widened.

"Well what is it!" Sherri asked.

"A few celebrities are going to stop by for the opening today!"

"Celebrities? Who, who, who!?" Terri asked excitedly.

"Yes, who?" asked Sherri.

"Well ... as your *super* publicist, I've been generating a lot of buzz about Sistah Knit, so the press is coming to cover the opening. A couple radio stations will stop by to cover the event, and maybe a couple – "

Sherri cut in, "Willa can you please get to the point about the celebs who are coming?"

"All right! Alicia Keys is coming!" Willa had a huge smile on her face.

"No way!" said Sherri. "Alicia Keys knits?

"Alicia Keys has *no time* to knit because she's busy making great music," said Terri. "This is great. Wow ... Alicia Keys."

Willa continued, "Also, Beyoncé will be stopping by to show her support." Terri and Sherri squealed like little girls with their excitement.

"No way! You can't be serious!" said Sherri. Willa laughed.

"Hold on! There's one more ... Miss Cicely Tyson, who is a knitter, will also be joining us."

"Are you kidding! Are you serious?" asked Sherri.

"Willa, are you for real?" asked Terri.

"I am not kidding, and I am serious. The Icon Miss Cicely Tyson is coming here today."

"I can't believe it. This is amazing Willa. I don't even know what to say ..." Sherri trailed on. "Thank you soooo much!"

"That's not all, ladies," Willa was getting a kick out of the looks on the twins' faces, "Guess who's coming to represent the knitting community?"

Sherri and Terri looked at each other and then back at Willa. She continued, with an even bigger smile on her face, "The Knitter, The Blogger, The Yarn Ho, Gayle aka GGmadeit!

Sherri screamed, "Oh my gosh GG?! She's the biggest name in the knitting community. Willa, this is awesome!"

"GG told me she was honored to get the invitation. She said she would not miss the opening of Sistah Knit for anything. She even sent something for you ladies." Willa reached into her handbag and handed a small ring sized box to each sister. They opened the little boxes.

"Wow, *We Knit Too* pins, oh my gosh!" said Sherri.

"This is really cool," said Terri, "I've been trying to get one of these pins for months, but they're always sold out."

"They're absolutely adorable," said Willa. "She wanted to let you know that she designed them herself and that her *We Knit Too* online publication will launch its first issue next spring."

"That is awesome!" said Sherri. Willa agreed. Both sisters put the pins on their dresses.

"All of your major guests read your bios and wanted to be a part of this wonderful opening celebration," Willa beamed. The twins hugged her.

"Willa, thank you! From the bottom of our hearts," said Sherri.

"Yes, thank you, Willa." Terri wiped happy tears from her eyes.

"You're both welcome. It's a pleasure working with you ladies to make your opening day special." Willa looked around the shop, "This is beautiful, amazing flowers and lovely colorful skeins of yarn. I keep telling myself I should learn to knit."

"Well you've come to the right place to learn! You know we'd be more than happy to teach you," said Sherri.

"Yes, you really should learn, Willa." added Terri.

"One day," said Willa. She was still looking around the shop. "It's so warm and cozy in here. Great job ladies, great job."

It was 9:45 A.M. *Harlem Weekly News Magazine*, *Why We Knit Magazine* and other print press media arrived, and were gathering outside of the yarn shop.

"Well, I'd better get out there and do my PR thing," Willa picked up her handbag and headed for the door. "See you ladies shortly," she winked.

"Thanks Willa, for everything. We love you girl," said Terri. Just then, an Asian lady tapped on the window, smiling, then rang the doorbell.

"Who's that?" asked Sherri.

"Oh, that's Miss Yoon from the cleaning service. She's here to give the place a final dusting. I spoke with her last week about coming over this morning. I forgot to tell you about her."

"Oh, that's great Terri. Good thinking, let her in." Terri opened the door.

"Good Morning, Miss Yoon." The woman stepped in and stopped in her tracks. She glanced around the shop.

"Oh my, Miss Terri, what a beautiful yarn shop ... I have never seen anything so beautiful in all my life." Sherri walked up to Miss Yoon to say hello.

"Thank you for that lovely compliment, Miss Yoon. This is my sister Sherri."

"Hello Sherri, nice to meet you. You are very pretty, you and your sister are twins, yes?"

"Yes, we are twins," smiled Sherri. "Thank you for coming."

"Congratulations on your grand opening for your yarn shop!" Miss Yoon smiled. She hung up her coat, opened her bag, and starting dusting. Terri looked through the window; more people were gathering on the sidewalk.

"Come look outside, Sherri. This is really exciting."

"My, look at all the people and the press. Can you believe it Terri?"

"I think I'd better pinch myself," replied Terri. The sisters were very excited. The waiters were setting out champagne glasses and napkins on trays. Miss Yoon, still dusting, kept repeating "What a beautiful shop."

The next forty-five minutes flew by. At 10:30 A.M. the doorbell rang again. It was Willa. "Half hour until grand opening time, you ladies ready?"

"As ready as we'll ever be," said Terri, smiling at her sister.

"Look!" said Sherri, looking through the window. "It's Mom and Dad, they're here!" Terri smiled.

"This is wonderful Sherri, Mom and Dad made it right on time." She opened the door. The sisters were extremely happy to see their parents. "Mom, Dad, it's wonderful to see you!"

"We are so happy you could be here with us today," said Sherri.

"We told you girls that we would not miss the grand opening," said their father, Mr. Constable.

"We are so happy to be here for this grand celebration," their mother added. They all hugged.

74

"Mom, Dad, you remember Willa, she's been our publicist since we started modeling," Sherri said.

"Nice to see you again, Mr. and Mrs. Constable," Willa smiled.

"Of course we remember Willa," replied the girls' mother.

"Willa, thank you for everything you have done for our daughters," said Mr. Constable. A waiter walked up to the group with glasses of champagne on a silver tray. Mr. Constable was the first to grab a glass. "I would like to make a toast." The others each took a glass and they held them in the air. "To our two lovely daughters who never gave up on their dreams. We love you very much, and we wish you much success with this beautiful yarn shop called Sistah Knit. May this venture bring you both splendid joy and happiness for years to come. We are very proud of what you two have accomplished. Cheers!" They clinked glasses all around.

"Thank you, Dad, that means so much to Sherri and me." The crowd outside grew larger. Media people of all sorts were packed in front of the shop: *The Amsterdam News, New York Daily News, The Times, Washington Post, Why We Knit Magazine, Cast On, Yarn on Our Needles* Magazine, *More Yarn* Magazine. Numerous Vloggers and Bloggers, *Knit Today, and Knit One Purl Two* Magazines. People stood outside knitting and crocheting. Others had brought their own knitted hats, shawls, gloves, and wraps to show off to the crowd.

"Well ladies, it's five minutes until show time!" announced Willa. She looked out the window. "I will monitor the press so you guys are not overwhelmed. This is going to be great." She turned to the sisters and winked. "Of course I'll let you know when your celebrity guests arrive. Time to go!" Their parents stood behind them, smiling and overjoyed with pride and happiness. The sisters walked hand in hand to the front door. Willa opened the door slowly. They stepped out to the cheering crowd. Camera lights flashed.

Sherri spoke first. "Harlem has always been a very special and soulful place filled with creative people. We sing, we dance, we build, and we create. The Studio Museum, The Schomburg Center for Research in Black Culture, the National Black Theatre, the famed Apollo Theatre ... and all the other wonderful places here in Harlem that support our culture and community. Now Harlem has Sistah Knit, right here on 125th and Fifth. A yarn shop that is home to those who love the crafts of knitting, crocheting, and fiber arts." The crowd cheered. Terri spoke next.

"As little girls, our mother taught us to knit as her mother had taught her when she was girl. Growing up we wore handmade sweaters, hats, scarves, and gloves. We love knitting. The Sistah Knit Yarn Shop will be an asset in this community. We hope to sponsor and lend support to other events and businesses. Our obstacles were many, but we remained determined to push our way through to get to this grand opening day." The crowd cheered in support. "The people of Harlem supported us all the way. We enjoyed modeling in Paris, but Harlem is our home and we are here to stay." The crowd, filled with Harlem natives, applauded loudly. "We are grateful to the press and especially grateful to all of you, the people of Harlem, for your love and support."

Together the sisters announced, "Good Morning everyone, welcome to Sistah Knit. *The first and only yarn shop in the history of Harlem.*" The crowd cheered even louder.

"Sistah Knit! Sistah Knit! Sistah Knit!" they chanted. The doors were finally opened to the public. People walked the long red carpet that stretched from the curb to front door of the shop. Smooth holiday jazz played as the waiters stood ready with trays of champagne and hors d'oeuvres for the guests. The crowd was filled with people of all kinds: young and old, black and white, Latino and Asian. Everyone was welcomed into Sistah Knit. The press people snapped pictures and jotted down notes. Glasses of champagne and wine disappeared from the trays. People were in awe of the beautiful skeins of yarns tucked neatly on the shelves and cubbies. Glass cases displayed unusual knitting needles and spindles made in Africa. Knitted garments hung on racks near the back of the shop. A beautiful velvet sofa and chair set looked dramatic against the mahogany floors. Several African bamboo baskets filled with skeins of yarn sat on the floor in every corner of the shop. Books about knitting, felting, crocheting, and yarn dying filled the shelves alongside books about African American history. The neighboring business people came by to wish the sisters good luck. Local community activists and politicians took advantage of the opportunity to have their photos taken with the sisters.

It was 11:45 A.M. when Michele and Ashley walked through the door. Terri spotted them from the far end of the shop. Waving a long slender arm, she called out, "Hey Michele, over here!" Michele and Ashley made their way through the crowd.

"Hi Terri!" Michele picked up a glass of champagne as she got closer to Terri.

"Hey Michele," said Terri. "Hi Ashley!" She gave them both warm hugs. "Ashley, you've grown into a beautiful young lady."

"Thank you, Auntie Terri," said Ashley. "You look beautiful too."

"Well thank you Ashley, but I have to work at looking good. You just have it naturally." Ashley giggled shyly.

"Yes, my baby is beautiful," Michele added. She looked around, "Terri this place is even more gorgeous now than it was earlier this week!"

"Well, yes, the flowers and a few other things really make a difference." A waiter came around with a warm tray of tiny salmon patties and chicken rolls. Terri continued as she grabbed one of each, "Sherri and I are very happy. Just look at all these people and press!" Michele bit into a salmon patty.

"My compliments to the chef, Terri. This is delicious."

Terri grinned, "If you think that's good, you should *see the chef*, he is fine for days!" They laughed together.

Sherri came over to greet Michele and Ashley. "Hello Michele. Thanks for being here. Hello Ashley!"

"Hi Auntie Sherri. Your shop is beautiful. I told Mommy that I would like to take some knitting lessons." The twins smiled.

"Well, you just let me and Auntie Terri know what your school schedule is, and we will arrange special times to teach you."

"Really?" Ashley beamed.

"Of course, and bring a classmate if you like. It'll be fun."

"Thank you, Auntie Sherri. I look forward to learning how to knit."

"Come in next week if you can and we'll pick out some yarn you like and look at a pattern for beginners. Okay?"

"Thank you. I would like that," said Ashley.

Michele smiled, "Well, it looks like my daughter might be knitting her mom and dad something for the holidays!"

Ashley looked at her mom. "Oh Mom. It'll take me a lot of time before I can make something."

"No, it won't," replied Terri, "You are a smart girl and you'll catch on quickly."

Sherri could see Willa escorting in more of the press. "Look Terri, more press is here."

"Ladies, go ahead and handle your business. Ashley and I will be fine." They waved goodbye.

People mingled around the shop enjoying the food and drink. Terri and Sherri relished being interviewed by the popular media people. Michele kept it a secret that GMN Network planned to stop by to do a story on the opening of Sistah Knit.

12:00 noon

Shante had not slept in this late in a very long time. She got out of bed slowly. She noticed the flyer for Sistah Knit sticking out of her backpack on the floor and reached for it:

> *Sistah Knit's Grand Opening. The first yarn shop in Harlem's history. A place for knitters to gather and share the love of creating handmade garments.*
> *Official opening time 11:00 A.M.*

She turned to Phillip and Cherise, who both slept soundly. Shante walked into the kitchen so as to not disturb them.

"*Good afternoon*," said Mrs. Brown, as she set hot biscuits on the table.

"I'm sorry Mrs. Brown, I didn't mean to sleep so late. I'll get Cherise and Phillip up right away."

"Hey! Slow down little missy. I was just kidding. You and Cherise have been through a lot over the past couple of days. You both deserved a good night's sleep. Please don't feel pressured while you are here." She sat down. "Shante, know one thing. I understand how things are. So relax yourself now, and eat some breakfast ... or should I say lunch?" They smiled. Shante took a seat across from Mrs. Brown.

"Thank you, Mrs. Brown." Shante took a bite of a biscuit and poured herself some coffee. "Hey, Mrs. Brown."

"Yes chile." Mrs. Brown buttered a biscuit.

"I was thinking ... it might be too much to take Cherise and Phillip to the yarn shop today."

"I thought about that too, Shante."

"Mrs. Brown, I can stay here and you can go."

"No chile. I'll stay home and you go. I can watch Cherise and Phillip for you." Shante frowned.

"Mrs. Brown, you've done so much for us already. I can't take advantage like that."

"You are not taking advantage, Shante. I want you to go. Tell me all about it later." Shante remained hesitant. "Go on, chile. It will be nice for you get out for a while with friends."

"Are you sure, Mrs. Brown?"

"As sure as I know I know my name is Mrs. Brown!" They both laughed. "I have some chores to do anyway. Cherise can help me, and you know Phillip is never a problem. You go on to the yarn shop. I might just have to find my old knitting needles and get back to making some things. Are you almost finished with that sweater you were knitting for Phillip?"

"Not yet. I still have little ways to go with it."

"You knit well, Shante."

"Thanks, Mrs. Brown. I learned how to knit at the library."

"Well good for you, it's good for young ladies to have a creative hobby. Keeps their minds off boys." Shante laughed.

"Do you really believe that, Mrs. Brown?"

"No, but it sounds good to say it. Now finish your breakfast and go on down to the knitting shop."

"Yes, Mrs. Brown, thank you." Shante figured she should tell her new friend she would be headed to the shop. "Mrs. Brown, would you mind if I used your house phone for a quick call?"

"Sure, Shante go right ahead." Shante picked up the handset of the beige rotary phone in the room she shared with Cherise. She dialed Justine's number and heard a voice pick up on the other end. "Hello Justine? It's Shante."

"Hi, Shante. How are you?"

"I'm fine. Are you going to the opening of Sistah Knit?"

"Yes, I'll be leaving my house in a little while."

"Okay great. Me too. I'm about to get dressed. See you later."

"Bye Shante, see you there."

Shante had never been to an opening of anything before. She did not want to embarrass herself by asking Justine what she should wear, so she decided on a simple red turtleneck sweater, a pair of black Calvin Klein jeans, and her ankle-high Jimmy Choo boots that Phil-Quan had given her as a birthday present a year ago. She was sure he got them hot off the street, but to her surprise he had actually purchased them from a store and gave her the sales receipt as proof. She spritzed her long thick braids with a honey-scented mist for some shine. She looked at herself in the mirror. She never wore much makeup, but for today, a touch of lip gloss would be nice. She put on a pair of large hoop earrings and her bronze bangle bracelet. Cherise started to wake up. "Hey Shante, where you going? "

"Well good morning, Cherise."

"Good morning."

"It's more like good afternoon, little sister. It's almost twelve thirty."

"What?" Cherise asked, rubbing her eyes. "I missed my morning cartoons. Why didn't you wake me up, Shante? Mrs. Brown said I could watch cartoons."

"Cherise, I just woke up at noon myself. Besides, it's Saturday, cartoons will be on all day. You better help Mrs. Brown out with some housework today."

"I will Shante, I promise," she paused, looking down at the floor. "Can I visit Mommy?"

"No Cherise! There's no way you're going up there alone." She saw her little sister jump at Shante's tone. She didn't mean to startle her. "Maybe I'll take you later ... but promise me you'll stay with Mrs. Brown all day. Okay?"

"But Shante, I just want to see Mommy for a little. I miss her."

"I know you miss her Cherise ... but this is the way things are right now. I'll take you to see Mommy later. Now get up from that bed and see what help Mrs. Brown needs." Phillip woke up from all the talking. Shante reached over Cherise and picked him up.

"Hey little man. Mommy is right here." She kissed him on the cheek. Mrs. Brown came to the doorway.

"I thought I heard the little fella. Give him here, Shante." Mrs. Brown reached for him. "Hello Cherise baby, come on and get washed up. I'll will fix you and Phillip some lunch. You two slept a long time."

"Mrs. Brown, I can stick around and help you out with these two," Shante said.

"No way. I got them, it's fine. Go on to the place. Where you say you're going?" Mrs. Brown asked. Shante giggled.

"To the opening of the new yarn shop in Harlem, Sistah Knit."

"Oh yes, you on to the Sistah Knit. We will be just fine here."

12:45 P.M.

Justine had been doing work all morning on her laptop. She looked at the clock on her night table, "Oh my gosh! It's twelve forty-five!" She quickly shut down the laptop and shoved it under her pillow on the bed. She rushed into the bathroom for quick shower. As soon as she finished, she rummaged through her closet, still wet from the shower. "Where are those new jeans I bought last week?" She took out a cream cashmere sweater from the dresser drawer. The smooth-sounding voice of Luther

Vandross singing "Any Love" played on the radio. Justine took a second to stop and think. The song reminded her of Ronald. She glanced at the engagement ring on her finger. "He's a good man ... " The song ended, and the voice of the DJ came on. Justine immediately went back to getting ready. Thoughts of her new record company pushed Ronald right out her mind.

1:00 P.M.

Rhonda had been feeling very tired over the past few days, and not hearing from Joe only made things worse. She placed her hand over her belly. Today she did not want to feel sorry for herself. She planned on going to the opening of Sistah Knit; she was not going to worry about her situation. Today she wanted to be free to enjoy herself with friends. She would have to tell them soon enough.

"One day at time" is what her mother would say. Rhonda knew each day that went by was a day closer to her becoming a new mother. The thought did frighten her as she imagined raising the child alone. She wanted to call Joe. She reached for her cell phone, but then put it back on the night stand. She looked at the flyer that was on the dresser. "Good for Terri and Sherri. I'm very happy for them." Rhonda got dressed and headed out the door.

1:45 P.M.

When Shante arrived at Sistah Knit, she was amazed at the size of the crowd. She moved her way through, searching for a place to sit. Waiters walked around with trays of finger food and drinks. Shante helped herself to a few tiny crab cakes and a glass of white wine. She noticed the beautiful skeins of yarn all around the shop.

The African art was not like anything she had ever seen before. She thought the entire place was beautiful. She noticed Terri and Sherri right away and figured they must be the owners, from the description Justine had given her. They were doing interviews with reporters. Someone tapped Shante on the shoulder.

"Hey Shante!"

"Oh hi Justine, you made it."

"Yes, I drove down. Traffic was not bad at all for a Saturday." She took Shante's hand, "Come on. I want to introduce you to my friends Sherri and Terri; they own Sistah Knit."

Rhonda was coming through the door when Michele noticed her.

"Hey Rhonda, over here!"

"Hey Michele! My, what a crowd. Hello Ashley, how are you, sweetie?"

"I am fine, Miss Rhonda."

"Ashley, you are growing up looking just like your mother. Beautiful."

"Thank you," replied Ashley with a shy smile.

"Ashley, why don't you go see if Terri and Sherri need any help."

"Mommy, they hired all the help they need."

"She's right," said Rhonda, smiling.

"Well then just go and look at the skeins of yarn for a while."

"Mom. Just say you want to have girl talk with Miss Rhonda," the ladies both laughed and Ashley waved bye to go mingle with the crowd.

"How are you? Really?" asked Michele.

"I'm all right Michele, I just didn't sleep well last night."

"Are you sure you're all right, Rhonda?"

"Yes, I just need to get a good night's rest."

"Has that young tenderoni been keep you up all night long?" Michele asked, smiling.

"Well, yes. I think Joe is the Energizer bunny. He just keeps going and going and going!" They laughed. "How is Charles doing?"

"He is okay. He's the energizer bunny at work. He keeps going and going."

"Michele, Charles provides very well for you and Ashley."

"Yes, he does, but I contribute to the household as well. I do all right at GMN."

"I know you do Michele, but you know Charles is an old-fashioned man who wants to make sure his family wants for nothing."

"Well if he really wants to take care of his family he needs to be home more and take care of me a little more between the sheets."

Rhonda frowned, "Michele, you work long hours as well. Do you think Charles is having an affair?" Michele shushed her.

"Rhonda! Don't say that too loud. I don't want any rumors to start." She looked around the room. "No girl, Charles is not that kind of man."

"You're right. I mean, Charles has loved you forever. You're the only woman for him."

"I love him too. We both just seem to be like two ships passing in the night. We had dinner as a family this week. It was nice. First time in a long time. Our relationship is different and I don't like it. I think we really need to find ourselves again."

"Have you talked to him about it?"

"No ... sometimes I tell myself that it's all in my mind and it'll work itself out."

"Has Ashley noticed anything?"

"She is busy with school and friends. Besides, she loves her father so much, she would never see any flaws in him." Rhonda took two glasses of wine from a tray as a waiter walked by.

She handed one to Michele and Michele took a sip. "I don't want us to grow apart because of our jobs." Rhonda handed back her glass, untouched, to another waiter as he passed. Michele looked at her and thought, *What an odd thing to do.*

"Remember Michele, you and Charles both chose your career paths."

"I know, and I want us to do better than just okay in our marriage. I want a great marriage." Michele took another sip of wine. "Why did you put your wine back on the tray? Was something wrong with it?"

"No there is nothing wrong with the wine ... I just realized I didn't want any." Rhonda, in need of a distraction, waved to Terri and Sherri across the room. They were still busy doing interviews.

"Are you sick, Rhonda?

"No, I'm not sick. I just need to ..."

"Need to what?" Michele frowned. "Are you watching your weight again Rhonda? Girl, one or two glasses of wine is not going to ruin your fabulous figure! How you've managed to keep that hourglass figure after having two kids is a wonder to me. I have to work out almost day and night to maintain my weight, and you know how much I hate working out. I wish I could take a magic pill and be thin for life. You know what I mean?"

She was about to take another sip of wine just when Rhonda blurted out, "Michele, I'm pregnant."

"You're *what*?" She was in disbelief. She lowered her voice to a soft whisper, "Are you serious Rhonda? How the hell?" Rhonda stayed silent, her eyes wide. "Rhonda, I don't know what to say. Talk to me girl."

"I found out a couple of weeks ago. I told Joe; he's freaking out." Michele waited for her to add more. Rhonda continued, "We got into a heated argument and he walked out. I haven't heard from him since." Michele put her hand on Rhonda's shoulder.

"What are you going to do?"

"I don't know. I have a lot to think about."

"What do you expect Joe to do?"

"I expect him to stand up and take care of his responsibilities like a real man."

"You're keeping the baby?"

"Michele, how could you ask me such a thing?"

"I'm sorry Rhonda, you know I'm pro-choice. It's just that I – "

"It's just what, Michele?" Rhonda crossed her arms.

"Rhonda, don't get me wrong, Joe is a cool guy and all, but I just don't see him as the father type."

"Well Michele, it's not what you see or don't see that matters, is it?" Rhonda was offended.

"I know, you're right. It's your decision ... I'm sorry. I don't want to see you get hurt." Rhonda sighed.

"I'm already deeply hurt by Joe's reaction," she paused. "I know he's younger and doesn't want to be tied down, and I knew that before getting involved with him. But I didn't expect to get pregnant!" She tried to calm herself, remembering they were at an event. "Michele you're the only person I've told besides Joe."

"Rhonda, I am here for you, anything you need."

"I know ... thanks Michele." Rhonda picked up a glass of wine from another waiter passing by. "One glass of wine won't hurt."

Justine and Shante were having a great time together. Justine pulled out her American Express Gold card to pay for the five hundred dollars' worth of yarns and needles. Shante was amazed at how much yarn Justine had put on the counter.

"What are going to make with all that yarn, Justine?"

"I don't know yet; I'll think of something. Are you buying anything today?"

"No, not today, maybe next week." The truth was, Shante didn't have any money to spend. Justine was feeling happy as she bopped her head to the mellow jazz music. Terri joined them.

"We'll hold your bag behind the counter, Justine," she said.

"Thanks Terri. This is a fabulous grand opening, so many people and press!"

"Sales are going great," said Terri. The photographers took hundreds of pictures of Terri and Sherri engaging with customers. The sisters answered questions about knitting, yarns, and stylish patterns. One customer asked about purchasing some of the beautiful art work on the wall. The twins apologized and told them it wasn't for sale.

"This is a wonderland for knitters," said another customer. "It feels like I am in the motherland of Africa or at a warm country home in South Carolina."

"Well that's the feeling we want our customers to enjoy when they visit Sistah Knit. This is home to all our customers," said Terri. A waiter placed a fresh tray of southern baked chicken fingers and crab cakes on the far end of the counter. The champagne and wine continued to flow. The crowd outside cheered with excitement as limousine after limousine pulled up alongside the curb. Willa motioned to Terri and Sherri, waving them toward the front door, "Sherri, Terri, look, your celebrity guests have arrived!" Sherri squeezed her sister's hand. All excited, Michele, Rhonda, Justine, and Shante hurried to the front door. The others inside gathered at the display window, trying to get a peek. The crowd was screaming as Beyoncé stepped out of the limo with her sister Solonge and their mother at her side. The paparazzi cameras flashed like bolts of lightning. The crowd went wild, calling out "Beyoncé, we love you!" Beyoncé waved at the welcoming fans while making her way to the front door of Sistah Knit. The crowd screamed with even more excitement as the next celebrities exited from the limos, one after the other: Oprah, Tyler Perry, and Miss Cicely Tyson stepped onto the red carpet. Alicia Keys stepped out of the next limo.

"Alicia, Alicia! We love you Alicia!" The cameras captured Alicia's beautiful smile and grace as she entered the yarn shop. Yet another limo pulled up, the chauffer opened the door, and the crowd cheered as they saw a beautiful black woman step out. She wore an autumn-orange thick wool knitted coat. Her one-of-a-kind orange diamond hoop earrings gleamed brightly against the backdrop of her natural afro, which was sprinkled with glitter.

"That's Gigi, that's Gigi of GGmadeit!" The cameras flashed as Gigi walked up the red carpet. The paparazzi captured pictures of Gigi giving hugs to her adoring fans.

The crowd was still calling her name. "Gigi, we love you! You rock Gigi, ORANGE FOREVER!" Several fans held up skeins of orange yarn and knitting needles while calling out her name.

Inside the shop, women from the Harlem Knitting Circle who met every Saturday at the George Library in Harlem came by to congratulate and welcome Sherri and Terri to neighborhood. The turnout of people made the sisters feel truly loved. They stood in the center of the store. Sherri clinked a knife against her glass.

"May we have your attention please! Hello! May we have your attention please!" The room fell silent and everyone focused their attention on the twins. The only sound that could be heard was the shutter clicks of cameras. Terri and Sherri looked around at everyone. Sherri looked to Terri, indicating that she should speak first. Terri smiled.

"Hello everyone. Once again, thank you so much for coming to the grand opening of Harlem's first-ever yarn shop, Sistah Knit. My sister Sherri and I are thrilled to be a part of this thriving community." Their parents looked on with pride as Terri continued, "There was no other place besides Harlem where we wanted to open this shop." The crowd clapped in agreement. "We will be a positive force in the community. Thank you to everyone who supported us. The elected officials, the churches, and the wonderful people of Harlem for opening your arms to us." The crowd applauded again. "Now I'll let my sister Sherri speak."

"Hello and welcome, everyone. On behalf of both of us, I would like to thank you all for coming out today and celebrating this joyous event with us. Thank you for your kind words and support. Sistah Knit has been a dream of ours for a long time. Today we are grateful that our dream has finally become a reality. We would like to thank our parents for being here today and for always encouraging us to follow our dreams no matter how big or small. Without their love and support, Sistah Knit would not exist. This store means a lot to us, and we sincerely wish to make it a place for knitters to come and relax while enjoying their craft. A special thanks to all our celebrity guests who have taken time out of their busy schedules to be here with us today ... Beyoncé and Alicia, you and your families have shown my sister and me so much love. We thank you for your lovely gifts of gold and pearl knitting needles." Willa held the needles up to the crowd's murmurs. Sherri continued, "Miss Cicely Tyson. You are truly an icon of beauty and strength. We are extremely touched that you have joined us here today. You have always spoken for women to have the right to be and to dream. We are humbly grateful to you." Some people wiped tears from their eyes.

"Miss Oprah, we grew up watching *The Oprah Show*. I don't believe there is anyone in this room today that has not learned something from you about living and being their best self."

"Sherri and I are thrilled beyond words to have you at this grand opening. Tyler Perry, you have proved that keeping God first and trusting him along with hard work and never giving up will prove positive results. Your personal story has motivated Sherri and me for years. We are so grateful that you could share this wonderful experience with us." Sherri smiled at her sister.

"And Miss GG, the queen of orange and class. Your story and blog keep us in the know on what knitting is all about. You have shared yourself like no other. That is why so many people love you. We are especially honored to have you join us today. Your Saturday questions, livestreams, and posts are amazing. We thank you for your being beautifully authentic in your own coco skin. We have learned that the honest and humble beauty inside is truly the beauty that shines outside. Our publicist Willa informed us that you will be part of our Knitting and Tea Time once a month."

The crowd clapped and cheered. "To the Harlem Knitting Circle, for holding down a loving environment for knitters at the library for so many years, we salute you for your longevity and undying dedication. Terri and I want to share in that environment of love and support. We have classes for all sorts of knitters starting next week. Please check out our website and find us on any social media platform." The crowd clapped and cheered again.

Sherri continued, "And last but not least, we would like to thank our mother and father, for years of love, life lessons, and support. To Willa, our publicist who stood by us for years. Our close friends Michele Nelson, Justine Whitaker, and Rhonda James, and to this community, for your tireless work of handing out tons of Sistah Knit flyers and spreading the word about Sistah Knit. Thank you to everyone for sharing this happy occasion with us today. Please know that Sistah Knit is a place where you can come sit and have a hot cup of coffee or tea or cocoa. This is a safe space."

"We are grateful to be a part of the heartbeat of Harlem. Sherri and I thank you all so very much."

The crowd cheered and gave a loud round of applause. The music resumed and people went on mingling. Shante could not believe her eyes. Alicia Keys was standing only a few feet away from her. Shante felt wonderful. She realized her newly found friends were women of class and achievement. They had career goals, they dressed well, and they lived in nice homes. They had celebrity status. Her determination to make a better life for herself and her loved ones became stronger than ever.

6:30 P.M.

The crowd finally started to dwindle down. The remaining six customers in the shop had purchased cotton, wool, silk, and cashmere yarns and signed up for knitting classes. Just then Miss Yoon returned to the shop.

"Miss Yoon, did you forget something from earlier?" Sherri asked.

"No, I came back to help clean up after the big event." The catering staff had already been picking up empty wine glasses and crumpled napkins. Terri and Sherri were pleased.

"Why thank you, Miss Yoon. That is very kind of you."

"My pleasure, ladies." Miss Yoon put on her rubber gloves and started cleaning.

"Whoa, what a fantastic day," Terri said as she turned the "closed" sign on the door. Sherri flopped down in a soft cushioned chair across from Michele and Rhonda.

"I am *exhausted*," she said, kicking off her shoes and rubbing her feet together. Justine and Shante were sitting on a large plush sofa with big multi-colored pillows. Terri joined them, sitting on the floor and resting her head back on a large pillow.

"This was just a wonderful event," announced Justine. "I mean, Beyoncé and Alicia Keys, Cicely Tyson, Oprah, Tyler Perry, and GG – who's coming next!? What's up with that, ladies? How did you get them to come?"

"Willa really hooked us up," Sherri said.

"She sure did," replied Justine. "By the way everyone, this is Shante; we met on the Metro North."

"Nice to meet you," Shante said. "The grand opening was beautiful!" Shante was excited to be a part of something so special.

"Thank you for coming, Shante. You're always welcome here," Terri said.

"Justine told us she was bringing a friend. Glad you enjoyed yourself," said Sherri.

Terri looked around the room. "Hey Michele, where's Ashley?" she asked.

"Her classmate Cindy and her mom came by to pick her up for a sleepover. They'll drop her off early tomorrow, before church."

"Good for Ashley," said Terri. Sherri looked over at Rhonda.

"Hey girl, how you doing? You look sleepy."

"I'm okay," said Rhonda, half groggily. "Just didn't sleep well last night."

"That young stud of yours keeping you up all night?" Terri asked. Justine and the twins giggled. Shante smiled, remembering how she and Phil-Quan would spend hours between the sheets.

"Well, something like that," Rhonda replied.

"That's what happens when you date younger men," said Sherri.

"Tell me about it," replied Rhonda. The catering staff was all packed up and headed out the front door.

"Good night everyone," waved the head chef. "Terri and Sherri, congratulations and best of luck." Terri stood up and held the door for them.

"Thank you all for a great job today! The food was just delicious. Sherri and I really appreciate the service and all you have done for us. Goodnight."

"You're welcome ladies. There's a bottle of champagne in the back. It was delivered earlier today. It's in the fridge on the top shelf. Looks expensive."

"Thank you," said Terri as she walked him to the door. Once he was gone, she headed to the kitchen and came back with the champagne and a tray with six glasses. Justine stood up to help. Terri opened the card that was attached and read it aloud:

> *Congratulations on the opening of Sistah Knit. All the best. From Bradford Wilson.*
>
> *P.S. Give my regards to Michele.*

Michele's heart skipped a beat when she heard his name. Bradford was her first love before she had married Charles. Bradford had become a football player with the Atlanta Falcons.

"Well, well, well Michele. It looks like you have a secret admirer," said Sherri. Michele blushed.

"You ladies know that Bradford and I used to date way, *way* back in the day."

"Yes, I remember," said Rhonda. "I recall you knitting a sweater for him."

"A sweater he never wore," said Michele.

"Well it *was* a very bright blue," Rhonda said, holding back laughter. Terri poured the champagne. Once she finished, she inspected the bottle,

"Holy ... this champagne must have cost about two grand!" Everyone was in awe, everyone except Michele. Sherri held up her glass.

"Well ladies, let's have a toast to *way* back in the day – Michele and Bradford."

"No guys," said Michele, "it's not like that anymore. I'm going to interview Bradford in a few weeks about his career with the Falcons. For work."

"Oh, so you're going see your old boo?" asked Rhonda with a big smile on her face.

"No, it's nothing like that and you know it girl. Strictly business!" Michele lightly punched Rhonda on the shoulder.

"Whatever," said Sherri. "Let's just toast to a brighter future for everyone here."

"Amen to that," said Justine.

"I hear you girl," said Rhonda.

"Me too. A brighter future. I'm all for that," said Shante. They clinked their glasses and took a sip. Rhonda barely let the champagne touch her tongue. Michele and Rhonda exchanged a glance.

Rhonda whispered, "Oh, what a tangled web we weave." Michele whispered back, "Look at the pot calling the kettle black."

"Hey, what are you two whispering about over there?" Sherri asked.

"Nothing girl," replied Michele. "Rhonda was just teasing me about Bradford." Shante felt lightheaded. She leaned forward a little.

"Are you all right Shante?" asked Terri.

"Uh yes, the champagne is good. I just don't want to drink too much. I want my head together when I take the train back to Yonkers."

"I understand what you mean," said Sherri.

"Hey no worries," said Justine, nonchalantly. "I'll drive you home, Shante."

"You don't have to go out of your way on my account, Justine. I can take the Metro North."

"No way," said Justine, "and it's not out of my way at all. It's on my way toward Tarrytown.

Shante was grateful. "Oh ... okay, thank you Justine."

"You're welcome, it's no problem!" Justine moved closer to Shante. "Hey, how's that sweater you're knitting for your son coming along?" she asked.

"It's coming along fine. I hope to be done in another week or two."

"How old is your son?" Michele asked.

"He is two years old and quite the handful."

"Oh, I remember those days," Michele said with a sigh.

"Terrible twos, exactly!" laughed Shante. Rhonda grew flush at the thought of chasing a toddler around, for the third time in life. She excused herself to the restroom.

"Rhonda, are you all right?" Sherri asked.

"She'll be okay," said Michele, trying to draw attention away from Rhonda. Justine stood up and stretched her arms out. She let out a muffled yawn. "Well ladies, it's been wonderful, but I need to get going."

"Yes, me as well," Michele said. Rhonda returned to join them.

"You too, Rhonda?" Sherri asked, concerned.

"Yes girl, I'm fine. Probably just a bit too much champagne."

"Rhonda, you hardly touched your champagne," Sherri said.

Rhonda quickly hugged her to keep her quiet. "Thanks so much for having us."

"Your shop is very nice," Shante said, "I'll be coming back."

"Please do!" said Terri. "Wait, before you go ... we have a little something for you all." Terri went into the oak-lined closet and pulled out four large gold-colored glittered bags with purple ribbons tied around the handles. The bags were filled with yarns, needles, and pattern booklets.

"What's all this?" asked Rhonda.

"What are you up to Terri?" Michele asked. "I just received a box of yarn from you and Sherri."

"And I just purchased some yarn from you earlier today," added Justine.

"I know you did, but this is a thank-you gift from Sherri and me." Terri handed each of the women a bag. Shante was so happy considering she didn't have any money to buy anything.

"Thank you very much, Terri and Sherri, this is very kind of you to do this." Shante couldn't help but feel a little embarrassed. "I ... I just met you today, I should be supporting your business," she said.

"No Shante, it's our pleasure," replied Terri. "Make something nice for yourself."

"I will," said Shante.

Sherri looked around the shop smiling. "Well, on Monday morning, Sistah Knit will be officially open for business."

9:30 P.M.

Rhonda was exhausted by the time she arrived home. She was having another restless night, tossing and turning while having vivid dreams of arguing with Joe about her pregnancy and then making passionate love to him. She dreamt she had married Joe and later divorced him. At one point during the night she dreamt she gave birth to twin boys that looked exactly like Joe but they never stopped crying. She dreamt she had twin girls that screamed day and night, and that they, too, looked exactly like Joe. She dreamt she had a dog and a cat that looked like Joe. She woke up in a cold sweat breathing heavily. She dashed into the bathroom and splashed cold water on her face.

She pulled a towel from the rack to dry her face and looked at herself in the mirror.

Back in her bedroom she noticed a green light blinking on her answering machine. Sitting on the edge of her bed, she played back the message.

"Rhonda, it's Joe." Hearing his voice somehow frightened her. She clenched her bathrobe tightly around her chest. "I've been thinking about your situation, Rhonda, and my feelings have not changed," he paused. "I can't promise you anything Rhonda ... I can't marry you, it's complicated."

"What the hell could be complicated about your girlfriend being pregnant with your baby?" Rhonda said. "I want you to do the right thing for the baby." It was 3:40 A.M. She got back into bed and soon fell asleep.

Sunday, November 2nd, 2008

8:00 A.M.

Mrs. Brown was getting dressed for church. Gospel music from the Christian television channel was playing so loudly it woke Shante from a deep sleep. Mrs. Brown, at the top of her lungs sang, *"Oh Lord Jesus, take my hand, lead me on!"* Shante entered the living room smiling.

"Good morning Mrs. Brown."

"Good morning Shante, praise the Lord! How was the grand opening yesterday?" She turned the volume of the TV down.

"It was great. The store owners are so nice. They're these beautiful twin sisters who used to be models in Paris. They gave me a gift bag filled with yarn. They treated me like they'd known me for years." Mrs. Brown smiled.

"Glad to hear it child. Praise the Lord for his favor!" She looked at herself in the mirror that hung on the wall above her faded blue sofa. She adjusted the wide brim hat on her head, making sure the large red bow on the front was perfectly positioned. "I made some breakfast for y'all, it's warm in the oven." She picked up her purse and strutted out the door singing. *"Jesus, my sweet Jesus, my savior come to thee!"*

"Enjoy the service, Mrs. Brown!" Shante giggled as she could hear Mrs. Brown's voice echoing off the cool brick walls of the hallway. Cherise shortly walked into the living room, also awoken by Mrs. Brown's singing. She sat herself in front of the television to watch cartoons. Phillip trailed directly behind Cherise, in little baby steps. Shante laid out the breakfast Mrs. Brown had prepared, "Come eat, Mrs. Brown made a good breakfast for us." Phillip struggled trying to climb into the chair at the table. Shante sat him on her lap. Cherise said grace and they began to eat. Phillip liked grape jelly on his toast; he always managed to get most of it all over his face. Cherise laughed at him, calling him jelly mouth. She handed Shante a napkin to clean his face.

"Shante, can we go see Mama today?" Shante took a moment to respond.

"Okay Cherise ... if you really want to."

"I really want to see her today."

"All right, after we eat and get dressed, we'll go upstairs." Cherise tried to hide her happiness.

"Thanks, Shante." Shante watched her play with Phillip at the table. *She's just a child who misses her mommy,* she thought.

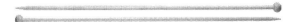

Shante dreaded the elevator ride to their mother's place. When they got upstairs, she wasn't surprised to find the door unlocked. They walked in slowly; Shante held Phillip's hand tightly, keeping him close by her side. Cherise looked around nervously; the apartment was unusually quiet. There was no television or radio playing and no people talking, and Debra was nowhere in sight. Shante led Cherise to their mother's bedroom. They could see a figure rustling under the covers.

"Mommy!" Cherise called out. Debra removed the blanket from over her head. Her bushy afro desperately needed washing and grooming.

"Hi baby," Debra lazily called out. Cherise hopped onto the bed and gave her mother a big kiss on the cheek.

"Mommy, I miss you."

"I miss you too, Cherise. You doing good in school?"

"Yes, Mommy. I got an A on my math test." Debra sat up and put her arms around Cherise.

"That's my smart baby girl." She glared at Shante. Shante pursed her lips to keep from saying something she would regret. Cherise was eager to explain herself to her mother.

"Mommy, there were so many people in our house the other day and I ... I was afraid, so I left. I tried to wake you up." Debra stared at her.

"You were worried about your mama?" Cherise looked away.

"Mommy, I don't like it here. I want to go back to Mrs. Brown's house." Debra was displeased.

"Why don't you want to stay here? This is your home."

"Mrs. Brown said we can stay as long as we want." Shante did not want this conversation to drag out, and she finally spoke up.

"Well, you know where you can find us. Not that you would ever come looking." Debra quickly clapped back at her.

"Don't start your mess with me this morning, Shante. I really ain't in the mood for your smart-ass mouth." Shante reached out and grabbed Cherise's hand. She had been holding Phillip on her hip.

"Come on Cherise, let's go!"

"Wait, Mommy!" cried out Cherise. Dante had overheard the talking and nonchalantly sauntered into the room.

"Hey family, what's going on around here this morning?" He turned to Shante. "Hey sis, how are you?" He lowered his face to Phillip. "Hey lil' man, how you doing? Give your uncle D a high five." Dante held up his hand and Phillip slapped his little palm into his uncle's dry and calloused hand. Shante wanted to leave as soon as possible; she turned Phillip away from him.

"Dante, you know how I feel about ratchet living. I want Phillip to shake a person's hand, not give them a high five."

Debra sucked on her teeth, "Yeah Dante, you know your bougie-ass sister thinks she better than us!"

"I am not bougie, Mama. I just want my son to have some manners!" Cherise had started to cry. She wiped away her tears and released her hand from Shante. She sat on the bed next to her mother.

"Okay Mommy, Shante. Please just calm down for a minute."

"Listen, sister," Dante said, "It's just a damn high five. Nobody around this neighborhood shakes hands. You know how we brothers get down around here."

"That is exactly what I don't want Phillip learning. How *y'all brothers* get down round here."

"Well who the hell is he gonna shake hands with around here?" asked Debra, rolling her eyes.

"This is why I don't like being in this house. Phillip will know how to greet people. You all are just small-thinking people!"

Debra laughed. "Oh, so now we small-thinking people?" asked Dante.

"Yes! You and your crazy-ass mother are two small-thinking people."

"Shante! Don't talk about me in my own house!" shouted Debra.

"Would you prefer I talk about you behind your back?"

"Shante, don't make me get up out this bed," Debra growled. Shante grabbed Cherise's arm once more.

"Come on girl. Let's go!" The rest of Shante's siblings had been awaked by the noise and were coming out of their bedrooms as she entered the hall.

Her sister Denise asked, "Hey what's going on? You and Mama going at it again?"

"What's up with all the shouting?" asked Michael. He tightened the du-rag on his head.

"Nothing going on," Debra replied, "just Shante acting like a damn fool again."

"Mama, why you always giving Shante a hard time?" asked Denise.

Debra glared at her. "Your sister thinks she better than everyone else."

"So what Mama? She can think of herself any way she wants," shouted Denise.

"Shut up girl, nobody asked you for your damn opinion!" said Debra.

"What the hell is wrong with everybody?" asked their sister Tracy. Dante raised his hands in defense.

"Ladies, ladies, can we have some peace in this house?"

"Dante, will you mind your damn business?" shouted Debra.

"No Mama, you're a damn drama queen sometimes!"

"Dante, don't be acting like your uppity-ass sister!" Debra then reached for the pack of cigarettes on her night table and lit one.

"Mama I told you about smoking around Phillip."

"Girl don't tell me who I can and cannot smoke around in my own damn house!" Shante pulled on Cherise's arm. "Come on Cherise, we're leaving!"

"Cherise don't have to go nowhere!" Debra shouted.

"Cherise, come on now!" Cherise stared at her mother as she was dragged along by her big sister. Dante put his arm around Cherise and told her to be good. She smiled with tears still in her eyes.

"I'll be good Dante."

"Come to your mama, Cherise," said Debra. "Mama loves you, sweetie." Cherise rushed into her mother's arms one last time, and Debra put out her cigarette. She hugged her baby girl tightly, knowing in her heart that she was not fully fit to care for her.

"Go on with your sister," she looked at Shante.

"Phillip, give your grandma a kiss before we go," said Shante. Debra hugged Phillip and kissed him on his cheeks. Dante started to slap Phillip five and then looked at Shante and decided against it. He reached out to shake his nephew's hand.

"Bye lil fella." Phillip shook his uncle's hand. Looking up at Dante with an innocent smile, he gurgled, "Bye-bye." Shante smiled.

"Thanks Dante."

"Good to see you, Sis."

"Good to see you too, brother."

"Cherise, come see your mama again soon. Maybe I'll come down to Mrs. Brown's apartment to visit you." Cherise looked back and smiled at her mother as she followed Shante out of the room.

10:15 A.M.

Charles saw Michele watching him as he adjusted his Italian silk tie in the mirror. He smiled at her using his reflection.

"Are you ready, Sweetheart?

"I will be, as soon you zip my dress for me." Michele walked up to the full-length mirror, admiring her handsome husband.

"New dress?" He pulled the zipper up her dress slowly and traced his finger against her spine.

"Yes, it is."

"I love the peach color against your skin." He smiled at her.

"Thank you, Charles." Michele called out, "Ashley, are you ready?"

"Yes, Mom, I'm ready to go!" Ashley came to her parents' bedroom door; she was holding her coat and bible. "Look Mom, I found the hat you knitted for me last winter. Doesn't it look cute?" Charles kissed his daughter on the forehead and tugged Michele on the arm.

"Come on ladies, we don't want to be late."

"Daddy, we're never late for church!" They laughed.

As he opened the car door for Michele and Ashley, Charles asked,

"Michele baby, how was the grand opening of Sistah Knit?"

"It was *fabulous,* Charles. The community really came out to show support. They got a lot of sales. Terri and Sherri were excited to see Ashley."

"Daddy, I'm going to start taking knitting lessons at Sistah Knit!"

"Good for you baby girl, that's great!"

"Charles, you have to see the yarn shop; it's absolutely beautiful. The twins did a marvelous job at decorating." Michele smiled as she looked over her neighborhood through the car window. "Sistah Knit will be good for the community. Knitting has become such a lost art." She glanced at her daughter. "You don't see many girls Ashley's age knitting. I learned to sew and knit when I was growing up. This shop will bridge the knitting community together, along with the Harlem Knitting Circle."

"Well honey, these are different times we live in today."

"Yes Charles, it is. I'm so happy to see girls playing sports and challenging their minds and physical abilities ... but there is still something to be said when a child is taught a craft using their hands to create something other than a text message." Ashley smiled at her mother as she pretended to send a text message.

"Come on, Michele. You know Ashley is a pretty well-rounded young lady. She gets good grades at school. She's liked by her peers and teachers. She spends time with her grandparents ... so what if she texts a few times a week?"

"How about several times, Charles." As he looked over his shoulder to squeeze the car into a parking spot, he winked at Ashley.

"I saw that!" said Michele, smiling at the both of them.

"Ten-thirty. See Daddy? This is the same time we walked into church last week. We're never late."

He held Ashley's hand as they walked toward the front steps. "Baby girl, you are right, we're never late." The family took their usual seats in the pew as the choir sang "Amazing Grace." Michele smiled at a few familiar faces. Charles focused on the choir. Ashley was seated next to one of her classmates and giggled softly. Michele glanced at the crowd to her right and suddenly felt as if she could not breathe. Seated in the row in front of her was Bradford Wilson, her ex. She closed her eyes to focus her breathing. She could not help but stare. Bradford caught notice of her and mouthed "hello." Michele just stared. He blew a kiss and she quickly turned away. She didn't want Charles or Ashley to notice her discomfort. She sang softly along with the choir, trying to look anywhere else but in Bradford's direction.

"Amazing grace, how sweet the sound ..." She could still feel Bradford's eyes on her.

The pastor took his place at the lectern at the side of the altar.

"Good Morning, everyone. This is the day the Lord has made. Let us rejoice and be glad in it." The congregation roared a singular "amen." Michele thought, *What the hell is Bradford doing here?*

"Oh Lord forgive me!" she whispered.

"What did you say?" asked Charles.

"Nothing sweetheart, I was thinking out loud." Charles held his wife's hand tightly. The pastor continued speaking.

"Without love we are nothing. For God so loved the world that he gave his only begotten son Jesus to die on the cross for us. God wants us to love one another. Love your neighbor as yourself. Husbands, love your wives as Christ loves the church." Charles squeezed Michele's hand a bit more. Bradford's attention was now on the pastor. "Wives, love your husbands. Children love and obey your parents, that is the first commandment of the Bible." Michele's mind wandered. She would be interviewing Bradford for GMN Sports Special in a few weeks. She couldn't help but wonder what her life would have been like if she had married him, an NFL quarterback.

"A good wife loves her husband," the pastor boomed. "*Let the church say Amen!*" The congregation clapped and shouted.

"Amen! Yes Lord, Halleluiah!" he continued.

"Divorce is running rampant among Christians. Couples don't want to work things out these days! You can get a divorce online in this fast-paced world of technology we live in. Meet your mate online and a few years down the road just divorce him or her online. That is not the Lord's way for his people!" The sound of Amen flowed through the church again. Michele was trying hard to stay focused on the sermon. The choir began to sing another song.

"Jesus, Jesus, Jesus is mine. Oh, Glory divine." The collection plate was passed around. She refused to look in Bradford's direction again. Church Announcements were soon being read:

" ... A bake sale to raise funds for the Annual kids' summer camp. Choir rehearsal is on Thursday evenings at 6:00 P.M. and Bible Study is on Wednesdays at 7:00 P.M. Please see Sister Mattie if you know someone who should be placed on our daily prayer list. The Sistah Knit Yarn shop had their grand opening yesterday. They gave a big offering from their first day of sales. We thank them for their generosity."

When the service was finally over, Michele simply wanted to get up and leave, but as usual, Charles had to greet and chat with the pastor and other parishioners. Ashley, too, was chatting with a few friends. Michele tried her best to avoid getting anywhere close to Bradford. Many of the congregation knew him as the all-star football player. He was surrounded by a crowd of boys asking for his autograph and picture. A few of the single ladies looking for a husband gathered closely around him.

Michele noticed Terri and Sherri near the door and quickly made her way over to them.

"Terri, Sherri, *praise the Lord*, it's good to see you."

"Hey Michele, nice to see you too," said Terri.

"Nice dress," Sherri said.

"Thank you. Where are your parents?"

"Oh, they're inside mingling with old friends."

"Where's Charles?" asked Terri.

"He's probably busy telling Pastor how much he enjoyed the sermon." Bradford walked up behind Michele and tapped her on the shoulder before the twins could alert her. She turned around and was startled to see him standing right in front of her. The twins cringed.

"Oh! Hello Bradford."

"Hello Michele," Bradford smiled, "nice to see you." Michele looked for any distraction.

"Um, Bradford, these are my friends Terri and Sherri." He smiled at them.

"Hello ladies, nice to meet you. Congratulations on opening your yarn shop." The twins' parents came over to join their daughters. Mr. Constable recognized Bradford right away. He extended his hand to him.

"Hey ... I know who you are, young man. You play for the Atlanta Falcons!"

"Yes I do Sir," Bradford was never one to shy away from attention. Mr. Constable chuckled.

"Well, I *am* a Dallas Cowboys fan, but I will admit you do play a mean game of football, Bradford."

"Thank you, Sir." Mr. Constable patted Bradford on the shoulder.

"Keep up the good work."

Charles walked up to the group. "Hello everyone!" he shook Mr. Constable's hand and gave Mrs. Constable a kiss on the cheek. He took Michele's hand and pulled her close to him. "Hey Bradford," he said pleasantly.

"Hello Charles, nice to see you and Michele again."

"What brings you to town?" Charles asked, eyebrows raised.

Bradford chuckled, "Does a brother need a reason to visit the place where he grew up?" Charles was about to respond when the twins' parents excused themselves. They told their daughters they would wait for them in the car. Michele stood between the two men trying to defuse the mild tension.

"I'm interviewing Bradford for the sports segment at GMN next week."

Terri jumped right in with her. "Yeah Charles! Michele was telling us about that. Bradford is an outspoken Obama supporter."

"Sounds exciting," replied Sherri, watching Michele. Charles stared at Michele; he was surprised she had not mentioned this to him. Bradford looked Charles directly in the eye.

"Well, I'm in town visiting some family and taking care of NFL business."

"We should get going," Michele said, pulling Charles' hand. She was anxious to leave Bradford's presence. "Where's Ashley?" Charles put his arm around her.

"Have a blessed day, everyone." The couple said goodbye to the group and began their search for Ashley. Bradford gave Michele's legs a long stare as she walked away. Sherri slapped him on his muscular arm.

"Bradford, stop it! Michele is a married woman."

"I'm just looking, no harm in that, is there?"

"Yeah right. It's the way you're looking at her," Sherri crossed her arms. Bradford grinned.

"Michele is a fine woman. Always has been, always will be."

"She's a fine *married* woman, Bradford. You remember that," said Terri.

Bradford thought, "Yes she is, and I never stopped loving her."

11:45 A.M.

"Justine, breakfast is on the table! Your father and I are going to the noon service, see you after church!"

Justine dashed out of bed to the balcony outside her bedroom so she could wave bye to her parents.

"Thanks for breakfast Mom! Enjoy the service. Give pastor and first lady Butler my regards."

"I will!" her mother shouted. "You should be coming with us." Justine, ignoring her, called "Bye Daddy!"

"When you coming to church Justine?" he called back.

"Soon Daddy, very soon." Her parents drove off in their brand-new Lexus. Breakfast smelled delicious. Scrambled eggs with cheese, bacon, grits, toast, and coffee. Justine poured herself some coffee. The house phone rang. She answered without checking the caller ID, assuming it was her mother calling about something she'd forgotten. "Hey Mom."

"Hello Justine, it's Ronald." Justine almost choked.

"Oh! Ronald ... why are you calling the house number?"

"Because you didn't answer your cell. How are you?"

"Um ... I'm doing okay. How are you?"

"I'm a man who misses his woman and I wanted her to know how much I truly love her." Justine sighed.

"I love you too Ronald."

"I'm not trying to push you, Justine. Just thinking about you."

"Thank you, Ronald. I appreciate your call. I'll talk to you soon." He remained silent. Justine hung up the phone slowly. She was not in the mood to wrestle with thoughts of getting married. She went back to the table and started to eat her breakfast. The phone rang again.

"Yes Ronald?" she answered, trying not to sound annoyed.

"Oh, hey Justine ... this is Shante." Justine giggled.

"Shante, hey girl! I thought you were Ronald."

"Justine, I just wanted to thank you for inviting me to the opening of Sistah Knit. I really had a great time. It was so nice meeting everyone, especially Michele. I've seen her on GMN many times. The twins are lovely and Rhonda is a beautiful woman. I hope I look that good when I get to be whatever her age is."

"Of course! And yeah, me too," replied Justine. "But you know the saying: *black don't crack.*" They laughed.

"I mean, they really have it going on. Not like the women in my neighborhood. They're all broke down or cracked out." Justine let out a small sigh.

"Yeah, I know it. It's sad what happening now in the urban communities."

"Yeah ... very sad."

"Anyway, I'm glad you had a good time. Come by the shop tomorrow?"

"Okay I will. I'll come around four o'clock. My last class is over at two forty-five."

"All right Shante, I'll see you tomorrow. Michele and Rhonda will be there too. I have some good news to share with everyone."

"What is it?" Shante asked.

"You'll have to wait until tomorrow."

Shante laughed. "Okay Justine, enjoy the rest of your day."

"Bye Shante." Justine hung up the phone and started again to think about Ronald. She decided to get dressed and go to church after all.

1:00 P.M.

Terri was signing the receipt for the cable service installation at the shop. "Whoa, this screen has great picture quality. I've never seen a ninety-inch screen before," said the cable guy. He flipped through the channels.

"Oh, leave it right there on GMN!" called Sherri from behind the counter. Terri handed the man back his clipboard and pen and he headed out the door.

"Good day, ladies. If you have any problems please give us a call."

"Thank you," replied Terri. Michele was on, reporting on the Obama campaign. Terri picked up a green cashmere scarf and started knitting. She'd memorized the pattern and knew it by now. Knit two, purl two, yarn over, knit two, purl two, knit two together. Sherri turned the volume up. Michele was anchoring the Sunday evening news.

"Obama is in the lead over John McCain forty-nine percent to forty-four percent among voters most likely to go the polls this November," Michele smiled professionally at the camera. "This is a very interesting Presidential race to follow. We will be back with more election news and updates. Stay tuned, we'll be right back."

The tiny bells over the door jingled as a pizza delivery man opened the door. "Soul Pizza!" he announced in a sultry Barry White voice. Sherri, sitting on the sofa, looked at him standing there with his wool cap over his head. His dreadlocks hung just above his shoulders.

"Now, *that's* a good-looking man," she thought. Terri paid him for the pizza and thanked him. He looked back and smiled at Sherri as he walked out the door; she smiled back and Terri didn't notice as she tried to balance the large pizza box.

"Time to eat!" smiled Terri as she brought the pizza to the kitchen. The doorbell jingled again. This time it was some customers, three ladies, apparently all churchgoers. The first was a tall lean light-skinned woman with a tight curly black wig and glasses that made her eyes look the size of boiled eggs. She wore a brown tweed coat and carried a purse that looked like it was from the 1940s. Next to her was a short, chubby lady also wearing a curly style wig that looked matted and tangled. She had fire engine red lipstick on her coco brown skin. The third woman was about five

113

feet nine had a head full of beautiful thick grey hair. Her mocha-brown smooth skin was flawless. She wore small pearl earrings and just the right shade of bronze lipstick that complemented her complexion. Her coat was beige with vibrant earthy colors of rust, brown, green, and orange around the collar and cuffs.

"Hello ladies!" said Sherri. "Welcome to Sistah Knit. How can we help you today?" The ladies all smiled and greeted her as Terri returned from the kitchen.

"Look!" said the tall lean lady. "They're twins." Sherri giggled.

"Yes, we are twins. I'm Sherri and this is my sister Terri."

"What pretty young ladies," said the woman with the bright lipstick. "Oh! Forgive my manners! My name is Louise Smalls, and these ladies are my friends Annie Mae Willis and Odessa Carrington. We're members of Fellowship Baptist Church."

Annie Mae Willis stepped up closer and pulled a floral print handkerchief from her purse so she could wipe her eyeglasses. She wanted to get a closer look at the sisters.

"Nice to meet you. Is there anything we can help you with?" asked Sherri. Odessa Carrington spoke first.

"I am looking for some stretchy sock yarn. Something colorful ... it's for my granddaughter."

Annie Mae Willis jumped in, "I need soft and thick yarn for knitting hats."

Louise Smalls looked around the shop and said, "I'm making scarves for some children at the church."

"Miss Smalls, if you will come with me, I can show you what we have for knitting scarves," replied Sherri.

Terri escorted the other two ladies, "Miss Willis, Miss Carrington, right this way."

"What a beautiful shop you have," said Miss Willis. "It's so warm and cozy."

"Thank you very much," replied Terri. "Ladies would anyone like some tea or coffee?"

All three ladies asked for tea. Sherri gave Miss Smalls a basket of yarn to look through as she went to prepare the tea. Terri hung their coats on the rack and proceeded to show the other two ladies yarns and bamboo knitting needles. The ladies giggled as they looked over several skeins of yarns. Terri and Sherri smiled at each other. They felt good about their hard work. Sherri set the tray of tea on the coffee table.

"I like these multi-colored skeins," said Miss Smalls.

"Ladies please help yourselves!" said Sherri. The ladies gathered around the table.

"Delicious tea! Peach and mint ... Mmm ..." said Miss Carrington as she sipped. Miss Willis and Miss Smalls agreed.

"Glad you ladies are enjoying it," said Sherri.

"You know, this is the kind of place that's been missing from Harlem for a very long time," said Miss Carrington. "I think this shop will do very well."

"Thank you, Miss Carrington. Terri and I do hope the shop will do well." Terri brought over another basket of yarn and placed it on a table next to Miss Smalls.

"Have you ladies been longtime knitters?" Terri asked.

"Oh, yes!" replied Miss Carrington as she pushed her grey hair from her eyes, "Miss Willis started a knitting circle at the church about ten years ago."

"Sure did," replied Miss Willis, sipping her tea.

"We have about twenty-five women that meet once a month," said Miss Carrington.

Annie Mae Willis nodded her head in agreement. "I'd say about thirty or more women now."

"But there was never a place in Harlem to buy yarn!" said Miss Carrington.

"We always had to travel to the city for decent yarn," added Miss Smalls, shaking her head. The twins both smiled.

"Well, that's why we chose this location for our shop," said Terri. "We wanted to fill the void."

"This place is lovely," said Miss Smalls. "We've spent hundreds of dollars on yarn in other shops all over the city, and never once did they offer us a cup of anything!"

"That's right!" said Miss Carrington, "They barely let us use the restroom. One yarn shop in midtown gave us three different reasons that we could not use their bathroom. The owner said 'Sorry Miss, the bathroom is out of order.' Then the salesperson behind the counter told Miss Smalls that the plumber was inside installing a new toilet!"

"Yes, they did, such nonsense," said Miss Smalls. Miss Carrington continued, "Another time that same clerk behind the counter said that someone was using the restroom. We purposely stayed in the shop another twenty or thirty minutes, and no one ever came out!" She shook her head, still displeased with their experience.

"We never went back to that place," said Miss Willis.

"And we don't ever plan on going back!" said Miss Smalls.

"What was the name of the place?" asked Terri.

"We re-named that store, something more fitting," chuckled Miss Smalls. The three ladies looked at each other and in unison they said, "Bitches and witches that do knitted stitches!"

"Oh, my gosh! That's funny!" laughed Terri.

"Well anyway, we are very happy Sistah Knit can be the yarn shop where you can buy yarn, use the restroom, and enjoy all the tea you want," said Sherri.

"This place feels like home," said Miss Carrington. "It has a warm loving feeling."

"That is exactly what we want our customers to feel."

"Are you always open on Sundays?" Miss Carrington asked.

"No," replied Sherri, "we just had some extra inventory to sort out."

"Please come visit our church whenever you can," urged Miss Smalls.

"Thank you. Terri and I would love to visit," said Sherri as she poured more tea for the ladies.

"Thank you for this wonderful time at Sistah Knit," said Miss Carrington. "I know the women of the Harlem Knitting Circle are glad to know your shop is part of the community."

"Yes," replied Terri. "Many of the women came to our Grand Opening."

"Wonderful!" said Miss Willis. "Some of those women are members of our church. They enjoy knitting."

"Just as we enjoy knitting," said Miss Carrington, "and there is always a baby shower at church or a hat or scarf that needs to be made for a teenager going off to college."

"Wow, there seems to be a lot of knitting going on in Harlem!" said Terri.

"Honey chile, there sure is!" replied Miss Willis. Miss Carrington got up from her chair. "Thank you for the tea and your warm hospitality."

"Yes, thank you girls so much for the tea," said Miss Willis.

"We wish you all the best of blessing with this shop," said Miss Smalls.

"Thank you," replied Sherri and Terri. The sisters helped the ladies with their coats.

"Thank you ladies for your purchase, and please come again," said Sherri. Miss Carrington had a big smile on her face.

"Oh, you girls can count on that. We had a lovely time. Your shop is beautiful and you have much better yarn than most other shops we've been to."

"Why thank you," said Terri. "We really appreciate that." Terri opened the door and the women exited, smiling happily as they carried their multi-colored Sistah Knit shopping bags.

Sistah Knit drew more and more customers as the days went on. The business was well received by the Harlem community; people enjoyed the warm hospitality and undivided attention the twins showed to each of their clients.

Two little girls came to the shop to ask about knitting lessons as well as purchasing some yarn. They each had five dollars. After they had a quick look around the shop, they realized they did not have enough money to buy even the smallest skein of yarn. Sherri and Terri overheard them talking about hats they wanted to make for themselves as the New York weather got colder. Sherri walked over to the girls.

"Oh, did I forget to tell you two young ladies that this basket of yarn is on sale today?"

"How much is the sale price?" asked one of the girls. She looked up at Sherri. Her thick pink wool hat covered her plaited braids

118

that hung just below her ears. Her friend wore red furry donut-sized earmuffs. Her curly afro puffs stuck out from behind her ears. Sherri remembered when she and her sister were that age.

"The sale special is just *fifty cents* for each skein of yarn and fifty cents for a set of knitting needles."

"Wow that's great! We can buy so much, Stacy!" shouted the first girl. They rummaged through the basket of yarn and needles. Sherri looked over at her sister. Terri winked and nodded her head in agreement. She had done the right thing for their little sweet customers. Sherri handed the girls a schedule of the knitting classes for their age group with the dates and times. The girls each picked out four skeins of yarn and a set of jumbo knitting needles. When Terri rang up their purchase, she looked at the two girls and decided to join in on her sister's kindness.

"Oh my, little ladies!" Both girls looked at Terri with sadness on their faces thinking that maybe there was no sale after all.

"I think my sister forgot to tell you that when you purchase four skeins of yarn, you get the knitting needles for free and these lovely *"We Knit Too"* pins by GG. Today only!"

The two girls giggled with excitement as they stuck the pins to their coats. They were thankful.

"We like it a lot here!" said one of the girls. Terri gave the girls their change and bags. "Thank you, we will be back for our knitting lessons."

"Have your parents call or come by the shop to give you girls permission for your lessons. Okay?"

"Yes, we will!" The girls waved goodbye as they ran out of the shop. Sherri and Terri high-fived each other and smiled.

"Sistah Knit is in business!" shouted Terri.

"Yes, it is," replied Sherri. "Sistah Knit is in business."

Michele and Rhonda arrived at Sistah Knit around half past three. Sherri put extra tea and hot chocolate on the table. Justine and Shante strolled in shortly after.

"Hey ladies, we're *here!*" Justine sang out. Everyone laughed at her girlish playfulness.

"Well, the gang's all here, then!" Terri said.

"Hello ladies," said Sherri, smiling as she blew kisses to Justine and Shante. Rhonda helped Sherri with the hot beverages.

"How is everyone doing?" Shante asked. Michele greeted Justine and Shante with hugs and cheek-to-cheek kisses.

"Hello ladies, good to see you. What's up Justine?"

"I'm fine, Michele."

"How are you Shante?" Michele lightly touched Shante's braids, admiring them.

"Doing good, glad to be back at Sistah Knit." Sherri waved her hand to get everyone's attention.

"Hey girls, how about I order a variety of soups from Maggie's Soul Soup?"

"Yes, that sounds good," said Terri. Everyone agreed. Sherri placed an order for yellow split pea, pumpkin corn, chicken and dumplings, and seafood gumbo. "Make sure to ask for extra sweet potato rolls," said Terri. Justine held up her knitting project.

"Look at the sweater I'm knitting for Ronald."

"It's looking really nice!" said Michele.

"Yes, it is," replied Rhonda. "I *love* that seed stitch pattern."

Shante could not figure out how to finish a pattern with a dropped stitch and asked Terri for help.

"You'll need a crochet hook. Come, I have some at the counter." Shante eagerly followed.

"The soup order will be here in fifteen!" Sherri announced. The ladies talked amongst themselves. All except Rhonda, who seemed to be in her own little world. Sherri sat next to her, concerned.

"Are you feeling all right, Rhonda?"

"I had a hard day at work, that's all." Michele looked at her.

"Would you like a cup of mint tea?" She poured and handed Rhonda the cup of tea before she could respond.

"You do look really tired. Sure you're okay?" asked Justine.

"Yes. I'm all right." Shante and Terri made their way back to the table. Shante sat on a large floor pillow, still focused on her knitting.

"Want some tea, Shante?" Sherri asked.

"Hot chocolate for me, please. Thank you." Michele looked at Rhonda and nodded toward the group, indicating that she should tell the others what was really going on. Rhonda turned to face Sherri.

"My kids will be home from college soon," she told them. "My mother keeps calling me every five minutes about this or that. Long hours at work ... you all know how crazy things can get. My plate is full."

"Rhonda, you should take a vacation! Some place warm and sunny," said Justine, smiling.

"I sure could use a nice long vacation," said Rhonda, sipping her tea.

"I'd love a vacation myself," said Shante, giggling, "I wish Phillip was in college too."

"Slow your roll, Shante," said Michele. "Enjoy your son now because before you know it, he'll be all grown. How old is Phillip?

"He's two years old."

"Girl you got a long way to go before Phillip is in college," chuckled Justine.

"That's what *you* think," said Rhonda. "That long way to go somehow comes around pretty fast. Enjoy the little fella while you can." She poured herself more tea.

The delivery man from "Soulful Soup" entered and handed gallon-sized soup containers to Sherri.

"Hot soup coming through, ladies!" said Sherri as she placed the containers on the table. Terri went into the kitchen and quickly returned with six wooden soup bowls and spoons. "Help yourself everyone, dig in!" They served the soup and passed around a basket of warm sweet potato rolls. Terri went back into the kitchen and returned with several bottles of water.

"Mm! This pumpkin corn soup is so good," said Shante.

"It's my favorite winter soup," replied Michele. Rhonda watched Shante silently for a moment before asking, "How old are you, Shante?"

"I'm almost twenty-one."

"And your son is two years old, right?" Rhonda asked, calculated. Michele knew she was about to reveal the secret.

"Yeah, he sure is a handful, though." Shante blew on her hot soup before putting the spoon to her mouth.

"I always loved kids," continued Rhonda, "and I miss that age. My college kids grew up so fast ... I miss knitting little socks and hats for them."

"You don't knit much for them anymore?" asked Shante.

"My son Tyree doesn't like anything knitted unless it has a designer label on it, and my daughter Twinkle has a sense of style I'm still trying to figure out."

"I think I was once like that," chuckled Shante. Everyone laughed.

"Who knows what it is. All I know is they do grow up fast," Rhonda continued.

"How old are they now?" Shante asked.

"They're nineteen. Second year in college, and both have full scholarships – from Spelman and Morehouse."

"That's great," said Shante.

"I'd like to have kids one day," sighed Justine.

"Maybe a little Ronald Junior?" asked Michele, smiling. Rhonda untwisted the cap off a bottle of water and took a long drink.

"Oh, right, I have to get married first," Justine laughed.

"Justine, why don't you – "

"I'm pregnant," announced Rhonda. The room fell silent. The ladies all stared at her. After a moment Terri rushed to the front door and locked it. She flipped the sign in the window so it read *"Sorry, We're Closed!"* Justine spoke first.

"What did you just say, Rhonda?!"

"You're pregnant?" asked Sherri.

"Rhonda. Oh my Lord, Rhonda!" exclaimed Terri. Shante and Michele remained silent.

"I am six and half weeks pregnant. I'm fifty years old. And the father is my forty-year-old boyfriend Joe," she said matter-of-factly.

"Rhonda, what are you and Joe planning to do?" Michele asked.

"Well, right now Joe and I have different plans."

"What do you mean different plans?" asked Sherri.

"I want to take responsibility and raise this baby ... with Joe at my side married or not. He's not happy about this pregnancy at all. He walked out on me the other night."

123

"What do you mean he walked out on you?" demanded Michele.

"You two always seemed so happy and in love ... " sighed Justine.

"I, I really thought Joe and I were on the same page," Rhonda tried to stop herself from crying. Michele squeezed her hand.

"You know we will support *whatever* you decide to do ... but Joe was never on the *same page* with you about anything. Girl, the man is a playboy."

"Michele! Don't say that. You just don't like Joe," Justine said.

"Someone had to say it! You're right, I don't like him. He has nothing to offer Rhonda."

"Well," Rhonda interrupted, "you're not the one dating him. I am."

"Ladies! Please let's keep our heads together now," said Sherri.

"What are you going to do?" Terri asked.

"I'm not sure right now. I feel ... alone and afraid."

"Is having a baby at fifty something you want to do?" asked Sherri. Terri looked over at her sister.

"Sherri, what are you saying?"

"I mean, let's be real here about this thing," Sherri crossed her arms, "Rhonda, is having a baby part of your life plans for yourself?" They all looked at Rhonda, waiting for her to respond.

"I mean, I never thought about having another child, but now that I'm pregnant it might not be so bad."

Shante spoke up. "Sometimes life just happens ... and suddenly your life plan just changes." She was looking up at Rhonda, who smiled in return.

"Thank you, Shante."

Sherri spoke again. "So, in other words, you don't believe in abortion?" Rhonda became defensive.

"*No*, I do not believe in abortion."

"I didn't mean to offend you."

"No offense taken," said Rhonda, crossing her arms to mimic Sherri.

"What do you think Joe is going to do?" Michele asked.

"I don't know. Like I said, he walked out on me."

"The man you love just walks out on you." Michele ground her teeth. "Rhonda, you didn't get pregnant on your own!"

"Joe was acting strange. I thought he would be happy for us." Rhonda lowered her head, and she started to cry, "I didn't expect that to happen. Joe was always so sweet and kind to me. We've been together for two years! He loved me like no other man ever has," she sniffled. "He never questioned any past relationships, not even my kids' father. He's passionate and gentle. I feel good when I'm with him. I feel good when I *think* about him. We've traveled together. Joe always treated me like nothing less than a queen. Yes, he's forty with no kids and never married, and that's part of the reason I was attracted to him. He was a man with no baggage! So, if any of you are wondering what or why I would think Joe would want a child with me, his girlfriend ... it's simply because he is a loving man, with love to give a child. So ... I think he has to think things over. This is new to him. He's probably just as nervous as I am."

After a short silence, Terri said, "Sherri and I are here for you; we all are."

"Yes we are, we love you Rhonda," added Sherri, although she was doubtful. Rhonda wiped the tears from her face and smiled.

"Rhonda," said Shante, "I haven't known you very long, but I do know that if a man loves you, truly loves you, he will be there for you no matter what."

"Thank you, Shante. You're very sweet. And so smart for your age."

"You're strong Rhonda, I admire you girl," said Justine.

"I just have to give Joe some time to figure things out."

Michele, who had been quiet, snapped at her. "Really? Give Joe time to figure things out!? A child, no, correction, *you and Joe's* child is coming into this world. *Responsible* parents prepare for that child's arrival into this crazy world."

"I never said Joe was not responsible," Rhonda tried to keep her cool. She knew Michele cared for her.

Michele spoke more softly, "All right ... yes that's right, my bad."

"So when are you going to see a doctor?" asked Terri.

"I have an appointment next week and I'm very nervous."

Michele was excited to call Charles at work. His secretary Gladys answered the phone.

"Hello Mrs. Nelson, Mr. Nelson is in a board meeting at the moment. May I have him return your call or take a message for him?"

"Please tell him I love the flowers he sent."

"Yes Mrs. Nelson, I will."

"Thank you, Gladys, have a good one."

"You too Mrs. Nelson." Charles often sent flowers to her at work, partly since their demanding careers didn't allow them much time together. She enjoyed the fragrance of the mixed autumn mums and marigolds as she opened the card. It read:

Can't wait to see you. Love, Bradford.

Michele's jaw dropped. She plopped into her desk chair, staring at Bradford's scripted handwriting. "Oh my Lord, this man is crazy! He knows damn well I am a married woman and what we had back in college is long gone and over." She tore up the card and tossed it in the trash bin under her desk. Her office phone rang. The caller ID showed it was Charles. She let it go on ringing. She would figure out something to tell him about the flowers later. Michele quickly sent an email to Terri and Sherri at the yarn shop: *"Hey twins, I will stop by after work, need to talk."*

Brenda, Michele's assistant, tapped lightly on the door before slowly entering. Michele swung around in the chair. "Come on in, Brenda." She walked in and handed Michele a folder of papers.

"Hey Michele. This is the bio on Barack Obama, along with other documents and information about his campaign."

"Thank you very much, Brenda."

"Also, your interview with Mr. Bradford Wilson is set for next week. He called to confirm."

"Oh, he did?" said Michele, trying not to show any emotion.

"Yes, he asked if the interview could be moved up sooner. I explained that we have certain protocols to our scheduling to follow."

"Good. Thanks Brenda. Oh, and I'll be leaving the office at four today. You can reach me on my cell if anything needs my immediate attention."

"Okay Michele," Brenda closed the door gently as she exited. Michele spoke out loud to herself.

"I'll settle things with Bradford tomorrow. The *nerve* of him sending me flowers *and* trying to reschedule the interview! Who the hell does he think he is?" Michele dialed in to her voice mail. It was Charles.

"Hello baby, I was in a meeting when you called. Things are very busy here. I love that you received flowers but, sweetie, I didn't send you flowers, at least not yet! I didn't forget your birthday is tomorrow. Also, I'll pick Ashley up from tennis practice today. I love you."

What? My birthday? Oh my gosh! I forgot my own birthday!

There was another knock at her office door, "Come in!"

Bill Johnson, her co-anchor, entered. "Hey Michele, wanna grab a bite to eat?"

"Sure, if we can have a glass of wine with lunch," Michele giggled.

He smiled, "My thoughts exactly!" Michele grabbed her coat and purse.

"Let's go Bill. It's been a stressful morning."

Joe showed up at Rhonda's apartment around three in the morning, and they made passionate love for hours. As they lay in bed together at last, she watched him sleep peacefully. Thoughts of Joe being by her side every night after their child was born made her smile. "I love you, Joe Miles," she whispered. It was noon when she checked her cell phone and saw a text from Michele:

Going to Sistah Knit after work, come by if you can.

Rhonda turned her phone off and snuggled up to Joe.

As the ladies gathered at Sistah Knit, Rhonda asked Michele, "Have you ever thought about what life would be like married to a professional football player?"

"Not *just* a football player, a six-foot-four handsome quarterback for the Atlanta Falcons," said Sherri dreamily.

"Girls, please. Those flowers are going in the garbage tomorrow. Have I thought about what my life would be like married to Bradford Wilson? Well, I can't really be sure. He never wanted children, he made that very clear." She glanced at Rhonda. Rhonda rolled her eyes. Michele continued, "Bradford enjoys splurging in the NFL superstar lifestyle, you know, fancy restaurants, and cars, and *women*. Traveling all the time and mingling with celebrities. Bradford was always clear on what he wanted."

"You could have been his prize trophy wife!" said Rhonda.

"Yup. Sounds like a good life to me," said Sherri. Terri shot her sister a look.

Michele went on, "I would *not* have been happy with that kind of life. Bradford was the most popular guy in college. He enjoyed the limelight back then and he's enjoying it now with a big ego to match. Yes, I still feel something for Bradford, but Charles is the man I married and truly love. Charles is a good man ... but we have been just a little out of touch lately with our busy work schedules."

"Which is not good for any couple," said Sherri.

"Yes, I agree, but it's gone on so long. We manage to keep up with Ashley's busy schedule and we make sure she has everything she needs. That's what matters."

"But do *you* have everything *you* need, Michele?" Rhonda asked. Terri and Sherri waited with wide eyes for Michele's answer.

"I think that I do." Michele paused. "Our eighteenth wedding anniversary is coming up soon."

"If you *think so,* then you're not really sure, Michele," said Sherri.

"That's right," added Rhonda.

"Are you missing closeness with your husband ... or is it a curiosity for Bradford?" asked Terri. Michele looked puzzled.

"I love my husband and daughter. I have the career that I always wanted. We live a good life. My family is all doing well. But at the same time, Charles and I haven't been on vacation in over a year. We talked about getting away some place tropical and romantic ... but neither of us looked into it, so it just fell off the radar and we never talked about it again. We just allowed work to get in the way of us. Things have to get better soon."

"Michele, fight for your marriage, girl!" said Rhonda.

"You and Charles are great together, just give it some time," said Sherri.

"No, she can't do *that,* too much time has passed already," said Terri.

"I've been in the communications business all my life, and yet I can't seem to communicate with my own husband lately. We're not mad or angry with each other, but we're aware that we haven't been spending our special quality time together," replied Michele.

"You have tried, Michele," said Sherri. "Life happens, too many marriages are failing because couples get off track."

"Yeah, you're right. But it's not like Charles and I are looking to separate."

"Well you damn sure don't want to go down that road, Michele, it's ugly," replied Rhonda, shaking her head.

"It is a little strange how Bradford just suddenly popped up," said Sherri. Terri looked at Michele.

"Ladies, the man did not just *pop up*. He's in town for business, and it just so happens that I am the anchor at GMN who will be interviewing him." Michele was very matter-of-fact.

"Girl, you're a foreign news reporter; since when have you covered sports?" asked Rhonda.

"Rhonda, I switched to regional and sports news over six months ago." She crossed her arms.

Terri asked, "Couldn't you get someone else to do the interview?" Michele's eyes widened.

"Well, yes ... if I had some kind of emergency, I guess. I have a lunch interview with Bradford set for tomorrow," she told them. "Honestly girls, I don't want to have someone else do the interview. I need to deal with some unresolved feelings with him." The ladies sighed and groaned.

"Girl you sound like you might be playing with fire," said Sherri.

"No, not at all," replied Michele. "I need to deal with this issue head on. You know, I forgot my own birthday is tomorrow?" A tap at the window interrupted their conversation. Terri got up from her chair and ran to unlock the door. Two customers entered the shop, rubbing their hands together from the cold.

Shante knitted as she explained her latest family ordeal to Mrs. Smith at the library. Cherise was in the next room getting help with her homework from a tutor.

"How is Phillip?" Mrs. Smith asked.

"He's doing great. He enjoys being at Mrs. Brown's during the day while I'm at school."

"Are you keeping up your grades Shante?"

"Yes, I got an A-plus on my last three assignments." Mrs. Smith smiled.

"You're a very bright young lady Shante. I am proud of you. I believe you are going to get a good job opportunity after graduation."

"I hope so, Mrs. Smith. The economy's pretty rocky right now though, people are getting laid off every day." Mrs. Smith spoke softly as she knitted a pair of socks using the magic loop method.

"Don't worry Shante, God will provide for you. Keep up the good work and it will pay off."

"That's exactly what the instructors at school tell me," Shante giggled. "Now on a different note, Mrs. Smith you *have* to teach me that magic loop method. I like how you're knitting two socks at the same time!"

"I love knitting on the magic loop cable needles. I'll teach you one day."

"Mrs. Smith, you have to go visit Sistah Knit. It's new yarn shop in Harlem," Shante said excitedly.

"Yes, I plan to visit the shop soon. I saw all the news coverage on the television. The owners are young and very beautiful."

"They're former models from Paris ... The shop really is beautiful Mrs. Smith. I have never seen anything like it before. Terri and Sherri have really put their heart and soul into the shop," she paused, thinking fondly of her new friends. "It's a warm and cozy feeling you get when you're inside. They even make tea and hot chocolate for their customers."

"Now, *that's* something different," said Mrs. Smith. "Tea and hot chocolate? Sounds like Terri and Sherri had some good up-bringing."

"Their parents are from the South."

"Well that explains it." They knitted in silence for a little while, until Mrs. Smith felt it was appropriate to speak up, "So Shante, what are you going to do about your living situation?" Shante sighed gently.

"Well, Mrs. Brown said me and Phillip – I mean Phillip and I – can stay as long as we need to. She understands our situation."

"You just let me know if you need anything. It sounds like Mrs. Brown is a good woman. But, if the situation ever changes and you can't stay there, you call me. Okay?"

"I will, Mrs. Smith."

"I know how hard you're looking out for your sister and Phillip." Cherise just then walked in from the other room, as if she knew she was being talked about.

"Hi, Mrs. Smith."

"Hello Cherise, how are you today?"

"I'm fine. I got an A on my spelling test today." Mrs. Smith put her knitting down and gave Cherise a hug.

"Well good for you little lady. You're smart like your sister Shante, aren't you?" Cherise had a big smile on her face.

"I am proud of my little sister," said Shante. "Cherise plans to go to college to become a doctor." Cherise's smile got even bigger.

"A doctor," said Mrs. Smith, smiling. "Well I think you will be the prettiest and best doctor in the world. You just keep on getting those A's on your schoolwork." She kissed Cherise's cheek.

"Thanks, Mrs. Smith. If you get sick, I will come take care of you."

Mrs. Smith chuckled. "I would not want any other doctor except you, Cherise. Are you all done with your homework?"

"Almost, my tutor Samantha went to the bathroom."

"Okay, you get back to the desk. Shante and I will be right here." Cherise quickly walked into the study room. Mrs. Smith waited a bit and then spoke again. "Shante you're a good role model for Cherise," she paused. "I want you to keep one thing in mind."

"What's that?"

"Cherise is growing up to be a beautiful young lady, sooner rather than later. You've got to keep an eye on her. Teach and talk to her as much as possible. Please let me know if I can be of help."

"Thank you, Mrs. Smith."

"Shante, you remind me of my younger self. Life was a struggle but I was determined to make it. I believe you will do the same."

Michele left the shop and went home to get started on dinner. Ashley was out, staying the night at a friend's house. Charles came home around 8:45.

"Hey sweetheart, dinner smells good," he announced as he hung his hat and coat on the wall rack at the door.

"Charles, I'm in the bedroom!" Michele called. He entered, pleasantly surprised to see Michele standing there wearing a lovely black velvet dress that hugged all her curves just right. Her thick black wavy hair hung over her right shoulder and rested on her breast. The flicker from the candles illuminated her hourglass figure. Her shadow was reflected onto the wall behind her, her left hand resting on her hip. Charles soaked in her beauty for a few seconds before he spoke.

"Michele, sweetheart. You look just lovely. I could stand here all night just looking at you." She sat down at the foot of their king-sized bed.

"Well handsome, come over here and sit down next to me. It's just you and me tonight, Charles." She kissed him gently on his lips and touched him below his waist. She whispered in his ear, "It's been a while since we had some alone time." Returning her tender kisses and holding her close to him, he whispered, "This is exactly what we needed, Michele. I know it's been a long time. We both have been – " Michele put her finger over his lips.

"Charles, let's not think about anything tonight but us, here and now. Let's find our way back to each other."

"You know I love you, Michele, and I want us to be strong in our marriage."

"I love you too, Charles."

As the evening went on, they enjoyed fine wine and talked about their college days. They looked at their wedding photos and pictures of Ashley when she was a baby. They talked about working fewer hours and trying to adjust their schedules to spend more time together. They laughed for hours and held one another. They made love throughout the night. She told him how much she missed and loved him.

"I love you Michele, I always have and always will. You are the love of my life, baby." They fell asleep wrapped in each other's arms.

The next morning, Charles kissed Michele softly on the lips, waking her gently.

"Michele, last night was amazing. I love you so much girl. Have a good day, sweetheart. I have an 8 A.M. meeting with some clients." He kissed her again, passionately this time. "Thank you for a wonderful dinner and a fabulous night. I love you."

"I love you Charles; you have a good day," Michele whispered. Charles looked back at her smiling as he left the bedroom. She wanted to stay in bed under the fluffy covers but she had to get to work as well. She turned on the television and began making the bed. Advertisements for the upcoming football season played; an interview with Bradford flashed on the screen. Michele's lunch meeting with him was scheduled for later in the day.

She quickly focused her thoughts back to Charles and the great night they'd had together.

She switched the channel for a few seconds then switched it back. She thought, *I can't allow myself to lose control. I will have lunch with Bradford and discuss the interview. And that's it.* She got in the shower and stood under the hot steamy water. She focused on Charles. *Jesus, help me Lord!*

The three ladies from the Harlem senior citizen center gathered around the coffee table at Sistah Knit. They each knit as Terri brought them a tray of tea and warm buttermilk biscuits. They discussed their personal views on current events.

Louise Smalls

"These days, parents acting like they want to be teenagers and teenagers acting like they have no parents to teach them anything. Girls go to school half-dressed ... boys walking around with their pants hanging below their butts and sneaker laces untied."

Odessa Carrington

"Young girls having babies every day. The welfare line getting longer year after year. The police officers acting like cowboys, shooting anything that moves in the dark. Cops selling more drugs than the drug dealers. Taxes going up and wages are too low. My grandson can hardly make ends meet. His wife even got a second job. The poor keep getting poorer and the rich keep on getting richer. Food prices are up and the quality of the food is going down!"

Annie Mae Willis

"Every other day the news reports on a new germ or poison found in fruits and meats. Don't eat that, don't drink this. FDA is recalling this and that. The landlords are always raising the rents. My social security check is stretched thinner than a piece of thread. I worked all my life and now I'm told that I have to *give* a little more because the deficit budget needs to be gapped. Well hell! I never borrowed a dime from another country, friend or foe. Working people are to be responsible for funds they personally don't owe, but because we are Americans that means we automatically owe monies to other countries? Our grandparents were born into slavery. Stripped of everything they knew and owned. They were brought to this land, given a new "slave name" and ordered to do backbreaking work from before the sun came up till after it went down."

Louise Smalls

"Yeah, and they were given scraps of food from the master's table. Beaten or whipped if you even looked like you're going to speak up for yourself. Black families were separated from one another and sold off like cattle to different plantation owners. Family division didn't start with us, it started with the white slave masters. Our ancestors were at peace on the west banks of Africa just minding their own damn business when they were stolen and had iron chains placed on their necks and ankles. Jammed on slave ships by the hundreds or thousands. Men and women and children. Shame on America! And the government will never apologize for the enslavement of black people. They act like we brought ourselves to the damn place called America."

Odessa Carrington

"The cruelty of slavery is a crime this world has never paid for. If you didn't be a good niggah, they would beat you half dead. Now this racist government we have today is always treating people of color like no-class citizens. Black people built this place called America, the U S of A and yet, to this very day, we are still told to remember our place in this world!"

Annie Mae Willis

"Ladies, we and our ancestors have cleaned, cooked and taken care of white folks' children and babies for generations while our children were left alone or with relatives to care for them. They want us to smile and be mighty happy when they hand us twenty dollars for a whole week of work."

They all shook their heads in agreement.

Louise Smalls

"Twenty dollars, wow, you got that much?"

Annie Mae Willis

"I am tired of this America selling us a bunch of bull crap year after year, decade after decade. Now at this age in my life, I really don't give a damn anymore. I have paid my dues. Our parents and their parents have paid their dues to this country many times over for a place they never ever asked to come to. So, yes I am pleased that a black man is running for the office of President of the United States."

Odessa Carrington

"He is highly qualified to do the job of running this jacked-up country. I will vote for him and wish him all the best because he is going to have to fight. The racist political government people who will smile in his face and behind his back beat him with their political whip, because they don't want a black man in the seat of president. He's educated, a good family man, and he does want to make a difference."

Annie Mae Willis

"*Yes We Can*" is what he says, and the people are hyped up and want him to win. I know the evil powers in Washington, the Republicans are pissing in their pants right now at the fact that

Obama's poll numbers are looking really good. Which means they will sit days on end until they master up a plan to bring Obama down, and they will blame whatever the status of America is on him. Watch and see ladies, what I tell you. *Everything will be Obama's fault."*

"If it rains – *It's Obama's fault,* If the sun shines – *It's Obama's fault.* If gas prices are too high *it's Obama's fault,* jobs are hard to find it's *Obama's fault,* the war is going on too long – It's all *Obama's fault.* The Yankees lose the world series, even, well *it's Obama's fault!"*

The ladies all laughed.

"I'm serious!" Miss Willis said. "You all watch what I am saying. If a member of the tea party gets a run in her stocking ... ," and they all said together:

"It's Obama's fault!"

"God bless Obama," added Miss Willis, "for even wanting to take on such a tough job. President of the United States of America. Lord help that man!" The bells on the door jingled and two ladies entered the shop.

"Hey! We in da-house!" The two women came in dancing and bumping their hips together. They snapped their fingers in the air.

"Sistah Knit, Sistah Knit, Miss Dove and Miss Peaches are now in da-hoouuuzz!"

"Sistah Knit! Hey! Sistah Knit Hey!" The seniors were speechless. They stopped their knitting and sat with mouths dropped open as they noticed the women were in fact two drag queens.

"What in the hell?" said Miss Willis as she glared over her eyeglasses. Miss Dove was a little over six feet tall with long blonde braids and colorful makeup that had been applied perfectly. She wore a fire engine red wool coat with black stretch pants and red leather boots.

Miss Peaches was a little shorter and wore a black wool maxi coat with a red seed stitch scarf that was just as long as the coat. She had matching red wool gloves with black fingertips. They both wore large hoop earrings with gold glitter. They did some kind of hand game and sang a patti-cake song:

"Miss Mary, Mac-Mac-Mac, all stitched in black, black, black!" They laughed and bumped hips together a few more times before they came to a full stop. Sherri cleared her throat, trying not to laugh.

"Welcome to Sistah Knit. I'm Sherri and this is my sister Terri. How can we help you today?" Odessa Carrington started laughing and held the baby blanket she was knitting to cover her face. Miss Willis and Miss Smalls were staring blankly.

"Hello ladies! I am Miss Dove and this here is Miss Peaches. We need to buy some yarn so we can get our knit on. We have some holiday gifts to make. We have to get busy soon because time is just moving!" she snapped her fingers, "You know what I mean girl?" she directed this question at Terri.

"Yes, I do," replied Terri, smiling. "Time is really moving fast!"

"Yes, it is girl!" said Miss Peaches. The two, in sync, snapped their fingers and said together:

"Hey! We in the hizzouse!" Miss Willis rolled her eyes at them.

"What's wrong with you, old lady?" asked Miss Dove, "You never seen such *beauty* as us in your life, have you darling?"

"What beauty?" replied Miss Williams. Terri quickly interjected,

"Step over here Miss Dove and Miss Peaches. We have a nice selection of yarn that might interest you for your holiday knitting." She motioned for the two to follow her to the shelves farthest away from the old ladies. Miss Dove snapped her fingers at Miss Willis and tossed her braids over her shoulders as they passed.

Miss Willis looked up. "Miss Dove, is what you say your name is? You better watch yourself or I'll – "

"Or you'll *what*, Grandma?" Miss Willis stood up and her knitting fell to the floor. She placed a hand on her hip and waved the other in the air.

"Or I will open up a can of old-fashioned grandma whupass! That's *what*!" The other two ladies stood up, and Miss Odessa Carrington pulled off her wig and slapped it on the table.

"Let's kick their asses!" Miss Peaches shouted. "So y'all old kittens trying to get granny gangster up in here? On us?"

"I can put this knitting needle where the sun don't shine!" shouted Miss Willis.

"Calm down everyone, just calm down," Sherri said. She nervously walked in between the two groups.

"Yes, please ladies, calm down," pleaded Terri. "We can all get along! That's what Sistah Knit is for!"

"Girl, don't play with us," said Miss Smalls. The doorbells jingled.

"Hello everyone!" said Justine, smiling as she pulled off her hat and coat. The ladies suddenly composed themselves, realizing how silly they must have looked. Miss Odessa Carrington quickly pulled her wig back on. Miss Dove and Miss Peaches fluttered their lashes at Justine.

"Um, hello Justine!" said Sherri, "I was just about to get more tea for the ladies, come give me a hand."

"Sure," said Justine. She followed Sherri to the kitchen. When they were alone, she whispered, "Sherri, what the heck was going on in here?" Sherri burst into laughter.

"Girl, it was about to be a serious beatdown between the diva ladies and the senior ladies. I think everything is okay now."

"Are you sure Sherri? I saw that old lady had her wig off! She was really ready to fight."

"Yes, everything is all right, we calmed them down," Sherri chuckled, "Anyway, I'm ordering lunch in a little while. Can you join us?"

"Yes, thank you." said Justine. She waited until Sherri was done steeping the tea before she continued, "So ... I came by to tell you and Terri some good news."

"What is it?" Sherri asked.

"Well ... I am officially owner and CEO of JW Records!"

Sherri smiled and gave her friend a hug, "Congrats! We have to celebrate! That's wonderful. You must be so excited."

"Yes I am. I signed all the documents last week. I have some upcoming talent I would like to sign to my record label."

"Justine, it sounds like you are finally on your way to bigger and better things." They hugged again. "Ronald must be very proud of you?" Justine shrugged, "Yeah, I think he is." Sherri frowned.

"That doesn't sound very convincing. What's up?"

"Ronald decided to give me some space," Justine sighed.

"What?" She handed Justine a tray of warm biscuits and cornbread to carry.

"I don't know. I think he's right."

"Justine, you're confusing me." They walked back into the shop and Justine set her tray on the table in front of the seniors, who were back to knitting and talking politics. Sherri offered some biscuits to Miss Dove and Miss Peaches, and they each took one. Terri seemed to calm everyone down; she was showing off some skeins of yarns and bamboo knitting needles. Sherri was glad. She motioned Justine to join her by the counter. She spoke softly, "Are you telling me you and Ronald broke up?"

"No. Well, not really." Justine pulled on her hair.

"Then what?"

"Ronald thinks I should take time to think about things before we get married."

"Think about what, Justine? You're talking but, girl, you're not saying much." Miss Willis and the other ladies looked over in their direction. Sherri lowered her voice. "What are you *really* saying, Justine?" Justine was about to answer when another customer entered the shop. "Hold that thought. I'll be right back," said Sherri, and she went to greet the handsome gentleman who had walked in. "Hello! Welcome to Sistah Knit. I'm Sherri, how can I help you?"

"Hey Sherri, my name is Carl."

"Pleasure to meet you Carl. Are you a knitter?" Sherri asked. Miss Dove and Miss Peaches looked over their shoulders to catch a glimpse of him.

Terri whispered, "Oh, my Lord, what a *fine-looking* man." Justine admired him from behind the counter. Even the seniors locked their eyes on him.

"Ain't he good looking?" said Miss Carrington, adjusting her wig.

"Yes Lord," replied Miss Smalls. "He is damn fine. Just my type."

"Y'all know I can still catch me a young fine beau like him if I wanted to," said Miss Willis.

Carl chuckled at Sherri. "No, I'm not a knitter. My sister Danita asked me to pick up an order she called in earlier today. She's working late this evening and won't be able to come by herself."

"What a nice brother you are!" Sherri said, smiling. Miss Willis coughed loudly and caught Sherri's attention. "Um, let me get your sister's package. She walked to the counter and pushed Justine out of the way. She grabbed a bag from behind the counter and walked back to Carl. "Here you go! Please tell your sister if she has *any* questions to give me a call." Sherri handed Carl a Sistah Knit business card with her cell phone number on the back.

"Thank you very much, Sherri. I will give Danita your message." He smiled and walked out the door. Sherri stood there watching him through the side window.

"Sher-ri! Earth to Sherri!" called out Justine. Terri laughed. Sherri turn around quickly.

"Girl, I'm sorry. Did you *see* that fine man?"

"I saw him really good," answered Miss Dove.

"I bet you did," mumbled Miss Willis. Terri rang up the orders for Miss Dove and Miss Peaches.

"We *have* to come back to Sistah Knit! Y'all have some very nice yarn," said Miss Peaches.

"And some handsome customers too!" said Miss Dove. They high-fived each other. Terri handed them their bags, giggling.

"Thanks for shopping at Sistah Knit. Please come again."

"Yes, we sure will," said Miss Dove, tossing her braids over her shoulder as she looked back at the senior ladies who were glaring at her.

"You two betta watch you don't catch something out there in them streets," said Miss Willis.

"Later for you, old lady," said Miss Dove as they exited.

Terri addressed the ladies, "Would you like to join us for lunch?"

"No thank you," said Miss Smalls. "We have an ushers meeting at church we need to prepare for." They were packed up and gone within the next ten minutes. Terri, Sherri, and Justine sat in silence, watching the three seniors wobble down the street adjusting their wigs. After a moment, Sherri burst into laughter.

"What a *wild* afternoon this has been! Please, let's order lunch, I'm hungry after all that."

Terri agreed. "How about Chinese food?"

"Fine with me," said Sherri.

"Me too," said Justine. Terri went to kitchen area to order while Sherri and Justine got comfortable on the sofa.

"Justine, tell me. What is going on with you and Ronald?" Justine held up her left hand and moved her fingers back and forth. Sherri covered her mouth with her hand, "No ring! What happened?"

"Well. Ronald feels I need time to think about our relationship. He says I always put my career before him ... I know how badly he wants to get married, and I do love him but – "

"But what?"

"Well, you know how long I've wanted my own record label."

"And you have that now! So what about you and Ronald?"

"I want Ronald, but I don't want to rush into anything." Sherri crossed her arms.

"What do you mean rush into anything? You and Ronald have been together for what? Three years?"

"I know ... I just want to wait a while and focus on my new record label."

"And what is Ronald supposed to do? Should he take a back seat and wait until you're ready to be a wife and mother?"

"Sherri, if he loves me, he will wait." Sherri pursed her lips.

"Do your parents know about this, Justine?"

"No, I didn't tell them. I want to see what happens first."

"You know how your mother is. You can't fool her. You know she adores him, and your father even likes Ronald a lot." Justine rolled her eyes. Sherri continued, "Look, all I'm saying is to put yourself in his shoes. Do you feel Ronald is right to give you time to think about things?" Justine paused,

"Yes, Ronald is patient and kind and he loves me."

Sherri sighed. "I know you'll make the right decision, Justine. I'm here for you anytime you want to talk." They hugged. "But seriously! Don't keep that poor man waiting. He's a good one. And girl, please put that ring back on your finger. Ronald is giving you some space. He didn't break your engagement."

Michele tried on several different outfits before deciding what she was going to wear for her interview with Bradley. She chose a black blazer, white silk V-neck blouse, and a charcoal pencil skirt. She clasped a pearl necklace Charles had given her as a birthday gift around her neck and matched it with a pair of pearl earrings that had once belonged her Nana Bea. Her thick wavy hair fell gently over her shoulders.

She put on a pair of heeled black boots and stared at her reflection in the mirror.

It's just a business lunch, she reminded herself. The cab she had ordered honked twice outside. She took one last look at herself before she met the driver downstairs. From the back seat on her way to the restaurant she sent a text to Charles: *"I love you."* He sent a text back: *"I love you more."*

Traffic was moving slowly down Madison Avenue. Michele giggled to herself; she didn't mind being fashionably late. Plus, she did not want Bradford to think she was overly excited to see him by showing up exactly on time, even though he was never late for anything. Everyone in college would tease him about it, especially the rest of the football team. He was that student who always showed up way too early for class. Even his NFL coach would count on Bradford to be the first one to show up for practice. Michele looked at her watch; it was a quarter past one o'clock. Perfect. The cab pulled up right in front of the Golden Gate Restaurant in lower Manhattan. Bradford had a table in the far right next to the window; he immediately noticed Michele exiting the cab and marveled at her beauty as she walked in.

Everything seemed to move in slow motion for Bradford. Her tall, lean, hourglass figure moved softly like a floating feather. Each step closer made him want her more. He stood up to greet her, taking her hand and gently kissing her on the cheek. The scent of her perfume almost gave him an erection.

"Hello, Michele," he said, smiling. He did not even care she was fifteen minutes late. He waited to sit until after Michele was comfortably seated.

"Hello Bradford, how are you?

"I'm well ... now that you're here." Michele was thankful a waiter came to the table to take their drink orders so she would not have to respond to his comment.

"Sir, may I get you and the lady something to drink?"

"Yes, can you bring us a bottle of your finest French wine."

"Yes Sir, right away." The Golden Gate's finest French wine was at least two thousand dollars. Michele tried to act nonchalant.

"Impressive."

"Only the best for you." He leaned back to get a better look at her.

"You look beautiful, Michele."

"Thank you, Bradford. You're looking well yourself."

"I didn't say you looked well, I said you look beautiful." Michele squinted.

"And I said thank you."

"Michele, you know I always thought you were beautiful." The waiter returned, pouring a small amount of wine for Bradford to sample.

"This is perfect, thank you," Bradford said. The waiter poured the wine into gold-rimmed crystal glasses. A second waiter brought a small tray of French hors d'oeuvres, placing it on the table. Bradford could not keep his eyes off Michele.

"I ordered these before you came." Michele could hear her heart pounding in her ears. She took a sip of wine trying to relax her nerves.

"So ... how long will you be in town?"

"Well, I plan to stay about a week or two. Maybe longer. I have some business endorsements to discuss with my lawyers. Plus, I'd like to visit my sister Lois and her husband. See my nieces and nephews while I'm here."

"That sounds great. Nothing like visiting family." Feeling a bit more relaxed, she sipped her wine.

"And how is your family, Michele?"

"They're wonderful. Ashley is doing very well in school. She's taken on a few sports now, too. My sister Robin and her husband Marcus just had a baby boy last month. Isaiah. He's beautiful ... " she paused. "And Charles is doing great. He's a partner at Carrington Engineering and Finance now." Bradford sipped his wine as Michele gave her order to the waiter who had returned. Bradford stared at her, waiting for her to continue.

"We're about to celebrate our anniversary in a few days. Eighteen years." Bradford stared into her light brown eyes. She looked so beautiful.

"Charles is a very lucky man," he paused for a moment. "You should have been my wife." Michele's eyes widened.

"Bradford!" She whispered, wanting to not o make a scene, "That was a *long* time ago. Please put it to rest." She quickly finished the remaining wine in her glass. Her cheeks turned flush.

"How can I put it to rest, Michele? You remember what we once meant to each other? We were – "

"Look, I did *not* come here for this," Michele glared at him. "We have an interview to do, remember?"

"All right, Michele. Here's the interview. My name is Bradford Wilson. I am the top ... no, I am the *highest* paid quarterback in the history of the NFL. I've been playing for the Atlanta Falcons for ten years. I have more championship rings than I have fingers. I played football in high school and college. I have endorsements with soda, sportswear, and sneaker companies, and two movie deals in the works. I have well over a million followers across my social media. Off the field, I enjoy movies, reading, traveling, and spending time with friends and family. Most of all, I enjoy looking at the woman I never stopped loving from the first day I saw her back in college. There's my interview." He took another sip of wine, put his glass down, and picked at the food in front of them. Michele was speechless, unsure how to respond. She mimicked him and took another sip of wine and started to eat.

"Did you hear what I said, Michele? I never stopped loving you." She put her fork and knife down on the table.

"Okay? What do you want me to say?"

"Michele, I want you to say what's on your mind. Did you really think I just wanted to talk about my football career? You're a top reporter, Michele. You know all the answers. I wanted to see you again, alone. That's why I agreed to do this interview."

"All right. I know that we have a past together ... but a *very* long time ago. I am a married woman now, who's in love with her husband. I have a daughter. Our college days are long behind us. You will always be a dear friend to me, Bradford."

"Michele! Stop the crap talk!" his voice was raised. The next table over glanced at them. He whispered, "You knew what was going to happen today."

Michele's reply was stern but low. "No, Bradford. *You* cut the crap! This is not college. We are adults with different lives. We are different people. I love Charles. What would make you think otherwise?" He sipped some wine before answering.

"The way you looked at me when you walked in."

Michele rolled her eyes. "Bradford, have you lost your damn mind? What the hell do you mean, *the way I looked at you*?" She stood up, grabbing her purse off the table, "Thank you for lunch."

"Where are you going Michele?" He rose swiftly to his feet.

"You gave me all the information I need, right? This interview is over."

"Wait, Michele," he pleaded. She walked toward the exit without so much as a glance behind her. She did not want to tempt herself. She knew deep down in her heart that Bradford was right. She did feel something for him.

Tuesday, November 4th, 2008

Election Night

President-Elect Barack Obama stood on a podium addressing Americans across the country:

"If there is anyone out there who still doubts that America is a place where all things are possible, who still wonders if the dream of our founders is alive in our time, who still questions the power of our democracy, tonight is your answer."

A crowd of people huddled around the television at Sistah Knit. They hung on to each of Obama's words as he spoke.

"It's the answer told by lines that stretched around schools and churches in numbers this nation has never seen, by people who waited three hours and four hours, many for the first time in their lives, because they believed that this time must be different, that their voices could be that difference."

The watchers passed around boxes of tissues. Tears flowed down their faces as they witnessed a black man become President of the United States.

"Is this really happening Daddy?" Sherri asked, resting her head on her father's shoulder.

"Yes, it is Sherri. History is being made this very minute." His voice was low and calm. His eyes became watery. He hugged his wife close to him. "Look at all the thousands of people there." The camera panned to show the faces of figures like Jesse Jackson and Oprah Winfrey. They too had tears in their eyes.

"Wow," said Terri, "America's history is unfolding right before us!"

"It really is a new day in black America," Sherri said. The twins stood close to their parents, arms locked together. The doorbells jingled as Ronald quietly entered the yarn shop; he scanned the crowd. Justine was happy to see him. Once he made his way to her, he wrapped his arm around her, "Can you believe it? A black President?"

"It's so exciting!" Justine snuggled up to him. Rhonda smiled at the young couple. She wondered what Joe was up to. She focused her attention back to the broadcast.

"This election had many firsts and many stories that will be told for generations. But one that's on my mind tonight's about a woman who cast her ballot in Atlanta. She's a lot like the millions of others who stood in line to make their voice heard in this election except for one thing: Ann Nixon Cooper is 106 years old. She was born just a generation past slavery; a time when there were no cars on the road or planes in the sky; when someone like her couldn't vote for two reasons – because she was a woman and because of the color of her skin."

"Look at all these people here tonight," whispered Terri, "This place is jam-packed!"

"This is something really special," replied Sherri. "These folks will always remember where they were when Obama was elected President. Sistah Knit has truly become a part of Harlem on this special night. Sistah Knit is a part of history!" She squeezed her sister tight. "This place of ours ... it's more than just a yarn shop. It's home."

"I agree." Terri teared up. "I totally agree. It's home."

"This is our chance to answer that call," continued Barack Obama. "This is our moment. This is our time, to put our people back to work and open doors of opportunity for our kids; to restore prosperity and promote the cause of peace; to reclaim the American dream and reaffirm that fundamental truth, that, out of many, we are one; that while we breathe, we hope. And where we

153

are met with cynicism and doubts and those who tell us that we can't, we will respond with that timeless creed that sums up the spirit of a people: *Yes, we can.* Thank you. God bless you. And may God bless the United States of America."

"Amen!"

"Thank you, Jesus!"

"This was a long time coming, Obama!" The people in Sistah Knit cheered as President-elect Obama ended his speech. Sherri turned on the shop's audio system and started her Ray Charles CD. His song "America" rang through the crowd. People were hugging, crying, laughing, and dancing. Red, white, and blue balloons were hung all around the shop. Sherri handed Ashley a basket filled with Obama buttons and asked her to hand them out. Rhonda helped Terri and Sherri serve champagne and trays of finger foods. Despite the noise, Phillip was asleep on Shante's lap.

"We have a bedroom in the back where you can lay Phillip down, if you'd like," Sherri told her.

Shante carried Phillip to the back of the shop, away from the crowd and noise. It was a cozy and dimly lit room. "This is lovely, isn't it?" she whispered to her sleeping baby. There were two queen-sized beds on the far end of the room. They were decorated with pink and purple comforters, throws, and pillows. She gently placed Phillip down on the bed closer to the bathroom and took some pillows to create a little fence around him. Shante checked out the rest of Sherri and Terri's homemade apartment. She looked in the bathroom; it was spacious and decorated in pink, purple, and gold. The carpet was plush and soft. There were some stuffed animals sitting in a box in the corner next to a basket filled with skeins of yarn and knitting books. Shante took a fluffy teddy bear from the pile and snuggled it next to Phillip.

"Maybe one day, you'll be President." She sat on the edge of the bed looking at her son.

"I want so much for you, Phillip. I want you to live in a better place and have a room of your own, filled with all your favorite toys. I dream of you attending a great school and learning all sorts of things ... like business, and science and math. And history, black history, real history. The truthful kind, the kind where black people aren't left out. I want you to love who God made you to be and live a life that he and you can be proud of." She paused and took a deep breath. "Tonight, my son, a black man became President. From this day on, Phillip, your mommy is going to start talking to you like you're already a doctor, a lawyer, even a President!" She giggled and kissed him on the nose. "Good night Doctor Phillip. Mommy loves you."

"It's great to see you, Ronald, I'm so happy you came tonight."

"I wouldn't have missed this for the world. I stopped by Kenny's barber shop up the street to hang out with the fellas for a little while. I figured you would be here." He paused, staring at Justine's smile, "It's good to see you too, Justine, but I gotta get going. I have to stop by my parents' house. My mom is probably crying her eyes out about Obama." Justine laughed.

"All right, give your parents my regards."

"I will," he hugged her tightly and kissed her softly on the lips. He made his way back through the crowd. Justine watched him until the door closed behind him. Sherri was standing behind Justine and whispered into her ear.

"So, what was that all about?" Justine quickly turned around.

"Girl! What are you doing sneaking up on me like that?"

155

"I wasn't sneaking! I just ... anyway, what's up with Ronald?"

"He came by to say hello. That's all."

"That's all?"

"Yes, that's all," Justine rolled her eyes. "Can we just enjoy the party? It's not about me and Ronald tonight. It's about our *new president!*" Justine did a little dance. Sherri laughed with her.

"Fine, but only because today is a special occasion." The doorbells jingled again. In walked Gigi of GGmadeit. She waved at the twins as she made her way through the crowd. Terri and Sherri were happy she could share this special evening with them.

Rhonda set a tray of finger sandwiches on the coffee table near the window. She looked out between the lace knitted curtains into the street. She saw two figures walking on the opposite sidewalk. She squinted; it was Joe, with another woman. Rhonda leaned forward, making sure it was actually him. That was his walk, his style, his manner. Rhonda felt her heart drop as she watched Joe passionately kiss the woman . Rage built up inside her; she wanted to scream. She leaned back and took a deep breath. She could not turn around and face the crowd with tears in her eyes.

"What's wrong?" It was Michele.

Great, Rhonda thought to herself. "Nothing," she said, still facing the window.

"Rhonda ... you're crying." Rhonda still kept her eyes on the window. She did not want to look at Michele. She did not want to look at anyone. "What are you looking at? Who's out there?" Michele moved the curtain aside and peered across the street.

"It's nothing," said Rhonda. Michele's nose pressed against the window. She gasped.

"Rhonda! Is that ... Joe? Who's that woman he's kissing?" Rhonda wiped the tears from her cheek before answering. She felt embarrassed.

"Yes, it's Joe."

"Well!" Michele put her hand on Rhonda's shoulder, "Don't you want to go kick his ass?"

"What can I do, Michele? Have you forgot I'm pregnant?"

"You can still shoot his ass!" Michele looked out the window again. "Ugh, they're gone. Where do you think they went?" Rhonda covered her face with her hands.

"Dammit Michele! Please! I don't know where they're going! I don't care. I can't deal with this right now."

"Okay, okay. I'm sorry, calm down."

"How– how could he do this to me?"

"Do you want to relax in the back room?"

"No, I think I'll just go home."

"Let me get my coat. Charles and I can drive you home."

"No, I can take a taxi. I just need to be alone for a while."

"No girl. You need to be with your friends."

"But I don't want to spoil the party. I'll be fine. I just want to go home." Michele sighed. Rhonda turned her face from the crowd.

"All right," Michele took Rhonda's hands. "Promise you'll call me later tonight. I don't care how late."

"Okay. Yes. I will."

"Rhonda, I'm worried about you being alone."

"Don't worry. I will be fine. I'll call you later, promise." They exchanged a loving hug. Rhonda sorted through the coat hooks, looking for her hat.

"Where you going Rhonda?" asked Terri as she approached them with another tray of snacks. "GG just got here. She's asking for you."

"I'm feeling a bit tired. I'm going home to rest. I'll see you and Terri later in the week. Please say hello to GG for me."

"Do you need me to go with you, Rhonda?" Sherri asked.

"I'm good. I'll be all right." Sherri hugged her. Rhonda got her coat from the closet behind the counter and left. Sherri and Michele watched her through the curtains.

As soon as she got into a taxi, Terri asked, "What happened? Is she all right?"

"No, she's not," replied Michele.

"Oh no! Is it the baby?"

"No ... Rhonda just saw Joe across the street kissing another woman."

"*What*? Are you sure?"

"I saw it too, girl." Terri sighed.

"What a shame. Rhonda is too good for him. She should leave him alone."

"It's not that easy," said Michele. "Sometimes it's just not that easy."

Saturday, November 8th, 2008

10:00 A.M.

Rhonda looked at herself in the mirror. She stared at her belly. The girls were right: Joe did not really love her like he proclaimed he did. Her twins would be home soon for the Thanksgiving holiday, and the thought of telling them about her pregnancy was just agonizing; she did not have the strength go to work. She called the hospital to have someone take her shift. The phone rang and Rhonda let it go to voicemail. A part of her wished it was Joe. Michele's voice echoed through her apartment:

"Hey Rhonda. Please call me. I hope you're okay. Love you, girl."

11:00 A.M.

Sherri and Terri's mother, Gloria, decided to spend the Saturday with her daughters at the yarn shop.

"You girls really did a wonderful job of getting this place together. It's beautiful. I am so happy to be here. Your father and I are very proud of our girls."

"Thanks, Mom," said Terri.

"It's great having you here with us, Mom," replied Sherri, kissing her on the cheek. Gloria began stacking yarn on shelves and in wicker baskets,

"What lovely yarn, and a hundred percent cashmere? You girls really have good taste."

"Well Mom, you always said nothing but the best for your twins," giggled Sherri. "We learned from you." Gloria smirked as she stood behind the counter, looking at her daughters with pride.

"Yes, girls. You're right."

Sherri smiled, "Mom, do you remember when Terri and I were six years old, and Auntie Maggie gave us those ugly beige knitted sweaters for Christmas? And you knitted little red flowers and put them around the collar to make them look better? Boy, was Auntie Maggie upset when she saw what you had done."

"Yes, I do remember that. I have to thank you girls for never telling Auntie Maggie what I really thought of those sweaters. May the good Lord rest her soul." They laughed as the doorbells jingled. Rhonda walked in; she looked worried and scared.

"What's wrong?" asked Sherri as she guided Rhonda to the sofa. Terri and her mother hurried over, and Terri poured Rhonda a cup of tea. Rhonda could no longer hold back her tears. She burst out crying.

"I've been trying to reach Joe for four days now. He won't return my calls. I saw him with another woman from the window during the Obama party the other night." She covered her face with her hands. "I'm hurt so badly, and I thought he would feel good about the baby and us being a family ... So many times he said he loved me and wanted a long-lasting relationship. I'm so ... I'm so embarrassed! What are my kids going to think of me? I can only imagine what my mother is going to say." Terri handed a box of tissues to Rhonda. Gloria took Rhonda's hands away from her face.

"Rhonda, calm down now. Having a baby is never a mess, it's a precious gift from God. I know relationships and matters of the heart can be painful. I been married over thirty years ... it's not pretty roses every day." Terri and Sherri looked at each other, and Gloria continued, "Rhonda child, if the man doesn't want you, then you should not want him! Your heart will heal. He hasn't

160

returned your calls in four days. Be smart enough to see the writing on the wall. Believe me, when I was younger, long before I married my husband, I would dump a man like a hot potato if he didn't return my call in four minutes. Let alone four days!"

Rhonda let out a little giggle and wiped tears from her eyes. Gloria handed her the cup of tea Terri had poured. "I understand when a woman loves, she loves hard. Oftentimes we give a man chance after chance after chance, wishing and hoping that he will change and see things like we do." Terri and Sherri remained silent, amazed at Gloria's words. They had never experienced her like this before; she had always been very quiet and reserved when they were growing up.

"You don't have to be ashamed of carrying a life inside of you. You can't live worrying about your two other children either, because sometimes children grow up and do as they want and not as they were taught. Don't worry about what anyone will say. Just take one day at time. Think about yourself and what *you* want. Stop crying and worrying about this Joe fella. He is not the important one right now. It's about you and that baby you're carrying." Rhonda sniffled and was about to speak when Michele walked into the shop.

"Hello everybody!" she exclaimed, but her smile quickly faded when she spotted Rhonda on the couch. "Rhonda! I've been trying to call you all week." Two Latina women walked in a few moments after Michele, and Terri intercepted them.

"Good Morning, how can I help you?" asked Terri.

"Yes," answered the younger woman, "We would like to see some yarn for crocheting baby blankets and booties." Rhonda started to cry again. Michelle waved at Gloria.

"Hey Miss Gloria, it's lovely to see you." Gloria smiled back.

"Hey Michelle. Look, Rhonda is upset about Joe. I'll go help Terri and Sherri with their customers so you ladies can talk." Michele rubbed Rhonda across her shoulders.

"Rhonda, what's going on with you?"

Rhonda sniffled, "You know, Joe just being an asshole, and not returning my calls." Michelle frowned.

"Rhonda, I'm sorry you're going through this ... rough patch. I really hope you hear from Joe soon."

"Yeah, me too," Rhonda composed herself and tried to change the subject. "So, what's going on with you?" Michelle looked away,

"Oh, nothing much at all."

"Now girl, one thing I know is that when a person says *not much* that means there is a *whole lot* going on. You might as well take off your coat and take a seat." The customers left the shop with their baby yarn and the twins and their mother rejoined the ladies.

"As you can see, Rhonda is not in any shape to give advice," said Gloria. "Now, I have known you most of your life, Michele. I can tell your problem without you even saying one word. You look exactly like your momma did when we were roommates in college and she had something going on. You're married to a fine man, good-looking too, and he works hard for you and Ashley. You and Charles are well educated with good careers. I was at your wedding so I know how long you been married." She paused, peering at Michelle. "You love Charles ... but something else is tickling your fancy right now. Am I right, young lady?" Michele looked at Terri and Sherri, as if to say: *how could your mother know this?* The sisters both shrugged their shoulders in amazement at their mother's wisdom. Michele motioned for Rhonda to move over so she could sit down.

"Michele ... you are treading on very thin ice if you decide to engage in something that might cost you your marriage," Gloria warned.

"With all due respect, how can you be so sure of this?" asked Michele.

"Because I was once in the same situation." Terri and Sherri looked at each other wide-eyed.

"Mother!" shouted Terri. Gloria raised her hands in defense.

"I have nothing to hide girls, so calm back down and settle your feathers. I haven't stayed married to your father for over thirty years by being a fool." As usual, Sherri ran to the door and locked it, flipping the open sign to closed. Gloria continued as the ladies listened intently.

"I once had feelings for another man when my girls were about twelve years old. His name was Sam. He volunteered at the election booths and did a lot of community events back in Richmond. We saw each other often. My husband ... well, he was always at work building his company. I did community service work while taking care of my children. So naturally, Sam and I spent a lot of time together working side by side. He was kind and sweet," she sighed. "And I loved my husband, but there was something I that adored about Sam. His charm was like the sunshine on the beach. I loved being with him ... Well, one day after helping out at the election polls Sam asked me out for a cup of coffee. I hesitated a bit. I smiled and said *'yes, I would like that.'* I was attracted to him. The reason I knew this is because I was looking for more, or so I thought. Sam was something different from my normal routine. He was the unfamiliar suspense that I wanted. Then it started. We would have lunch together two or three times a week. We went to different places most of time because we knew rumors would start up if were seen twice in the same place. Meanwhile, my husband never called or came home for lunch. All he did was work and work all day long. He came home just about the same time every night, which was late, and you girls were already in bed. Once in a while he did come home to have dinner with us – for special occasions. Trust me, I never stopped loving my husband, even the slightest bit, but if a husband or wife is not careful ... they can fall into something that can have your head spinning." Gloria looked directly at Michele.

"Mother, why didn't you ever tell Sherri and me about this?" asked Terri.

"I had no reason to tell you. Some things are better left unsaid unless there is a good reason to bring it up," she paused. "In many ways I loved Sam and he loved me. He was the person I could talk to about anything. We laughed at each other's silly jokes. We exchanged small gifts all the time, little things like a money clip, a lace handkerchief. If you spend enough time with someone you can end up loving them. After a while I learned that Sam was in the process of getting a divorce from his wife of five years. They had no children. He said she never wanted any kids."

"Mother ... you really fell in love with Sam?" Sherri asked.

"Yes. I was in love. I didn't mean for it to happen, but over time my heart began to feel love for Sam. I loved your father, too."

"How is that even possible?" asked Sherri.

"I can't explain it, but it is completely possible to love two men at the same time in totally different ways. You girls and your father were my life. Sam was just someone who brought me a certain happiness I was missing. Our relationship never became physical, but the desire was always there. When Sam's divorce was final and he was free to remarry, I was not willing to leave my husband or my girls. I remember having that kind of love for your father and I wanted to have it again."

The twins stared at her in shock. "Your father had done nothing wrong. He only wanted the best for our family. He believed that hard work was the only way to do that. I would watch your father staying up late working on business ideas and plans. I felt neglected, but in all honesty it was not fair to your father ... Your father was my first love, and nothing will ever replace that."

Michele frowned as the twins' mother looked at them and then went on.

"I decided to help my husband find me, and us, all over again. Your father loved me very much. He always had a loving heart and strong family values. He worked and worked because he loved his family and only wanted to give us the best. I was not willing to give up the man who I knew deeply and truly loved us so much. I mean, Sam filled some empty spaces in my life, but your father *is* my life. He chose me as his wife and we vowed to love each other until death do us part."

Gloria took a deep breath. "I began to make time for my marriage. Yes, it was tough, but love kept me where I truly belonged, which was at home with my husband and children. It might have been easier to say *I'm leaving you for Sam and I'm taking the girls,* but I would never take you girls from your father. I wanted my family together. I wanted my husband next to me at night no matter how late he came home from work. I would talk to him and listen to him, caress him, make love with him. After I expressed my concern with him, and let him know, he started coming home earlier and earlier. We found our way back to each other. I was never unhappy with your father, and I was not willing to give up everything for a temporary fix."

She looked at Michele. "So Michele, take some advice from an old woman who's been around the block and back. I know I look like I been in church all my life doing nothing but serving the Lord, but it's the crooked path that usually sets you on the right path in life."

"Mom," Terri said, "Sherri and I are happy you made the wise choice."

"Girls, that wise choice was simply the best choice. I am madly in love with your father. He is everything to me. God put us together. Michele, Rhonda, you are big girls now. Take a long look at your situations. One of you needs to stop chasing and crying over a no-good man and the other needs to keep her good man." The ladies sat in silence, absorbing her words. Gloria stood up from the sofa. "Now I have some work to do around this yarn shop. You ladies can talk amongst yourselves." She looked over at Terri. "Girl, you turn that sign back around. Sistah Knit is open for business!" Sherri followed her mother. Rhonda turned to Michele and meekly asked,

"What do you think?" Michele took a moment before answering.

"I respect her very much is what I think. She's right, I would never leave Charles and Ashley ... but Bradford is always on my mind."

Rhonda sighed, "Yes, and Joe is always on my mind." A few customers came into the shop. Terri and her mother guided them along the shelves. Sherri returned to the sofa.

"Hey, I'm sorry if my mom came on too strong."

"Don't apologize," said Rhonda. "Your mother is a wise woman. We needed to hear every word she spoke."

"Yes, we did," said Michele.

Rhonda touched Sherri's hand, "You know we just adore your mother. She was open and cared enough to share some parts of her personal life with us."

"Yeah, that was a shock! Terri and I have a lot of questions for her. Let's see what else we can find out about our *reserved* mother."

11:30 A.M.

"No! I am not bringing Phillip to see you in jail!" Shante paced back and forth in her bedroom as she yelled into her phone.

"He's *my* son, I want to see him!" insisted Phil-Quan.

"What the hell do you plan to *say*? Daddy's doing fine in jail?"

"Don't play with me Shante!" Phil-Quan was losing patience with her. "I want to see my son!"

"No fool, don't *you* play with *me*! I don't plan on wasting my time with your broke, drug-dealing ass anymore! You can see your son when you get out of jail. Hopefully by then he'll be a grown man, running his own legal, *drug free* business and living overseas far away from your no-good ass!"

Phil-Quan sucked at his teeth and lowered his voice, "Shante, you are wrong, girl. You don't gotta treat me like this. I messed up. Can't I get a second chance with you?"

"Phil-Quan, are you crazy or you just can't count? Your ass has been in and out of jail for years now and you're only 24 years old. I took you back too many damn times now. I'm done with you!"

"Shante, what the hell you mean you're done!?"

"What the hell is wrong with you Phil-Quan! Are you stupid? I am done means I AM DONE, FOOL!"

"You're not serious Shante. You're kidding me, right?"

"I am very serious Phil-Quan. Are you listening to me?"

"Yeah girl, I'm listening. Your man is listening to you, baby boo." He softened his voice, trying to win back her pity and tender affections. She was not buying it.

"Phil-Quan. I am only going to say this one more time. Listen up really good and I will explain." She said, strongly and sternly:

D – I don't want you.

O– over. your. ass.

N– not worth my time.

E– exit your no-good ass *the hell out of my life*!

"Shante, no, baby boo. I love you girl! Don't – " Shante hung up. Mrs. Brown had a smile on her face as she stood in the hall, eavesdropping proudly on the conversation. She whispered to herself, *Good for you Shante. I never liked that Phil-Quan anyway. He's no good for you.* When she heard Shante packing up her things into a shoulder bag, she hurried back to her bedroom and picked up her bible, pretending to be reading scriptures.

"Excuse me, Mrs. Brown. Would you mind watching Phillip for a while?" Shante stood in the doorway looking drained. "I want to go down to Sistah Knit for a while."

"No trouble at all, Shante, you go right ahead. Phillip will be fine here."

"Thanks Mrs. Brown. If Cherise wakes up before I get back, please tell her I'll be back soon."

"Don't worry about anything, Shante. You go enjoy yourself."

Shante walked into Sistah Knit about an hour later. Terri handed her a cup hot ginger tea on the spot.

"Thanks Terri, perfect timing." Terri frowned at her.

"I can tell something is wrong, what's up girl?"

"Hey Shante!" called Sherri from across the room. Shante took a few sips of the tea before sitting down on the sofa. Before she even got the chance to take off her coat, she announced in almost a whisper, "Phil-Quan is in jail."

"Jail? Are you all right girl?" Terri asked.

"Yeah ... I'm fine. I really am done with him this time."

"Girl you missed our mother giving words of wisdom about relationships earlier this morning. Rhonda and Michele got a life's lesson from her."

"Where are they?" asked Shante, looking around as she sipped her tea.

"They left about five minutes before you walked in," Terri paused, "Shante, are you sure you're okay?"

"Yeah girl. Phillip and I will be fine. I just can't take this mess with Phil-Quan anymore."

"You don't have to, Shante. I can tell you're a smart woman and there's no doubt how much you love Phillip."

"Thank you. I just wish I could go far away from here and start a new life. I've lived in Yonkers city housing all my life, seen things I wish I could un-see." She took a long drink. "Sometimes I close my eyes and dream of being somewhere peaceful and living a good life ... I want so much for both Phillip and Cherise. Can you understand what I mean?"

"Yes, I do understand. And you'll get to that peaceful place. One day soon. Cherise has a beautiful big sister and Phillip has a wonderful mother."

"Thanks, Terri."

"How is Cherise doing?"

"She's doing fine. I taught her how to purl stitch!"

"That's great," Terri smiled.

"Yeah, she really picked it up fast. She realized that purling is just knitting, only backwards."

"Good for her! Bring her to the shop on a Saturday. A few little girls about her age are coming in for beginner lessons."

"Thanks, she'll like that." The doorbells jingled and Justine walked in, smiling. Sherri and her mother waved hello to her as they helped some customers select yarn and needles. Terri gave her a hug, "Hey Justine." Justine sat next to Shante on the sofa and they greeted each other with a sisterly kiss on the cheek. Terri asked her, "Can I get you something warm to drink?"

"Sure Terri, thank you. Hot cocoa will be fine."

"All right, I will be right back," answered Terri. Justine rubbed her hands together to ward off the winter chill.

"How are you Shante?"

"Phil-Quan is in jail."

"Oh no! I'm so sorry to hear that. Are you okay?"

"Yeah, I'm all right, dumped him for good this time. I just want to raise my son and take care of Cherise. I graduate in June next year and Phil-Quan is *not* a part of my life's plan."

Justine smiled, "I hear that. Good for you Shante!"

"Terri said her mother was sharing words of wisdom about life and relationships earlier this morning."

"Really?"

"Yes girl, I guess we both got here too late." They laughed. Terri returned with the cocoa.

"Here you go ladies, enjoy. I added some pumpkin-spice-flavored marshmallows."

"That sounds so good, thank you Terri." Justine pulled a small wooden spoon out of the mug. The Sistah Knit logo was carved along the handle. "How cute!" exclaimed Justine.

"Yes, these are very nice, where did you get them?" asked Shante.

"Gigi of GGmadeit told me about this wood carver she met at the sheep and wool festival upstate in Rhinebeck. They do beautiful wood carving designs. Sherri and I ordered a couple dozen.

Aren't they adorable?" A new customer walked in, and Terri stood up. "Excuse me ladies, let me go help them."

Gloria and Sherri were still chatting with the others.

"Go on Terri, handle your business girl," said Justine. "You know we're not going anywhere. We will be right here on this sofa when you're done."

"Oh, I'm sure you will," replied Terri, laughing. Justine pulled out a project from her large Coach bag and began knitting.

"Holiday socks?" asked Shante.

"Yes. For my father, his Christmas present. I finished a nice pair of gloves for my mother."

"And ... Ronald? What are you knitting for him?" Shante asked, hesitantly.

"Well, I started a sweater, but it'll probably not be finished before Christmas," she paused, then said under her breath, " ... if we're even still together by Christmas." Shante gasped.

"Justine, girl! You *know* you are going to marry that man."

"I love him, but our paths are not going in the same direction right now."

"You'll work it out. I know you guys are taking some time apart but you might want to just get him something for Christmas. You know he will get something for you."

"You're right. What are you getting Phil-Quan for Christmas?" Justine laughed and Shante playfully shoved Justine's shoulder.

"Girl you better stop playing like that!"

11:30 A.M.

Rhonda's mother Barbara sat stoned-faced at the kitchen table staring at her daughter. Rhonda had just explained that she was eight weeks pregnant with Joe's baby, and she had tears flowing down her face.

"Mom ... I'm afraid I'll have to raise this baby alone." Her mother was quiet for a few minutes before she spoke.

"Rhonda. You are fifty years old, what were you thinking?"

"Mom, I know how old I am. You don't have to remind me."

"Hush, don't you interrupt me when I'm speaking!" She glared across the table. "I am not going to sit here and judge you, even though I just can't understand how you could let something like this happen at your age." Rhonda looked away and wiped tears from her eyes. "Hey! Look at me when I talk to you! I am still your mother." Rhonda sniffled. "You have got some decisions to make. What are the kids gonna think? They're both well into college. By the time they graduate you'll be starting all over with a new baby? You know I will stand by you no matter what, but you have to tell Tyree and Twinkle before Thanksgiving. If you wait any longer, you'll be showing and they'll know what's going on."

"Mom, I plan to tell them as soon as they come home."

"I know the tears are not because you're pregnant. Is there trouble in paradise, Rhonda?" Rhonda didn't answer her. She was still heartbroken over Joe. "I know tears of hurt when I see them, Rhonda. I had a few in my lifetime too." She raised her voice, "I never liked Joe for you. I told you a long time ago, that boy is no good!"

"Mom please!"

"Rhonda, you a grown-ass woman. Joe is nothing more than a very fine dressed-up garbage bag."

"Dressed-up garbage bag? What are you talking about Mom?" She could not stop the tears from falling.

"Rhonda, some men are nothing more than a well-dressed garbage bag, see? They're handsome, well-groomed, and smelling good on the outside, looking like they just stepped off the cover of a magazine. They wine and dine you and have you so wide open that you lead him directly into your bedroom every chance you get, which is exactly where he wants to be led because it's time for YOU to pay for all that wining and dining money he's spent on you. You're thinking, *wow this is the man of* my *dreams.* He says all the right things. He has no baggage or baby mama drama. Which, by the way, is a lie half the time, but because some women believe every damn thing a man tells them she can't see that. After some time has passed, and he's dipped in your cookie jar a few times and got his pleasure on, suddenly you don't hear from him as much and you begin to wonder why he hasn't called or stopped by." Rhonda's stomach dropped.

"Friends with benefits," continued her mom, "always works out much better for the man and never for a woman. Women have emotional soul ties after sleeping with a man. Pretty soon she attaches his last name to her first name. She feels like she's in love and thinks the man feels the same way. Oh no, he NEVER feels the same way. A dog can always get up and shake his tail!"

"Mom ... it's not like that with me and Joe."

"And how is it then, Rhonda? You need to wake up from thinking Joe is your *dream man.* You see, my daughter, your dressed-up fine looking garbage bag man is now starting to stink, and you don't like what you're smelling. He doesn't come around like he used to, he doesn't call as much. You're always on the hunt for him. He makes promises that he barely keeps."

"But Mom, Joe is different."

"Different from what, Rhonda? I could smell Joe's stink long before you even introduced me to him. Keep in mind, Joe being

173

younger than you has nothing to do with what I am saying. Most men are garbage bags. Your father was a garbage bag man too." Rhonda looked directly at her mother.

"Daddy?"

"Yes, your daddy. When I met him, he was dirty and greasy from his construction job. He literally was a stinky garbage bag man. The first time he tried to get my attention I thought he had *some nerve* trying to talk to me, looking and smelling so bad. Every day I walked past that construction site and he continued trying to get my attention until finally, I agreed to have coffee with him. He had to meet my parents first. That's the way real grown folks handled things back then. When he came to the door, he smelled good and he looked good. He had to have me back home in three hours. Whatever my father had said to him had Luke behaving like a nervous schoolboy. I continued to date your father, and each time we went out he was kind, loving, and most of all, very respectful. We got to know each other's morals and values. We talked about marriage, life, money, children, death. What I'm trying to tell you is that your father was not stinking on the inside. His heart was like the smell of fresh flowers. He was strong and had more confidence in himself than any man I ever knew. He had a good reputation wherever he went. People respected him. So, you see, Rhonda, my garbage bag man was a pure gem on the inside. The only tears I shed over your father was on the day he died. He made me happy for years, and our marriage was blessed. He loved life and he adored his family. You should have learned by now, Rhonda. At this point in your life you deserve to be happy. Lord knows I wish I could change things for you. I don't want to see you hurting like this. But I could see Joe is a man that only wants to do what Joe wants to do."

"How could you tell?"

"Your daddy taught me a lot about what an honest, loving man is. Besides, your eight uncles beat up a few of my other boys for me until your father came along." Rhonda smiled, just slightly. "Come here, Rhonda." Her mother squeezed her. "It's going to be okay. We will get through this." Rhonda cried hard in her mother's arms.

11:45 A.M.

Joe enjoyed his breakfast while reading the morning newspaper.

"Honey, you want some more eggs?" asked his wife, Erika. She poured her husband a second cup of coffee.

"No thank you, sweetheart. I've had enough. I'm always telling the boys: *nobody can scramble eggs like my Erika.*" She blushed as she rubbed him across his shoulder and kissed his forehead. He kissed her back and rubbed her pregnant belly. "How is my little man doing in there?"

"Your son is doing just fine."

"Good, that's what I like to hear."

"When is the next doctor's appointment?"

Erika's eyes widened, "It's today at three o'clock. You *said* you'd go with me. Ann is coming too."

"Oh ... baby, I have a very important meeting at three o'clock. Have your sister call me after or ... during the appointment, especially if anything is wrong. Okay?"

"All right ... but nothing will be wrong. I just really wish you could go with me," she smiled shyly. He kissed her on the belly again.

"I know. Me too, trust me. It's rare I have to work on a Saturday but this meeting is really important. I can pick you up around four or four-fifteen? You should be done by then, right?"

"Yes, I think so. That would be wonderful, Joe."

"All right then. I'll meet you at the doctor's office this afternoon."
He stood and took one last sip of coffee, "I better get going, I have
a lot to do at the office for a few hours."

Forty-five minutes later, Joe was sitting at his desk at Glen-Barns
Advertising Agency on Madison Avenue and 23rd Street. He
shuffled through some papers on his desk and made a few
business calls. He thought about Rhonda. He even felt sorry for
her; there would never be a serious relationship between them.

His office phone rang and startled him out of his thoughts. Mary,
the weekend receptionist, informed him he had a package
delivery at the front desk. When he went to pick it up, Mary
handed Joe a large gold and silver envelope. Joe examined it for a
moment. There was no return address. Mary watched him; she
was very nosy.

"Maybe it's a holiday card? Or party invitation?" she asked.

"I'll find out soon," Joe replied. He started to open the package in
front of Mary, then quickly decided to return to his office.

Who could this be from? He picked up a letter opener and ripped
across the top of the thick envelope. He pulled out a gold and
silver business card clipped to an invitation that read:

> *The BWB Organization of America cordially invites you to*
> *our Annual Thanksgiving Gala on Tuesday, November 22nd*
> *at the North Road Island Resort in Hill Crest, New York.*
> *Please respond by November 19th.*

Joe was excited to attend this event; working at BWB was his dream job. Only the best in the advertising industry got invited. He knew he had made good connections and would soon be a member. He sent his RSVP right away by both email and phone. He would let Erika know that he would be out of town for just that one day. His cell phone rang. He thought it was Erika calling from the doctor's office. It was Rhonda. *Damn. What the hell does she want?* He ignored the call and continued staring at the BWB invitation. A few seconds later, he got a text. He knew it was Rhonda. Joe deleted it without reading it.

1:30 PM

Rhonda put her phone on the coffee table. "Can't he just answer once? I just need to talk with him before I tell the kids about the baby." She thought about everything her mother had said and the advice the twins' mother had given her. She sighed, *I have the strength to bring up another child, and to have a happy life with Joe. It will be nice having a little baby around the house again. I know Joe will come around soon ... he's just scared. This is all new to him. At least Mom is supportive.* She rubbed her belly. "I love you baby girl, or baby boy. Can you hear your Mommy speaking to you? I love you and your daddy and he loves you too. We can't wait to see you soon."

2:15 P.M.

Erika listened to the voicemail her sister Ann had left on her cell phone: *"Hey baby, I'm on my way to pick you up. Be there in few minutes!"*

"Oh, my Lord," said Erika, "the time just flew by." She brushed her hair back and put it in a ponytail. She dressed herself in grey sweat pants and a navy-blue Morehouse sweatshirt. Erika retained her slim athletic figure throughout her pregnancy. She went to the gym three days a week and still ran three to five miles twice a week. She walked into the baby's nursery room she had prepared, looking around at all the beautiful things she'd set up for the arrival of her baby boy.

She opened the dresser drawer and pulled out a little pair of blue baby socks. She gently sorted through some of the other clothing, holding up a light blue sweater and matching hat. She picked up a soft brown teddy bear that wore a Yankees baseball cap and t-shirt. Erika smiled and rubbed her belly, "Your daddy is a big Yankees fan. I hope you'll be a Mets fan like your mommy."

She and Joe had painted the room pastel green and blue. Erika was a professional interior designer for celebrities and was able to design her nursery just as she dreamed it. The sunlight beamed perfectly into the room, just as she'd designed. She spoke to her belly. "I can't believe Joe and I still haven't chosen your name yet!" The doorbell rang. "Coming!" Erika hustled to the door to open it. She greeted her sister with a hug and kiss.

"Hey Ann! How are you?"

"I'm fine. How are *you* doing is the question."

"I feel good ... Hey, I even look good!" Erika rubbed her belly.

Ann laughed, "You would look better if you took off those ugly sweats." Erika scoffed.

"Girl, you know I'm comfortable in sweats pregnant or not. It's no big deal."

"Okay, you're right! I know how it is."

"I'm sure you do with four kids running around the house," Erika smiled. She loved children. She and Joe planned to have a least three more babies. Ann laughed.

"I only have one little six-year-old running around the house. Your other nieces and nephews are busy with their teenage business."

"Like I said, you know how it is," and they laughed together.

"Come on Erika, get your coat and let's get going."

"Yes ma'am, big sis, ma'am!" Erika saluted Ann, who had spent ten years in the military.

"You are too silly. Come on. You know Dr. Robert doesn't like patients being late."

2:30 P.M.

Joe called his best friend Kenny and bragged about his invitation to the BWB Thanksgiving Gala.

"No way man! You actually got invited? Kudos to you, man."

"Thanks Kenny ... I'd really love to know who recommended me."

"Hey, does it really matter? The point is you got invited."

"That's right," Joe smiled. "Listen man. I got to run and pick up Erika from the doctors. I'll holla at you later."

Joe stopped at a flower shop and bought a dozen red roses for Erika. While paying at the register, his cell phone rang. Again, he expected it to be Erika, but it was Rhonda. He ignored her call.

4:15 P.M.

"Everything seems to be fine," said Dr. Roberts. "I want to see you again in three weeks, so please see the receptionist on your way out." He scribbled on his prescription pad. "Here's a refill for your prenatal vitamins. Remember, just one a day. See you soon."

"Thank you, Doctor!" Erika smiled; she felt great. Ann had been talking with a few of the other expectant mothers in the waiting room when Erika came out.

"Everything good?"

"Yes, thank God." The receptionist handed Erika a little card to remind her of her next appointment. Ann helped Erika with her coat and they exited. In the elevator, Erika said, "Joe is supposed to meet us downstairs."

Ann raised her eyebrows, "But I thought he couldn't come with you today?"

"He couldn't. He had some work he needed to get done, but he said he was going to leave early."

"Good. I know he puts in long hours during the week."

"I love a hard-working man."

"Don't we all?" said Ann, smiling. When they stepped out of the elevator, Joe was standing in lobby with the roses. He spotted the ladies.

"Hey baby!" He kissed Erika gently on her lips. "Was everything okay?"

"Yes Joe, Dr. Roberts said everything is fine."

Joe greeted Ann with a friendly kiss to the cheek, "Hello my *favorite* sister-in-law."

"Hi Joe, nice to see you."

"These are for you honey," and he handed Erika the roses. "I love you and our baby so much." Erika giggled.

"Thank you, Joe, that's so sweet of you."

"Joe, you treat Erika *almost* as good as my Bobby treats me." They laughed, "Sis, your roses are beautiful, enjoy them."

"How about a late lunch, ladies?"

"I don't know Joe, it'll be five o'clock soon," said Erika, "Besides, Ann and I are going uptown to that new yarn shop, Sistah Knit. She needs some more yarn to finish the blanket for our son." Joe smiled, loving the pregnant glow of his wife.

"All right then ladies, I don't want to get in the middle of your yarn shopping plans. I'll take the flowers home for you." Erika pulled one long-stemmed rose from the bunch and smiled, "I'll take this one with me."

"Joe, how about making dinner for your wife?" laughed Ann.

He winked, "I already planned on doing that." He hailed a taxi for Erika and Ann. Waving goodbye, he watched the taxi drive off. He decided to head to the nearest bar before going home.

4:45 P.M.

The cab pulled up directly in front of Sistah Knit. The chilly winter breeze made Erika fasten the gray cable knit scarf tighter around her neck. It was her favorite item Ann had made for her. They rushed into the shop wanting to get out of the cold. Ann wore a thick pair of red knitted mittens and vigorously rubbed her hands together to shake off the chill. Sherri greeted them.

"Hi ladies! Welcome to Sistah Knit. My name is Sherri, how can I help you today?"

"Hi," replied Ann, still rubbing her hands together, "I'd like to see some wool and silk yarns, please."

"Sure, but first, may I get you ladies some tea or hot cocoa to drink?" Ann smiled.

"Oh wow. Yes please, cocoa."

"Cocoa sounds great, thank you," replied Erika.

"Okay," smiled Sherri. "Please, make yourselves comfortable. Have a look around." Terri came from the back of the shop to see who had arrived. Sherri motioned toward her, "This is my sister Terri. We're the owners of Sistah Knit."

"Nice to meet you Terri. I'm Ann and this is my sister Erika." Erika looked around the shop in awe.

181

"Very nice to meet you Terri. You and your sister have a beautiful shop," she said.

"Let me take your coats," said Terri, smiling. She noticed the cable knit scarf around Erika's neck. "Did you knit that beautiful scarf?"

"No. Ann is the knitter of the family. I might learn one day after I have this baby or ... after he goes off to college," Erika laughed.

Terri giggled, "Knitting is very relaxing. Definitely something worth learning." Ann looked around the shop, admiring the eclectic artwork on the walls.

"That's what Ann says about knitting. I just don't have the time to learn right now, but I do enjoy all the nice things Ann makes for me. Receiving is just as nice as giving!"

"I agree," laughed Terri. Sherri returned with a tray of cocoa.

"This a beautiful yarn shop. It's not like most yarn shops in the city," said Ann. "I saw your grand opening celebration on the news a couple of weeks ago. I'm sorry I didn't get here sooner." She sat down and picked up a mug of cocoa to take a sip. "Oh wow, this is good. It really knocks off the chill!"

"Enjoy, ladies," said Terri. "Sherri and I are very proud of Sistah Knit. It's been a lifelong dream of ours." Erika had been staring at the twins, "Hey ... I know who you are. You're those famous twin models from Paris. Terri and Sherri Constable, right?"

"Yes, that's us," said Sherri. Terri sat next to her sister with a big mug of cocoa.

"If my sister Ann watched the news more often, she would know who you guys are." The twins laughed. "Was modeling fun?"

"Yes, it was. Sherri and I enjoyed it for a long time. Sistah Knit is the next chapter in our lives."

"I've heard a lot of good things about this shop. It's really nice to finally have a yarn shop in Harlem," said Ann.

"We're happy to be here," said Sherri. Terri smiled in agreement. "You came at the perfect time. We have a thirty percent discount on baby yarns and twenty percent off everything else."

"Great!" replied Ann. "I do need some more soft baby blue yarn to finish a blanket for my new nephew." Ann patted Erika's belly.

"I am due January third," said Erika. "But we might have a New Year's baby! According to my doctor, at least."

"Wow. A New Year's baby. Is this your first child?" Terri asked.

"Yes, and I am very excited." Erika had been holding the rose Joe gave her. She set it down on the coffee table.

"Beautiful rose," said Sherri.

"My husband gave it to me after my doctor's appointment today," replied Erika.

"That's very sweet. I love roses," said Sherri.

"Come Ann, I'll show you our selection of baby yarns," said Terri.

"Sure, I would love to see what you have, lead the way!"

Sherri kept Erika company, "Have you and your husband picked out any baby names?"

"No, we haven't. I suppose we'll just look at our baby boy after he's born and decide what to call him right there and then!" They laughed. The front doorbells jingled. Sherri turned to see Shante, Justine, Michele, and Rhonda.

"The whole gang's here!" announced Sherri with a big grin. "Hello ladies, come on in, nice to see you all. I'll get some more cocoa."

Terri called out and waved, "Hello ladies!" They each removed their coats and got comfortable as usual. Terri introduced everyone, "Ladies, this is Ann and her sister Erika." Hellos and other greetings were exchanged. Shante, Michele, Justine, and Rhonda had their knitting projects in hand. Sherri returned with a larger tray of cocoa and some oatmeal cookies. Ann and Terri marveled over the different baby soft yarns.

"This is a nice surprise," said Sherri. "How is everyone doing?"

"Girl, you know it's not a surprise when we come by. We practically live here," said Michele. Everyone laughed.

"So, you ladies come here often?" asked Erika.

"Yes, we do. It's literally our home away from home. We've known the twins for years," said Rhonda.

Erika smiled, "It's good to see so many knitters. My sister Ann is making a baby blanket for my baby."

"That's so nice," replied Shante. "How far along are you?"

"Seven months."

"Do you know what you're having?" Rhonda asked.

"A boy," Erika looked down at her belly.

"That's great," said Shante. "I have a two-year-old son. His name is Phillip." Erika looked toward Michele, Justine, and Rhonda.

"Do you ladies have children?"

"I have a 14-year-old daughter, Ashley. My pride and joy," Michele smiled.

"I don't have any kids ... but maybe one day," Justine replied.

"I have two kids in college," said Rhonda firmly. The ladies waited for Rhonda to mention that she was pregnant. She said nothing.

Terri and Ann joined the group. "I got some nice yarn so I can finish that blanket for you Erika," Erika held up a skein to show her sister.

"Thanks, Sis," Erika smiled. Ann held up her mug of cocoa and toasted Terri and Sherri, "I can see why you ladies come here; this is a beautiful place. Such warm hospitality."

Rhonda asked, "Do you have children, Ann?"

"Yes, I have four. Two girls, sixteen and seventeen, and two boys, fourteen and six."

"Wow, a six-year-old?" replied Rhonda.

"Yes, three teenagers and a little one! Devon is a good boy. He sure knows how to work his siblings' nerves," she nodded at her sister. "They tell me I spoil them too much. Honestly, they spoil him just as much as I do." The ladies giggled.

"Was it hard adjusting to having a little child and teenagers at the same time?" Rhonda asked her.

"No, not at all," said Ann. "Everything fell right into place. My husband is a tremendous help. He loves kids, but I told him four is enough. He comes from a family of twelve." She paused. "How old are your kids?"

"They're both nineteen. Twins, Tyree and Twinkle. She attends Spelman College and my son is at Morehouse."

"Oh! Those are young adults. They'll be entering the workforce in a couple years," said Ann. Michele could see Rhonda did not know how to respond so she interjected, "Well, I don't know what I'll do with myself once Ashley is out on her own!"

"Believe me, you will find a brand new you," smiled Ann. "Life is full of surprises. You never know what's around the corner."

"Now *that* is very true," Michele replied. "You just never know what life will bring." She looked over at Rhonda. Justine picked up the rose from the table and admired it.

"Who's the lucky lady?"

"It's mine," said Erika, smiling as she took the rose from Justine. "My husband gave me a dozen roses today."

"That's sweet," said Justine.

"Joe is always giving Erika flowers," laughed Ann. "One day last spring her living room looked like a flower shop!"

"Yeah ... Joe used to give me flowers every day of the week," smiled Erika. Rhonda's heart stopped. She thought, *Don't be silly. It can't be your Joe.*

"How long have you and Joe been married?" Michele asked.

"Almost five years," replied Erika. Michele noticed Rhonda's blank stare.

Erika continued, "I knew from the first time I saw Joe he would be my husband. He always treated me like a queen since the day we met."

"Yes, a man that treats a lady like a queen is always a good catch," replied Rhonda. The other ladies went quiet as they finally caught on. They stared at Rhonda. It couldn't be him? Could it?

"That's right. And Joe's remained the same throughout our marriage," said Erika, giggling, "He is *very* romantic." Rhonda felt weak. Her mind raced. *There is no way,* she thought. Erika kept talking, "Joe and I love to take long walks. Actually, a few weeks ago, we even walked past your shop! It looked like there was a party going on. It was election night." She paused and waved her arms in the air, "Yay for our new President Barack Obama! We were *so* happy about Obama becoming President."

Rhonda quickly stood up, but she felt faint.

"Are you all right Rhonda?" Sherri asked.

"Um ... yeah. I just, I think I need to lie down for a few minutes." Sherri took Rhonda's elbow and escorted her to the back room. Justine laughed so as to not make Ann and Erika suspicious. Terri went behind the counter and bagged Ann's yarn. Michele stood up to retrieve Ann's and Erika's coats.

"It was so nice meeting you ladies. Please do come back again. Sorry to rush you out, but we have to help our friend."

"Oh, of course. We understand. I hope Rhonda feels better soon," said Erika.

"Yes, I hope she'll be okay," added Ann.

"Thank you for coming. Enjoy that yarn!" Erika and Ann got their stuff together and left. They were taken a little off guard but were happy they'd come. Ann waved once more through the display window before they walked to the corner of the street to hail a cab. Terri quickly locked the door and flipped the door sign from open to closed. The women huddled around Rhonda in the back bedroom. Sherri patted Rhonda's forehead with a cool cloth. Rhonda twisted and turned. She was frantic.

"Oh my God! Oh my God! That was Joe's wife! Oh my God Jesus!"

"Calm down Rhonda," said Terri.

Rhonda cried, "Joe is married? Oh my God!" She beat her fists into the mattress, "He's married! Erika is about to give birth to Joe's son. Oh God help me!" Rhonda sobbed from the deepest parts of her soul. She screamed, "Jesus how could he lie to me like this!" Michele tried to calm her down.

"Try to relax, Rhonda." Justine cried; she could not believe what she was witnessing. Shante also started to cry, feeling incredibly sorry for Rhonda.

"How could he do this to me?" screamed Rhonda. Terri tired to grab Rhonda's arm but she was out of control.

Shante yelled out, "Look she's bleeding!"

"Oh my God, call 911 Terri! Hurry!" shouted Sherri. Michele ran into the bathroom and snatched the purple bath towels from the rack. Rhonda continued to scream.

"God damn Joe! He's married! Oh God help me, help me please!"

8:00 P.M.

The ladies sat with Rhonda's mother in the waiting area for more than three hours at Harlem Hospital. Michele put her arms around Barbara.

"Don't worry, Mrs. James. Rhonda will be all right." Shante was on the phone with Mrs. Brown explaining everything that had happened. Justine cried softly. Terri and Sherri sat closely together with their arms locked together. The doctor entered the waiting room. "Is there a Mrs. James?"

"Yes! That's me!" Barbara quickly stood to meet the doctor. The other ladies trailed behind her.

"Are you all family?" he asked. The six of them were all huddled around him.

"Um, yes," replied Michele. The doctor stared at Mrs. Woods.

"Yes, it's fine," she said, "Please doctor, how is my daughter?"

He pulled the group near the corridor for some privacy, "I regret to inform you this, but she lost the baby." The women gasped. Justine cried harder. "Fortunately, your daughter is okay," the doctor continued. "Her condition is stable right now, and she's resting. She can have visitors tomorrow." Barbara frowned.

"Tomorrow? Is there any way I can see her for just a few minutes right now?"

"It's best if she has some rest. She's still recovering ..."

"Doctor," said Barbara, "she needs someone." The doctor looked at the women and the concern on their faces. They all seemed to really care about what had happened to Rhonda. He sighed.

"I guess ... all right. I understand. But only ten minutes, okay? She really needs to rest."

"When can Rhonda go home, Doctor?" asked Michele.

"Possibly in two or three days. Come this way, ma'am." The doctor escorted Barbara down the corridor.

Once they could not be seen, Michele asked the others, "Did you all see the look on her face when the doctor said Rhonda lost the baby?"

"What the hell is going on with Joe?" Justine asked, still wiping tears from her eyes.

"We're all shocked over this whole situation," replied Sherri.

"My heart ..." Justine sniffled, "just breaks for Rhonda."

"It's a damn shame," said Shante.

"Wow, I guess she really did love Joe. This broke her heart and mental state, literally," said Terri.

"This is crazy, how did she not know Joe was married?" asked Sherri.

"Because he has a master's and PhD degree in dishonesty and lying! Joe graduated from the university of *NOT A GOOD MAN,* that's how!" said Michele. "He was lying to Rhonda from day one. She believed every damn word his trifling ass spoke." Michele was visibly upset, her fists were clenched, and her face was tight; she felt like she could kill Joe.

Shante, in a tough tone, said, "Joe played Rhonda like a pimp plays his whores. He should be strung up to a fence with his legs spread-eagled, while the pit bulls chew away at his balls. That'd teach him a lesson." Everyone looked at Shante, surprised at her very brutal comment, but they agreed. Barbara returned to the waiting area.

"Here comes Rhonda's mom," said Shante.

"How is she doing Mrs. James?" Michele asked.

"She's resting. She's under some medication so she didn't know I was there. The doctor said she was under a lot of stress mentally and physically," she sighed. She sat down, feeling exhausted, "I'll have a long talk with her when she's better. I never liked Joe for my daughter," she paused. "Did you all know she was pregnant?" She looked at her daughter's friends, waiting. The ladies looked at Michele.

"Yes, she told us," sighed Michele.

"Rhonda does not need another child. What the hell was she thinking?"

11:05 P.M.

Joe had dropped off the flowers at home earlier, but he didn't stay for long. He went to his favorite club called Champs in the East Village. The music was always right and the drinks seemed to never stop coming. He returned home an hour before midnight. Erika had been sleeping for a few hours. He went to the kitchen and made himself a turkey sandwich. He looked at his cell phone and saw another message from Rhonda. For some reason, he decided to listen.

"Hello Joe ... please call me when you can ... I *need* to talk with you." She sounded really desperate. He dialed her number.

"Hey Rhonda ... I've been very busy. I'll come by your house in a few days."

11:45 P.M.

Michele entered her apartment and dropped her bag on the floor. She was exhausted from all the drama earlier in the evening. Ashley was asleep. Charles woke up when he heard her come into their bedroom. The book he'd been reading fell to the floor.

"Hey Babe," he said groggily, "How was your day?"

"I just left the Harlem hospital a little while ago." Charles sat up in bed.

"The hospital? Are you sick? Why didn't you call me? I thought you were at work! Are you okay?" He got out of the bed and rushed over to his wife.

"No honey, I'm fine. It's Rhonda."

"What's wrong with Rhonda?"

"She became ill this afternoon when we were at Sistah Knit. We drove her to the hospital."

"Well, what's wrong? They figure it out?" Charles asked. Michele thought before answering. She felt she could not go into the details.

"The doctors ... are running some tests. She is resting now." She felt bad lying to her husband, but she knew it was best for Rhonda. Charles kissed her on the forehead.

"Well it's time for *you* go get some rest, sweetheart." Michele settled down in her favorite chair. Charles massaged her shoulders. She leaned her head back, enjoying her husband's strong hands releasing the stress of the day.

"Thank you, Charles. That feels so good. What a crazy day."

Sunday, November 9th, 2008

1:05 A.M.

Justine stared at the clock on her night stand. She was unable to sleep, thinking about Rhonda. She went down to the kitchen and made herself a cup of tea. Her mother came down a few minutes later.

"Can't sleep?"

"Not a wink, Mom," replied Justine. "Rhonda is in the hospital."

"In the hospital? What happened?" She poured herself a cup of tea and sat across the table from her daughter.

"Mom, Rhonda was ... pregnant. She had a miscarriage ... and I think a nervous breakdown."

"Rhonda was pregnant? Are you serious, Justine?"

"Yup. Rhonda. Fifty-year-old Rhonda was pregnant. And the worst part of it all ... the man she loves is married!" Justine felt as if she were going to burst into tears again. Mrs. Whitaker was stunned. She tried to process all the information.

"Rhonda, your friend with two kids in college, was pregnant by a man who is already married?"

"Yes Mom. And we met his wife today. She came into the yarn shop." Mrs. Whitaker put her tea cup down on the saucer and then held up her right hand.

"Wait a damn minute. What do mean we met his wife today? Who is he and who is his wife?"

Justine spoke slowly, explaining the whole story. "Rhonda has been dating him for a while now."

"She did not know he was married?"

192

"Correct. Rhonda did not know he was married. Anyway, Joe's wife Erika came into the shop with her sister who needed to buy some yarn to finished a baby blanket –"

"Let me guess," said Mrs. Whitaker, "the baby blanket is for Erika?"

"Yes. How did you know that, Mom?"

"Never mind that, Justine. Finish the story."

"His wife is expecting their first child with Joe and ... so was Rhonda."

"Oh, my Lord. What a hot ghetto mess."

"Mom, how could you say such a thing?"

"Because that's what it is, Justine. A ghetto mess, stupid is as stupid does. At some point in life, and hopefully by fifty, a woman should have learned a few things!" Justine replied quickly in defense of Rhonda, "Well mother, she did not get pregnant by herself."

"Exactly my point. This Joe could not have gotten that far if she didn't allow it." Justine frowned.

"Okay, I guess I understand that."

"Let me explain to you in a clear, old-fashioned kind of way. Life will give us all ups and downs. Women, in my opinion, *always* take the blunt in most relationships. Good and bad. There is a difference between being *smart* and being *wise*."

"What do you mean?" Justine looked into her mother's eyes, searching.

"Starting when I was young, I played by the rules most of my life. Yes, I'd been hurt by a man or two before your father came along. But I never *forgot* that hurt. I tossed and turned; I wasn't able to sleep. I couldn't think straight! All I did was sit around waiting for the phone to ring, hoping for the man I thought was the love of my life to say he was sorry and couldn't live without me."

"Well, guess what, that phone call never came, but I survived and kept my chin up. I swallowed the hurt, and I moved on. I dealt with whatever cards life brought my way regarding relationships."

"Insecure women are always concerned about a man ... doing everything to make sure he's in check all the time. Honestly, we just want to make sure that the man won't leave us. Some women feel they need validation from a man to feel complete or important. Am I saying there is something wrong with doing and loving your man? Not at all. So long as all you're doing is being returned back to you lovingly." Justine listened carefully as her mother continued.

"I once felt like I needed validation from a man. Maybe because I watched my mother wait on my father's approval like a child waiting for a lollipop. Some would consider that *smart* because the woman allows the man to be the lead. He gives his approval on everything she does, but she never questions anything *he* does because a *smart* woman keeps peace with her mate. Well, *in my book,* that woman is a smart-ass fool because she can never make a decision on her own. She loses who she really is to gratify a man."

"A wise woman has learned from her past hurt and pains. Her eyes are opened, and she has no room in her life for foolishness or to be fooled by any man. No man created her so he can't truly validate her. Only God can do that."

"A wise woman knows what she is worth before a man tells her. Life has taught her wisdom. She is not moved by slick words and false love talk whispered in her ears. You can't get into her panties just for pleasure and fun and later have her sitting by the phone for a call that never comes. Ask God for wisdom, Justine."

Justine sat in silence, absorbing everything her mother said.

"Well, it's two in the morning. We better get some sleep now," Mrs. Whitaker announced.

"All right ... thanks Mom. Goodnight."

Shante was telling Mrs. Brown everything that had happened at the yarn shop when Cherise walked into the living room rubbing her sleepy eyes.

"Why are you up, Cherise?" Shante asked.

"I heard you talking."

"Go back to bed," Shante said softly, "I'll be there in a little while."

"Go back to sleep honey," said Mrs. Brown. Cherise yawned. She wanted to stay up and talk with her sister, or just listen. She slowly turned around and went back to their bedroom.

"Shante, you looked tired. You girls really had a rough night. I hope Rhonda will be okay." She stood from the sofa and started walking to the kitchen. "Come. Let me make you a hot cup of tea before you go to bed." Shante followed.

"Thank you, Mrs. Brown. It was awful Rhonda had to find out about Joe's marriage like that. You should have seen her screaming and crying. We were all so scared." Mrs. Brown put a tea kettle on the stove and turned up the flame. She reached into the cabinets for tea cups and saucers and set them on the table.

"That man should be ashamed of himself," said Mrs. Brown. Shante could see that Mrs. Brown was saddened by the story. "I might be old, but I am *not* dumb. I see what goes on with some of these no-good men ... and the so-called *good* men too." The tea kettle began to whistle. Mrs. Brown put a tea bag in each of their cups then poured the hot water before she returned the kettle back to the stove burner.

"It sounds like you've seen a few things in your time, Mrs. Brown."

"I sure have, Shante. A woman has to do her best to be smart. Women in some other countries do not have the rights to do what they want when they want. The man rules and laws are in place to keep it like that. In some places, young girls are married by ten years old to men old enough to be their grandfathers. Some are married off into rich families for money, and the girl grows up unhappy and often beaten if she does not give the husband a son. She has to *obey* her husband twenty-four seven! She cannot even think for herself. Many of those women would love to have the freedoms we have. To love and marry anyone you choose, to educate themselves, to own a business, to be free to be all they can be."

"But you know what I see in some women today, Shante? I see them disrespect themselves for the attention of a man. They are half-dressed or wearing something four sizes too small. They have every boyfriend or baby daddy's name tattooed all over their bodies. Fake fingernails so long that it looks like cat claws, and makeup so thick they look like Bozo the clown's sister. You know how many times I seen torn out weave tracks and braids all over the streets? All they want is a man, any man, it doesn't matter if he's somebody else's man, just give them a damn man so they can feel good about themselves."

Shante could not stop laughing. "Mrs. Brown, you're crazy."

"Shante. I am *just sayin'* and this is my opinion on how I see things today." She sipped her tea thoughtfully. "Don't get me wrong, in my day we had some characters too, but mostly, a woman took pride in herself. She was not loud with the mouth like a sailor on a weekend leave. We liked looking pretty and wearing clothes that actually fit us. We wore our own hair pressed and curled or rocked our natural hair in an afro. We didn't have names scrolled across our arms and legs in that ugly jai-house green ink. We carried ourselves like ladies of class and style. Look at pictures of Ruby Dee, Dorothy Dandridge, Lena Horne – look at Ella Fitzgerald. The women in Harlem back in the day were nothing like these women today. I know it's a different time, and things have changed, but Shante baby, always remember that class in a woman is a beautiful thing *and that never changes with time.* A man, whether he has class or not, will notice a woman with class right away. Always carry yourself with class and with dignity. That does not mean you stick your nose up at others as if you're better than other people. You carry yourself with elegance and class, weather you are wearing a ballroom gown or a pair of jeans and a t-shirt. You are a woman of class and you present yourself well. Try to make wise choices in all that you do. Get rid of old things and people that mean you no good in life." Shante paid close attention to Mrs. Brown.

"Life is just too short for the drama most women put up with to say they have a man. Yes, we will all make mistakes, but we should learn to do better from them. However, mistake after mistake after mistake tells me that that person is not learning anything, or they are just a damn fool altogether. Have a plan in life Shante, know what you want, and know what you're worth. It's okay to change your mind while you are on life's journey, because what works today may not work tomorrow." Shante nodded attentively and hoped Mrs. Brown would keep on.

"I miss my late husband Leroy. He was a good man, and I loved him. We had a good marriage. Forty years. He was man who knew what he wanted in life. He was loving and kind and always supportive of everything I did. He was not rich, but he gave me all of himself. He had pride and enjoyed life. I never had to search his pockets looking for phone numbers or sniff his clothes searching for the scent of another woman's perfume. I never had to wonder where or what he was doing when he was not at home. Leroy told my father his plan was that he wanted a wife, not just a *wifey* as some guys say today – which we both know means you have the duties of wife without marriage, until he gets tired of you and moves on to another woman who will happily take on that title. Part of my life's plan was to have a husband, and when our plans lined up together, we were married with the blessings of our parents in a church before God almighty. We had two sons, and they learned to be good men because their father taught them what being a man is. He never told them not to cry or that they should man up when they felt upset or hurt. I could never understand how one man can tell another to *man up* when they're both standing on the street corner holding their crotch with their pants hanging off their asses! They got no jobs, so how can they afford to wear two-dollar sneakers?" At this, Shante thought of her siblings. Mrs. Brown continued.

"Probably selling drugs and speaking slang like it's an exotic foreign language. They have babies with three and four different girls that they don't take care of and yet they always want to talk to the next pretty young girl that walks by. Hey Shorty come here! Let me holla at you a minute! What the hell kind of way is that to speak to a young lady? To anybody? My sons learned from their father how to address a lady, and how to find a respectful woman, not a home girl from around the block. Mr. Brown taught them well, may the Lord rest his soul. Shante, you deserve a good man to love you and help raise Phillip to be a good man. I pray that God will let that good man find you." She had finished her speech and her cup of tea and was obviously weary. "It's late child, let's go to bed."

2:00 A.M.

"Ann and I had a wonderful time at Sistah Knit," Erika whispered to Joe as they cuddled in bed. He had his right arm around her and his hand rested gently on her belly. Erika loved to talk with Joe during the late-night hours. "The owners, Terri and Sherri, were *so nice* to us. We were served tea and hot chocolate. Isn't that so sweet? Have you ever been to a place like that? ... Joe are you listing to me?"

"Yes honey, I hear you sweetheart. Nice," his voice was low and calm.

"Ann got some nice yarn to finish the blanket she's making for the baby. We met some friends of the owners. They said they come by the shop so much it's like they almost live there."

"Sounds like you had fun, sweetheart," Joe wished his wife would go to sleep, but Erika continued.

"We did, we had a really good time. Ann and I sat around getting to know everyone. They're so fun! They're all knitters. Shante is the youngest, she's a doll. She has a two-year-old son, Phillip. They live in Yonkers. She goes to school in Manhattan. I think she's really inspired by being around the older ladies. Then there's Justine, she works in music, and Michele ... and who else? Oh, and Rhonda." Joe banged opened his eyes, suddenly very interested in what Erika had to say.

"What young girl wants to be around older ladies?" he asked. He did not know what else to say. He knew it could only be one Rhonda that Erika was talking about. He grew nervous as he lay next to Erika.

"I don't see why not. Shante is a sweet young lady. A single mom trying to better herself. I suppose she sees them as mentors. I think that's nice, don't you?" Before Joe could answer Erika continued talking, "Anyway, Justine is a few years older than Shante. Michele and Rhonda are both older. Michele works for GMN. You've probably seen her on TV. She has a daughter named Ashley and Rhonda has two kids in college. They all were *such* a pleasure to talk to." Joe sat up quickly, suddenly remembering that he had left his second cell phone in the pocket of his bathrobe.

"What's wrong, Joe?"

"Oh, nothing baby, I just have to go to the bathroom." He scrambled out of bed and sped to the bathroom, locking the door behind him. He frantically searched the pockets of his bathrobe for the phone he'd hidden from Erika. That was the phone he used to call Rhonda. He turned on the faucet and flushed the toilet to drown out any suspicious noise. Erika kept talking all the while, a little louder so he could hear.

"Ann wants to go back next week just to have tea and knit. I suppose I could learn a thing or two. Ann always wanted to teach me how to knit. Wouldn't that be cool? I can knit our own clothes." Joe spoke loudly from behind the bathroom door.

"Yeah baby, that sounds nice." He found the cell phone, shut it off, and tucked it inside the side pocket of his boxers. He stepped out from the bathroom wearing his bathrobe. Erika was no longer in bed. *Is she onto me?* he wondered.

"Where are you going Erika?"

"I'm hungry, going to make a peanut butter and jelly. You want one?"

"Oh, no thanks. I'm good, baby." Erika walked out of the bedroom, headed for the kitchen. Joe removed the phone from his pocket and sent a text to Rhonda.

I will get in touch with you in a few days. I've been busy.

He quickly turned the cell off again and stashed it in his briefcase. He crawled back into bed. As he lay down, he whispered under his breath, "Damn Rhonda, this shit is really messed up."

Monday, November 17th, 2008

12:30 P.M.

"Rhonda. You've been out of the hospital for a week now. When are you going to pull yourself together?" Barbara asked. Rhonda felt numb. She had been lying in bed for days. She noticed the red flashing light on her home phone. She thought it might be Joe, but for the first time, she did not want to talk to him. Rhonda's mother figured she would not receive an answer to her question, and instead said, "Rhonda, you need to eat something."

"I will, Mom. I will."

"I brought some vegetable soup. I can make you a sandwich to go with it." Rhonda rubbed her temples and closed her eyes.

"Okay, thanks Mom." Her mother sighed.

"Rhonda, I don't want you worrying about Joe. Your kids will be home tomorrow and I don't want them seeing you like this. Please, pull yourself together. Things could always be worse." She left to fix a lunch.

Rhonda sat up in the bed and pushed her hair back from her face. She took a deep breath and said to herself, "How could *anything* be worse than this?" She got out of bed and looked at herself in the mirror. She placed her hand over her belly, rubbing in small circles, "No baby, no baby anymore. Joe is married and his wife is pregnant. Damn Joe, this shit *is messed up.*"

She looked at the red flashing message light on the phone. She was tempted to check the message but her mother interrupted her thoughts.

"Oh, you're out of bed. Good, here's your lunch." Barbara entered the room and set the tray of lunch on a table near the window.

"Thank you, Mom." Rhonda sat down at the table. Barbara kissed her on the top of her head. "Rhonda girl, you are gonna be fine."

"I know Ma. You always said everything happens for a reason." Barbara sat down across from her.

"Remember there is always a lesson to be learned from every situation, Rhonda." She smiled, "Well, I'll be back this evening to check on you. I have some errands to run and I told Terri and Sherri I'd stop by the shop and let them know how you're doing." Rhonda felt bad about avoiding her friends' phone calls. She knew how much they cared about her, but she just didn't feel up to talking. To anyone. Not yet.

"Thanks Ma ... Tell them I said hello and that I'll see them soon."

"I will. See you this evening." Barbara blew her a kiss before she left, and Rhonda waited to hear her lock the door behind her. As soon as her mother was gone, Rhonda walked over to the night stand and pressed the play button on the answering machine.

"Hey Rhonda. It's Joe. I left you a few messages ... please call me. I been thinking about you."

"Yeah, I bet you were thinking about me," Rhonda rolled her eyes. She skipped through the other messages and deleted them without even listening to them. "The hell with you Joe. I'll call you when *I* am good and ready." She went back to the table to eat her lunch.

Bradford sent Michele a text message asking her out to lunch again. She ignored it. He decided the best way to reach her would be to show up at her job. After charming his way through the lobby and front desk secretary, he knocked on her office door and slipped in without waiting for a response.

"Hello there," he announced, smiling. Michele was stunned.

"What the hell are you doing here?" she asked in a low voice, not wanting anyone else in the office to hear. She quickly got up, pulled him inside, and closed the office door behind him. When she turned around to face him, though, he grabbed her and kissed her passionately on the mouth. He had a strong grip on her waist. She felt mixed emotions. She wanted him to stop and continue at the same time. She reluctantly pushed him away.

"Bradford! You have to stop this. I'm married." He stared at her and tilted his head.

"You asked *me* to stop ... but you didn't say that *you* wanted to stop." Michele took a step away from him and shook her head.

"Bradford, *don't* put words in my mouth."

"C'mon. Let's go to lunch."

"No. I can't. I have to prepare for the evening news."

"Okay. I won't interrupt a lady while she's at work," he winked. Michele grew more frustrated.

"Bradford, why are you even here?"

"Michele, I had to see you. You wouldn't answer my text messages; I just ... I wanted to talk with you," Bradford sighed.

"Why are you acting like we're back in college? We have been over this before."

Without hesitation, he said, "I know what I feel, Michele. I love you." Michele turned away from him.

"Bradford, stop it *please*. You know I'm married. There is nothing more for us."

"Tell me how you really feel, Michele."

"I love my husband very much. That's how I feel," Michele said firmly. She walked to the door and opened it, waiting for him to leave. He hesitated.

"All right, I see. I'll call you later. Have a nice day."

"No, don't," Michele whispered. "And please do not show up at my office unannounced again." Bradford smiled. She looked him directly in the eye. "I mean it. I *will* call security."

"Well who do you think let me come up here unannounced? Security!" he winked and sauntered out of her office. She quickly closed the door behind him and returned to her desk. She closed her eyes and rested her head in her hands.

Oh God, help me. She had wanted to fully embrace his kiss. His arms wrapped around her felt good. A flush of sensual heat and sexual desire ran through her entire body. She wanted Bradford.

Wednesday, November 19th, 2008

5:30 PM

Two days had gone by before Rhonda decided to give Joe a call. When he answered, she put on a brave voice.

"How you been baby? I really been missing you." Joe let out a sigh of relief.

"I been missing you too, Rhonda. I called you several times." Joe was nervous. She paused for a second, thinking before answering him.

"Oh, I know ... I'm sorry. You know my kids will be home for Thanksgiving, so I have a lot to do." Joe figured that indeed made sense.

"All right, well can I come over to see you tonight?" He regained his confidence and his voice had its usual tone of relaxed assurance.

"Sure, Joe. I'd love to see you. It's been a while ... and you know how much I miss you when we're apart for a while." She tried to sound sexy, knowing that he'd respond and would fall right into her hands.

"Okay baby girl. I can come over around nine. I'll bring a bottle of wine to get our night started."

"Sure Joe. That sounds lovely; I'll see you later," she slowly hung up the phone, smiling.

6:00 P.M.

"What do you mean you have to go away for work?" Michele shouted. "It's our eighteenth wedding anniversary! You have other plans?"

"Michele, sweetheart," Charles sighed, "this is not my plan. It's work and I can't get out of this meeting. I have a presentation due in Los Angeles. The dates got changed around several times. I'll fly out and do the presentation, and I'll be back on the nineteenth." Michele was silent. "Michele, it's only one day. We can celebrate when I return."

"Charles ... you promised we would have a special anniversary."

"And we *will* have a special wedding anniversary. That has not changed." Michele said nothing. "Hey, why don't you come with me to L.A.? We could celebrate there."

"I can't. I'm on special assignment for the network. It's not easy to just pick up and leave." Michele was visibly upset. Charles looked her directly in the eyes.

"Well sweetheart, it looks like we're going to have to wait a day before we can celebrate."

"Yup. I suppose we'll have to wait." Michele replied, passively. They continued with dinner with few words spoken between them.

6:30 P.M.

"Mom I am *so* excited Stanley is coming home for Thanksgiving. We have so much to catch up on!"

"Yes, it will be good to have everyone together for the holidays. It'll be nice having both of my children home again ... more coffee, Justine?"

"Thanks Mom, yes, I'll have another cup, please." Justine held the mug steady as her mother poured the coffee slowly. Mr. Whitaker came into the kitchen smiling.

"My two favorite ladies."

"Hello Daddy."

"Hello baby girl," he kissed Justine on the forehead.

"Honey, would you like some coffee?"

"Yes, dear." Mrs. Whitaker poured her husband a hot cup of coffee. He sat down next to his wife.

"Did I hear a someone say Stanley?"

"Yes! Stanley will be coming home for Thanksgiving this year," said Justine excitedly.

"I'll get his room ready in a few days," said Mrs. Whitaker. Justine smiled, "Mom, you always keep Stanley's room clean and fresh."

"You sure do," replied Mr. Whitaker, sipping his coffee and winking at Justine.

"I know ... but I should change the linens. Maybe hang new curtains ..."

"Mom," Justine giggled, "Stanley won't care about new curtains. He won't even notice."

"Well that doesn't matter at all. I just want to make sure everything is perfect for him."

"Oh! I forgot to mention," said Justine, "Stanley called last week to say he's bringing home a friend for dinner ... maybe *they'll* notice the curtains." Mrs. Whitaker looked surprised.

"A friend? Is Stanley dating someone?"

"I don't know, maybe," said Justine as she raised an eyebrow.

"Well, he hasn't said anything to me, so don't go jumping the gun," said Mrs. Whitaker.

"Look, all he said was that he was bringing a friend for dinner," said Justine.

"Hmm. You know Stanley has never brought anyone home during the holidays."

"I hope he is dating someone," said Mr. Whitaker, firmly. "That boy needs to settle down." He paused. "Speaking of settling down and starting a family ... What about you, Justine?"

"Um, what do you mean, Daddy?"

"Justine, you know I'm talking about you and Ronald. When are you going to settle down and start a family? Your mother and I would like to have some grandchildren."

"Oh Daddy, you and Mom will have grandkids one day," she sipped her coffee.

"Well, I hope it's within our lifetime," said her father, chuckling.

"Justine, your father is right," said Mrs. Whitaker, more sternly. "You and Stanley are so business-driven ... and that's good but you have to take out time and live your life and build a family." Justine didn't feel like having this conversation once more.

"I am *just* getting started with my record business. I want to be able to provide for this *family* you're always talking about." Her father looked confused.

"Provide for your family? You sound like you're planning on being a single parent." Justine tried to be polite.

"No Daddy. I want to be able to provide for myself and my children if I have to."

"What do you mean if you have to? Is Ronald not able to provide, did he lose his job?"

"No Daddy, that's not what I mean, and no Ronald did not lose his job." Mrs. Whitaker cleared her throat as if she wanted to say something. Justine continued, "I want to focus on one thing at time. First my business ... and *then* marriage. Lots of people have careers and marry later on." Mrs. Whitaker sighed.

"But Justine, those people don't have anyone. You have Ronald. He's a good man." Justine grew frustrated.

"I don't have to rush into anything, Mom." Justine could not bear the thought of her parents knowing that she and Ronald were taking some time apart.

"We understand Justine," said her father. "However, we want some grandbabies. And we want you to be happy."

"Justine is a smart young woman," added her mom, giving Mr. Whitaker a look. "We know you will make the right choices."

"And I *will* make the right choices," said Justine. They sat in silence for a moment before Mr. Whitaker spoke up.

"Well ladies, good night. This old man needs his rest so he can live long enough to see his grandkids someday." Justine smiled at her father as he got up from the table. Mrs. Whitaker laughed.

"Honey, I will be up soon."

"Goodnight Daddy, love you."

"I love you too, Justine."

7:00 P.M.

"Shante, will we ever go back home to Mommy's house?" Cherise asked. Shante avoided looking at her little sister's face.

"You don't like it at Mrs. Brown's house?" she asked.

"I do ... but I miss Mommy. I saw Dante today. He said I can come home anytime I want." Shante sighed and bent down so she was face to face with her.

"Cherise, listen to me. I miss Mommy too, but she is not well and she needs help. She can't look after you properly right now."

"I can take care of Mommy, Shante. I could do it; she needs me."

"Cherise, I promise you, Mrs. Brown and I are gonna do our best to get Mommy all the help she needs to get better."

"Then ... after ... can I go home?" Cherise had a sad look on her face. Shante stood and rubbed her sister's neck.

"Let's talk about it when Mommy is better, okay?"

"All right Shante."

"Cherise, you are safe at Mrs. Brown's house. Everything is going to be fine. I want you to trust me." Cherise hugged Shante; she did not want her to see that tears were forming in her eyes. "Little lady," Shante said, smiling, "you just keep your mind on your school work and keep your grades up."

"I will Shante."

"You know Phillip loves you and needs you very much."

"I can take care of Phillip for you, Shante."

"Yes, you can. You already do a great job of looking after him and helping Mrs. Brown. We both *really* appreciate your help." Shante kissed Cherise on the forehead. "Okay, homework time, young lady!" Cherise smiled and went into their bedroom to start her schoolwork.

Shante moved toward the windows in the living room. She looked out into the darkness of the winter season. The stars above shone through all the smog of the city. She wished her problems were as far away as those stars. Shante got a text message that broke her thoughts. It was from her sister Denise:

Hey Shante can you meet me at the coffee shop on the corner in 15 min?

Shante stared at the screen. She hadn't spoken to her sister in a while; she was surprised to hear from her.

"Hello everyone," Mrs. Brown announced as she bustled into the apartment, carrying grocery bags in each hand. Shante quickly texted Denise back.

Be there in a few.

Shante hurried over to help Mrs. Brown with her load. "Hey Mrs. Brown. Let me help you with those bags."

"Thank you, sweetie. I thought the elevator was broken, it took so long to come." She pulled her coat off and hung it near the door. "Where's Cherise? I got her some cookie dough ice cream."

"She's doing homework. Phillip is napping." Shante hesitated. "Mrs. Brown ... I need to go out for a while. My sister Denise wants to talk to me." Mrs. Brown looked concerned.

"Sure Shante, go on. You do what you gotta do. You know the kids will be fine."

"Thanks Mrs. Brown. I won't be very long." She grabbed her coat and headed down the hallway. To her surprise, the elevator came quickly. Once she got outside, she walked fast, wanting to avoid the local drug dealers and catcalls. She said to herself, *I have got to get the hell out of this neighborhood.*

The scents of Chinese food, spicy fried chicken, and French fries lingered in the air for blocks. When she arrived at the coffee shop, Shante saw her sister sitting in a booth near the window. Denise waved at Shante as she walked in. The two hugged. Shante sat.

"What's up Denise, you okay?"

"Yeah ... I'm fine, Shante. I miss you and Cherise."

"We miss you too," Shante sighed, "Cherise told me she saw Dante earlier today. He told her she can come back whenever she wants." A smiling waitress came over to their table to take their order. Once she was gone, Denise lowered her voice.

"Shante ... you did the right thing by getting our little sister out of that place. The police were up in there the other night." Shante rolled her eyes.

"Again?"

"Yeah. Mommy was fighting with one of her boyfriends and some of her friends tried to break it up ... Mommy's left arm is broken."

"I hate to say it Denise, but even if both her arms were broken, she'd still find a way to get high." Denise looked worried.

"Shante, I– I don't know how to help her." Shante sighed.

"Neither do I. I just know that I have to keep Phillip and Cherise out of that environment."

"Shante ... I think I'm gonna move out after Thanksgiving."

"Good for you Denise. What are your plans?" Denise hesitated.

"Well ... Derrick and I are gonna move in together." The waitress brought their coffee, setting two steaming mugs on the table, along with a small plate of cornbread.

"Ladies, the hot cornbread is on the house, enjoy."

"Thank you," said Denise, sipping her black coffee right away. Shante raised her eyebrows.

"Derrick? Didn't he just have a baby last month with Kiesha?"

"Yes ... but they're not together anymore ... It's just something that happened between them." Denise avoided her sister's eyes.

"Is that what Derrick told you? *Just something that happened?*" Denise was silent. "Are you kidding me girl? That's bull crap Denise, and you know it." Shante started to raise her voice.

"Shante," Denise said calmly, "I have been dating him for a year and a half now."

"Oh yeah? And nine months of that year and a half he had a baby with someone else." Denise said nothing. "Look. I'm planning on moving out of Mrs. Brown's house as soon as I can get a job and save up some money. I graduate in June ... so maybe we can work on getting a place together? What do you think?" Shante was looking deeply into her sister's eyes, hoping she would agree.

"Shante, I can't wait that long, I need to get out of Mommy's house as soon as possible. You don't know what it's like there anymore. It's *so* bad. I'm surprised the housing authority hasn't thrown her out yet."

"So you really think moving in with Derrick is the best answer for you?" She put her hand on her head, thinking about other options for her sister. "What about moving in with Auntie Grace?" Denise sucked her teeth and gave Shante a scowl.

"Shante, she lives all the way in Long Island. I can't be going all the way out there."

"Why not? You know she'd love the help. She offered that Phillip and I could stay with her. I know she would welcome you." Denise looked down at her chipped pink nail polish.

"Well, Derrick said he would – "

"Girl, the hell with Derrick!" Shante said, "He's just a boyfriend. He is *not* your whole life." Denise sat back in her seat.

"Well Shante, Phil-Quan is *your* boyfriend, right?"

"No, he is not my boyfriend. He's Phillip's daddy and that's all. I told him what to kiss and where to go!" She lowered her voice. "That man is headed nowhere fast ... Anyway, enough about me. I'm not the reason you called." Denise looked away. Shante continued, "So you really going to leave Mommy's house after Thanksgiving?"

"Yes. I am."

"Denise ... maybe you could stay with a friend for a few days until we figure something else out."

"I already *have* something figured out, Shante. I'm going with Derrick."

"All right so, if you move in with Derrick, who's going to pay the rent? I assume you'll be doing it because he has no job."

"He said he would find a job right away." Shante stared at her sister for a moment before she sighed once again in frustration.

"Denise, don't you see that moving in with him is a bad idea?"

9:00 P.M.

Rhonda was not a smoker, but she lit a cigarette and took a long drag as she stared ahead. She took a sip from a glass of wine she had poured herself. Joe sat across the table from her. "What are you doing, Rhonda?" he asked, eyebrows raised. Rhonda exhaled the cigarette smoke slowly.

"What the hell does it look like I'm doing?" Her voice was low and calm. Joe fidgeted in his seat.

"But Rhonda ... you're pregnant. You shouldn't be drinking and smoking."

"And? What do you care about what I should and shouldn't be doing?" She blew smoke rings from her lips. She remembered she used to be really good at them in college. "Why do you look so confused, Joe?" She poured him a glass of wine and he drank it quickly.

"I ... I don't understand. Why you are drinking and smoking, is something wrong?"

"I am drinking and smoking because I can. And no, nothing is wrong, not anymore." Joe tried to lighten the mood.

"Well, whatever it is, you know I am here for you baby." He reached for her hand but she pulled back, looking sharply at his big brown eyes. Joe sat back and ground his teeth.

"Look Rhonda. I am tired of playing games with you."

"Oh yeah? *You're* tired of playing games?"

"Yes, Rhonda, I am." She rolled her eyes.

"Well, you *should* be tired of playing games with me ... and your *wife*." Joe's heart skipped a beat and then pounded. He heard it throughout his entire body.

"Rhonda, what the hell are you talking about?" He tried to remain calm and appear unmoved by her remark.

"Joe don't try to play stupid with me. You are a married man and your wife is pregnant!"

Joe was shocked. So, it really was the same Rhonda that Erika had been talking about.

"Rhonda, I was going to ..." his voice suddenly became shaky, as if he'd lost his usual confidence.

"Don't say a *damn* word Joe!"

"But Rhonda, really! I was – "

"Shut up Joe! Just *shut the hell up*! I met your wife Erika last week at Sistah Knit." She remained cool and collected, even though she raised her voice. She looked Joe straight in the eye and crushed the butt of her cigarette in the ashtray on the table. Her knitting basket was sitting on the dining room table next to the bottle of wine. She reached under a pile of yarn and pulled out a Smith & Wesson .38 revolver. She held it delicately in her right hand and pointed it right at Joe. He quickly jumped up and shouted.

"Rhonda! What the hell are you *doing* girl!"

"Sit your handsome monkey ass down, Joe. I'm playing games now, *player*." Joe hesitated. "I said sit!" Rhonda yelled. Joe sat down slowly; his legs trembled.

"Rhonda, I can explain everything. Sweetheart." She poured more wine into her glass as she kept the gun pointed steady in her right hand.

"No Joe, you don't have to explain a goddamn thing. I don't want to hear your sorry ass stories. Tonight I'm going to tell you a story." Sweat ran down Joe's face. "Relax Joe, take it easy. Isn't that what you always told me? Relax, Rhonda, take it easy."

"Rhonda baby. I never meant to hurt you."

"Then tell me Joe, what did you mean to do?" For once, Joe was at a loss for words. He was genuinely frightened, thinking Rhonda seriously was going to shoot him. "What's wrong Joe, cat got your tongue? Or is your mouth full of cotton?" Joe stared at her with wide eyes. "You are usually a man of many words. Here, have some more wine." She leaned over and poured more wine in his glass. His cell phone rang. He slowly reached in his pocket to answer it.

"No, no, no Joe. Don't answer it. It's probably your wife. You never returned *my* calls right away, so I think you can let her wait." She kept the gun pointed at him. Once the phone stopped ringing, she spoke again, "So, here is *my* story, Joe. You were never going to tell me you were married. I know that now. And yeah, I was a fool for a minute, Joe. You thought you was the big man. Got a wife at home and me and all my loveliness as your side chick. Is that what you tell your home boys in the club, Joe?"

"Rhonda, it's not like that at all."

"Then how is it Joe? You can't talk your way out of this mess. I mean, what do you think you could possibly tell me?" Rhonda waved the gun around as she spoke. "Were you going to say, 'Oh, by the way Rhonda, I have a wife and a baby on the way.' Huh? Were you gonna wait till I went into labor?

"*Honestly* Rhonda I – "

"Honestly what, Joe? You don't even know what being honest is, so stop it!" Rhonda was full of rage but kept a straight face as she pushed the gun closer to Joe and pulled the trigger. Joe jumped and screamed.

"Rhonda!" No explosion, just a loud click.

"Are you scared Joe? The next shot might be real."

"Rhonda, stop it please! I never meant to hurt you!" His voice cracked as if he were about to cry.

"Didn't I tell you to shut up? You're gonna listen to me and don't say one damn word!"

Joe trembled. Rhonda went on. "You know I really loved you Joe. I cared about you." Joe tried to look away.

"Don't turn your damn head! Look at me when I'm talking to you!" With his head lowered, he turned his eyes to her. "You just wanted sex, and you tried to make a fool out of me."

"Rhonda I – " she raised the revolver closer to his face.

"Be quiet Joe! Just listen! Don't make me tell you again. I really cared about you, Joe, and you played me for a fool. Did you laugh about it with your home boys? You led me to believe that you were a single man. I should *kill* your black ass right now. It's a hell of a thin line between love and hate, isn't it, Joe?" Joe was like a deer in headlights; he couldn't move or say a word. He nodded his head in agreement. "It's okay Joe, you can talk now. Go ahead. What have you got to say before I shut your ass up permanently?"

"Rhonda, I really never meant to hurt you. I never wanted you to find out."

"Yeah I sure bet you didn't want me to find out."

"I did love you Rhonda," he wiped sweat off from his forehead with the back of his arm.

"You *did* love me? That was past tense there, Joe."

"No Rhonda. I still love you. I love you, really. I do love you." Rhonda rolled her eyes.

"Joe, stop lying! You don't know what to say right now. Look at you, sitting there sweating and shaking. What happened to mister cool-smooth Joe?" She lit another cigarette with her left hand. "I suppose you want to know why I'm smoking and drinking?" He stared. "I'll tell you why, Joe. Because I am not pregnant anymore with your child. She took a long hard drag on the cigarette. Joe looked puzzled but was too afraid to speak. "If you're wondering how, it's because I had a miscarriage a few hours after I met your wife. I went into shock after I found out you're married and about to have a son." She paused, expecting him to speak up, but he said nothing. "It was just such a slap in the face, Joe. Because I really thought I could get you to love me enough to marry me and raise our child together." Joe of course was secretly relieved to hear that Rhonda was not pregnant.

"I did a lot of thinking over the past few days, and I learned that I must have been a damn fool to ever think that you and I could make something real of our relationship in the first place. All the signs were right there in front of my face. You would only call or answer your cell phone on *your* terms. I know you have two cell phones, and that should have told me something right there!" Joe looked shocked that she knew about his two cell phones. "Does your wife know about your two cell phones, Joe?"

"Rhonda I'm ... very sorry about all this."

"Yeah Joe, you're so damn sorry now. What else can you say? Your ass is just sorry you got caught. Your wife thinks she's the only woman because she has a ring on her finger. But little does she know that her little Joey has Rhonda, too." Joe's eyes widened.

"Rhonda, you won't tell her, please?"

"Maybe I did already Joe," Rhonda smirked. "If you make it home tonight, you'll find out."

"Rhonda, please!" he had tears rolling down his face now. "Please Rhonda, please don't."

"Oh, you begging now? I should make your ass get on all fours and crawl around like the dog that you are. You disrespected me Joe. You lied and you stole my love and broke my heart. I will get over you but I will *never* forget it." She extended her arm and aimed the gun directly at his chest.

"Rhonda no! No! Rhonda! Please don't do this! Please! Yes I'm begging! I'm begging you! I'm not worth it Rhonda!"

"Finally! Now you're talking the real truth. You are not worth it. As a matter of fact, you ain't worth *nothing*." She spun the gun around on her index finger. "I might be upset and angry but I ain't about to lose my entire life and children on your worthless, no-good black ass." Joe clenched his fists. "All right, this is how it's gonna work. There is one bullet in this gun. I pulled the trigger once, so that means you have five more chances in the cylinder. So, Joe, if you can run faster than I can pull the next five rounds ... then you'll live. On the count of three, I am going to pull this trigger." Joe stood up quickly.

"Sit your ass down! I said on the count of three, you fool." Joe's heart was beating fast. He even peed himself. Rhonda noticed and started to laugh hysterically.

"One," she lit another cigarette and slowly inhaled and exhaled the smoke. Smiling, she asked, "Joe would you like something to eat?" She waited for him to respond. He swallowed hard.

"Uh, no. No, no thank you, Rhonda," his voice was squeaky, barely above a whisper.

"Two. Are you sure Joe? I don't mind preparing what might be your last meal." She took pleasure in watching him tremble like a withered leaf. "Three." Aiming directly at Joe, she pulled the trigger. Joe ran so fast his right shoe came off as he fell over the coffee table. He scrambled to unlock the door, his sweaty hands making it hard for him to get a good grip on the locks. She pulled the trigger once more. Another click. Joe ran out screaming down the hall. He had left his coat on the sofa. Her apartment door was wide open. Rhonda could not stop laughing as she closed the door and locked it. She took another puff of her cigarette and stubbed it out, saying to herself, "It was good to shake his unfaithful ass up," she smiled. "He'll never know the gun wasn't loaded ... truth is, I love him too much to kill him."

Friday, November 21st, 2008

7:00 P.M.

Michele, Shante, Justine, Terri, and Sherri sat in a circle with their knitting projects in their laps as they listened carefully to Rhonda tell her story on how she "scared Joe out of his shoes."

"Rhonda, are you out of your mind?" Terri asked.

"Yeah girl! Joe could press charges on you or something," Michele said.

"What the hell is he gonna tell the police?" asked Rhonda.

"The gun should have actually been loaded," said Shante, who was getting a real kick out of Rhonda's storytelling skills. "He treated you wrong."

"Hell yeah! Joe *should* be shot!" Sherri said as she looked at Shante, nodding.

"I am so *done* with him," smiled Rhonda.

"Well, good for you," Michele said. "Lord knows you deserve better."

"My mother thought I was crazy for what I did. She thinks Joe got off too easy."

"That's what I'm saying! You should have popped a cap in his ass with that gun," said Shante. They all laughed.

"Ladies, I thank all of you for standing beside me through this crazy ordeal. I really appreciate everything you did for me ... I love you guys," Rhonda glowed.

"That's what good Sistah friends are for," replied Michele.

"Yeah, we're glad you're all right and feeling better every day," said Justine.

"Me too," said Rhonda, relaxing in her seat. "Thanksgiving is next week. My kids will be home ... I just want to hug them and tell them how much they are loved. It's almost a new year and I want a fresh start of working on *myself*."

"Nothing is wrong with a woman wanting to improve herself," said Shante. Rhonda smiled at her.

"Well ladies, speaking of Thanksgiving ... Sherri and I have been working on the Sistah Knit pre-Thanksgiving dinner," Terri announced.

"It's not going to be the whole neighborhood, just us girls," added Sherri.

"Sounds lovely, what can we bring?" Michele asked.

"I could bring collard greens!" said Justine. Terri waved her hands.

"No, no, no ladies. You don't have to bring a thing. Sherri and I are taking care of everything."

"You two are gonna cook?" Michele asked. The twins laughed.

"No way!" said Terri. "Make My Plate Soul is fixing the entire meal for us."

"Ooh! I heard their food is great," said Justine excitedly.

"Yes, people are always saying how good the food is," said Michele.

"Sherri and I thought it would be a good idea for all of us to spend some time together before Thanksgiving. So, on next Tuesday we'll close the shop early." Sherri smiled.

"Tell them about you-know-who!"

"Oh, yes," Terri smiled. "And we will have a *special guest* joining us this year."

"Who did you and Sherri invite?" Michele asked. The others looked very curious.

"Gigi of GGmadeit!" said Terri.

"Omigod, that's wonderful!" Justine said.

"Yes, Sherri and I have been following her on social media. We reached out to her a few times after she attended our grand opening and the election party. She's awesome and would love to join us for dinner."

"Wow. Gigi is actually going to have dinner with us. I'm so thrilled," said Michele. Shante cleared her throat.

"Ladies, I just wanted to say that ... I'm happy to be a part of your pre-Thanksgiving dinner. It has been so much fun hanging out with you all over the past weeks. You've all made me feel so welcomed and loved. It means a lot to be a part of this great *Sistah friendship*. And I'm excited about Gigi coming next week, too."

"Shante, you are forever family with us," said Terri. The others agreed as they stood to form a group hug.

Saturday, November 22nd, 2008

4:00 P.M.

Shante slowly walked toward her mother's apartment. As usual, the door was open. She stepped in with caution. Surprisingly, the house was quiet: no music, no crowds of people in the living room, not even the television was on.

Cherise sat at the kitchen table, licking chocolate cake batter off a wooden spoon. For just a second, it felt like old times when her mother would bake cakes and cookies for the whole family. Debra noticed Shante right away.

"Oh, hello Shante. Come on in." Shante walked into the kitchen and sat down across from Cherise. Before Shante could open her mouth, her mother spoke.

"I went down to Mrs. Brown's and got Cherise." She poured the cake batter into the bake pans.

"Who's the cake for?" asked Shante.

"Anyone who wants to eat it," her mother replied. Cherise's eyes moved from left to right as she listened carefully to the conversation between her mother and sister. There was cake batter all around her mouth. All she could say was, "Hi, Shante."

"Hi, Cherise." Shante looked around, "Mama, where is everyone? It's so quiet."

"I told them all to leave," replied Debra, without looking up from her baking pans.

"What, why? For how long, Mama?"

Debra raised her voice slightly, "Until I say they can come back. Okay, Shante?" Shante tried to remain calm. She didn't want to make a scene in front of Cherise.

"I didn't mean to upset you Mama."

"I am *not* upset," she turned to Cherise. "Cherise baby, go in the living room and watch some TV while Mama talks to your sister." Shante handed Cherise a paper towel.

"Here girl, wipe your messy mouth." Shante could no longer stand the smell of cigarette smoke. She kept quiet as her mother lit a cigarette and took a long drag before speaking.

"Your twin brother Dante is doing drugs," she announced. "That boy is wrecking my nerves, Shante." Shante was unsurprised. She thought to herself, *With all the drinking and drugs that goes on around here, why are you surprised Mama? Duh?*

"I *told* that boy he better not be selling drugs from my house."

"Mama you said he was *doing* drugs."

"Well he's selling drugs so he probably using 'em too. And I think your other sisters and brothers doing drugs also." Shante knew that was not true; she had just spoken with Denise.

"Mama, are you for real?" Debra took another quick puff of her cigarette.

"I know what I know. That's all I can say." The oven beeped indicating it had preheated.

Not wanting cigarette ashes to end up in the cake batter, Shante got up and put the two cake pans in the oven. She closed the oven door gently. Her mother stared at Shante for a moment.

"You got any money, Shante?" She put out the cigarette butt in the small ashtray on the kitchen table. Shante frowned.

"Why, do you need something from the store, Mama?"

"I don't want anything from the store."

Shante spoke carefully, "Then what can I get you, Mama?"

"You can get me ten or twenty dollars," Debra replied. Shante looked down at her hands.

"No Mama. I don't have any money."

"Well what the hell do you use to get to school every day if you have no money, Shante?"

"That's why I don't have any money. Because I go to school every day."

"Then why you not in school today Shante?" Shante stared at her mother's eyes; they were wide.

"Mama ... it's Saturday." Shante realized she was high. She stood up and walked to the living room.

"Come on Cherise, it's time to go."

"But Shante, I want some cake," said Cherise.

4:30 P.M.

Michele stood in the bedroom doorway and watched Charles pack his suitcase. He sighed.

"Don't look so sad, Michele it's just for *two days*."

"Yup, and one of those two days is our eighteenth wedding anniversary."

"I know, and I feel awful, but we can celebrate when I get back." Michele stared at her nails.

"I suppose you're right."

"Baby, we haven't made it this far in our marriage for nothing." He reached out his arms to embrace her. She held him tight.

"I love you Charles."

"I love you more, Michele." Ashley came into their room.

226

"Hey you guys. Mushy mushy, kiss kiss. Can I spend the night at Sharon's house?"

Charles still held Michele. "Sure, if it's okay with your mother."

"Did Sharon's mother say it was okay?"

"Yes, Mom. She said it's fine. If it's okay with you and Dad they'll pick me up in half an hour."

"All right, you can stay over. I'll check on you later," said Michele.

"Thanks," said Ashley as she turned to leave. When she got to the doorway she turned back around and said, "Oh! Happy Anniversary, Mom and Dad. Love you mushy kissy guys."

"Thanks sweetheart," smiled Michele.

"Thank you, baby girl. We love you too," said Charles. Ashley left the room as quickly as she'd come in. Michele looked at him.

"What time is your flight?"

"At nine tonight, from LaGuardia." He put a couple extra silk ties into his suitcase.

"Do you need me to drive you to the airport?"

"No honey, the company is sending a car to pick me up around six-thirty." Charles leered at her, "We still have some time ... How about we celebrate before I leave?"

Michele locked their bedroom door.

Rhonda sat quietly with a glass of wine. Her head rested against a soft satin pillow on her sofa. The sultry soul sounds of Sade's

"This Is No Ordinary Love" played in the background. In spite of everything Joe had put her through, she did still love him.

Justine lay in bed working on her laptop as she spoke with Ronald on the phone. A large bag of potato chips rested on her right thigh. She put several chips into her mouth.

"I love you too Ronald ... I know you're the man for me," she smiled from ear to ear as she told Ronald her feelings, "and I am ready to be your wife. You know I love you, and my parents adore you."

"Baby, you know *I* love *you*," said Ronald, "I've thought about you every day for weeks. I missed you so much ... We should set a date, Justine." Justine cleared her throat to speak clearly, wiping tiny bits of chips from around her mouth.

"Oh of course we'll set a date. How about ... June of 2010? I always wanted to be a June Bride."

"Baby that sounds good but I was thinking maybe a bit sooner."

"Like April or May 2010?" Justine asked.

"Well, more like right after Christmas." Ronald was excited.

"You mean ... December twenty-sixth of 2010, Ronald?"

"No Justine. How about December thirty-first?"

"Of 2010 ... ?" Justine asked slowly.

"No. New Year's Eve next month. We could have a nice intimate service. Our family and close friends." Justine was silent. "What do you think, Justine?"

Sunday, November 23rd, 2008

11:30 AM

Michele was eating breakfast and watching television when the doorbell rang. She opened to door to find the biggest flower arrangement she had ever seen. The delivery man was completely hidden behind the flowers. Michele could hear only his voice.

"Good Morning! I have a delivery here for ... Michele?" She was looking around the flowers trying to find the man's face.

"Um, do you need me to sign?" asked Michele.

"No signature required." Michele took the flowers from the man's hands, still unable to see his face. Weird, she thought. She closed the door behind her and carried the flowers to the table, just barely finding the card. It read:

> *Happy Anniversary, I love you with all my heart.*
> *Love, Charles*

The phone rang. Michele was happy to hear her husband's voice.

"Charles the flowers just arrived. They're beautiful. Honey, I love you."

"Happy Anniversary sweetheart. I love you. I miss you," said Charles. Michele smiled.

"Happy Anniversary to *us*, Charles. I love you and miss you too."

Michele and Charles spoke throughout the day, giving each other well wishes and kisses over the phone. As Michele was getting ready for bed, Charles gave her one last call.

"Maybe we can take a nice vacation to Paris in the new year."

"Oh, Charles! I would love that. It would be like a second honeymoon."

"Exactly. I have plenty of vacation time, and my next business trip won't be until April."

"Charles, I would be so happy to get away," Michele said as she slipped into bed. "I love you so much. Good night."

"Sleep well, Michele. I'll be home Monday night. I love you baby."

11:30 P.M.

Michele could not believe she was having drinks with Bradford in the lobby at the Waldorf Hotel.

"I didn't force you to come here, Michele," said Bradford as he looked at her with concern.

"I know," she took a big swallow of wine. She felt wrong. "My husband is in Chicago ... and I'm here with you." Bradford moved closer to her.

"Why *are* you here?" He looked into her eyes. Michele took another long drink of wine and waited a moment before she responded.

"Because ... I still have ... a *curiosity* about you." Bradford's eyes widened.

"What *kind* of curiosity?"

"The same curiosity you have about me, Bradford. What if?"

"I know you're a married woman."

"Well you never seemed to let that bother you before. You've expressed your feelings for me. *Many* times."

"I never stopped loving you. I always wanted you to be my wife." Michele sighed.

"I loved you once too, Bradford. A long time ago. We simply cannot relive our past lives." Bradford was silent. Michele drank the last of her wine and asked, "Why have you never gotten married?"

"Simple. I never found anyone besides you that I wanted to marry." Michele looked away. He continued, "We could have worked together, Michele. If we had only tried a little harder." He reached out and touched her hand. This time she did not pull back. He looked at the five-carat diamond ring that sparkled on her finger. "Charles is a very lucky man, Michele. I wonder if he realizes how lucky he is."

"I know he does realize how blessed he is," replied Michele.

Bradford was still holding her hand. "Come with me, Michele."

She held her breath. She could not explain why, but she was drawn to him. She did not know even how she got there, but in the blink of an eye, she was suddenly in his room.

"Lovely suite," she announced. She walked around and admired the beautiful décor and the view of the city from the balcony. "You football players really know how to live it up," she joked, trying to calm her nerves. She walked to the door that led to the balcony and peered through the glass. "Wow, the stars are beautiful from up here," she said.

"Michele, *you* are beautiful," Bradford replied. He walked up behind her and gently moved his hands around her waist. She loved the strong touch. He kissed her softly on the side of her neck, catching the scent of her expensive perfume. She leaned back and rested her head on his chest. He nestled his nose in her thick wavy hair. "Michele ... " he said quietly, "I've wanted you for a long time. I love you." He gently squeezed her breasts.

231

Michele was silent. He turned her around so he could see her face. He pulled her body close to him. She felt warm all over.

He slowly slipped his hand up under her midnight-blue dress, touching her inner thigh, carefully moving closer between her legs, caressing her intimately. He could feel she was anxious. "Michele, I want you." He kissed her passionately on the lips. Her breathing became heavy as Bradford unzipped the back of her dress and let it fall to the floor. He ran his hands through her long soft hair, kissing her on the neck and shoulders. She stood in front of him completely naked. Bradford stared at her. "You're so beautiful, Michele." She could hear her cell phone ringing in her purse. Her heart raced, thinking it could be Charles calling once more to tell her how much he loved her. She tried to pull away but he held her tighter, lifting her up and settling her on the bed.

"Michele, you are such a beauty. I have wanted you for such a long time." She felt like melting ice on hot summer day. She wanted him just as much, and all she could do was say his name as he entered into her ever so slowly. Michele was drowning in heat and passion as she lay under his warm strong body. His big hands lifted her hips up as he thrusted deeper. She moaned with pleasure. She called out his name again. He held her tighter, thrusting harder.

"Bradford!" she moaned.

"Michele, I love you," he whispered. He kissed her breasts as she held tightly to his shoulders. He imagined her as his wife, making love to her every night. Michele enjoyed him. They made love over and over again. She left the hotel early the next morning.

Monday, November 24th, 2008

9:30 A.M.

Michele's cell phone rang over and over; it was Bradford. He had left her several messages:

"I love you Michele."

"You were wonderful last night. I can't stop thinking about you."

"I can't wait to see you again. Call me back, baby."

Michele locked her bedroom door and lit a cigarette; she'd bought a pack on her way home from the hotel. She felt sick to her stomach. She had made love to another man on the eve of her eighteenth wedding anniversary. She looked at the clock beside her bed: 9:30 A.M. She texted Charles. An ocean of guilt washed over her:

"Good Morning honey, Happy Anniversary. I love you so much."

Her phone rang seconds later. It was Ashley. Michele was only slightly relieved.

"Hey Ashley," Michele tried to sound cheerful.

"Hi Mom. I am calling to let you know I'm all right. Sharon and I are on our way to school. Classes start late this morning."

"Oh, okay sweetheart. Enjoy your day ... I love you."

"I love you too Mom. See you later."

Her phone buzzed as she received multiple texts. Five from Bradford. And one from Charles:

Happy Anniversary Michele. I love you and can't wait to hold you in my arms. I will be home in a few hours.

Michele began to cry. *How could I have betrayed my husband?* Her cell phone rang again. It was Bradford. She ignored it and headed for the shower.

6:00 P.M.

Michele's stomach was in knots. She sat on the edge of the bed watching Charles unpack his suitcase and listening to him talk about his business trip. Every time he mentioned how happy he was to be home, she felt sicker.

"We are going to have a *wonderful* time this evening, Michele," he smiled. "I made reservations at a great new French restaurant downtown."

"Yes ... Wonderful!" said Michele, forcing a smile. She tried to act as normal as possible. "What time, honey?"

"The reservations are set for eight. Can Ashley stay over with a friend?" He walked over to his wife and kissed her gently on the lips. "I planned for us to stay at a hotel for the night," he winked. Michele felt a lump in her throat,

"Oh did you ... ? Which hotel?" she asked.

"Now baby, you don't want me to give it all away, do you? I want to surprise you!" he took a step back and carefully admired Michele's face. "I missed you so much, Michele. I know how badly you wanted me to be home for our anniversary."

"I understand Charles. I know you needed to do those deals for the company."

"That's why *tonight*, I want everything special for you. Because *you* are so special," he paused, "I love you Michele. You are my life. I married the best woman in the world. There is no man on earth luckier than me."

She stood up and gave him a warm hug. "I love you Charles. God knows ... I love you so much."

Michele kept checking her cell phone as she dressed for her evening out with Charles.

She deleted four text messages from Bradford, realizing she would have to change her cell phone number within a day or two if he kept this up. She wanted to completely forget what had happened with him. Everything she thought she might have felt for Bradford was gone now. She felt numb. She wanted nothing more to do with him. Tonight was about her and her loving husband celebrating their wedding anniversary. She thought, *I must have been out of my damn mind. What the hell was I thinking?* She could hear Charles singing happily in the shower. *How do you tell your husband you slept with another man ... on your anniversary?* She could not even imagine telling him. Their life together would be over. This would be the secret she would take to her grave. The thought of hurting Charles by being honest and telling him was too much to bear. He would be hurt to his soul if he ever found out. She spoke out loud, staring at her reflection,

"I love my husband. I vowed to be with him. Until death do us part." Tears filled her eyes.

"Well, I love you too, sweetheart." Michele's heart skipped a beat. She hadn't realized Charles had walked into the bedroom. He continued, "And I vowed to be with you until death do us part. You going over wedding vows, honey?" he laughed.

"This is a lovely restaurant, Charles. Great choice." Her eyes ran up and down the walls, admiring the French artwork. She did everything she could to avoid looking into his eyes. She felt ashamed to be here with him. He took her hand, holding it gently.

"I am happy to be home with my lovely wife," he kissed her hand. He lifted his glass and she did the same. "Happy Anniversary Michele. You are the love of my life. You and Ashley complete me."

"And we love you a thousand times more, Charles," Michele's eyes became watery. One tear slowly fell down her right cheek. She knew in the deepest of her being that she loved Charles. She knew that the man sitting across from her was all she needed in this world. She was heartbroken over what she had done. "Happy Anniversary, Charles." She squeezed his hand tight. "I love you." They clinked their glasses and took a sip.

"I love you too, Michele." He reached over and traced a finger across her cheek and softly wiped away the fallen tear.

They made love throughout the night.

Michele woke in the early morning. She rolled over in bed and stared out from the large ceiling-to-floor window at a star-filled sky.

God please forgive me, she thought. *What would Charles think if he knew I was in this exact bed with another man the night before?*

236

Tuesday, November 26th, 2008

3:00 P.M.

Sistah Knit Pre-Thanksgiving Dinner

The aromas of turkey, greens, yams, mac and cheese, and sweet desserts filled every corner of Sistah Knit. The Sistah Friends sat silent as they listened to Michele tell the story of her encounter with Bradford. She tried her hardest to remain composed.

"I don't understand, Michele. Charles is good man," Rhonda said.

"I know ... I don't know! I was curious with lust and I crossed a line that I would not dare cross ever again. I put myself in a place that will pain me for the rest of my life."

Terri put her arm around Michele's shoulders to comfort her, "It will be all right, Michele. We're all human. No one is perfect."

"No one is judging you," offered Shante. She reached out and clasped Michele's hand, squeezing it.

"That's right," said Sherri, "It's important we learn from our mistakes."

"Sherri's right," added Rhonda. "I learned from *my* mistake. Next time I'll use a loaded gun on Joe's black ass," she laughed, and the others laughed with her, easing the tension a bit. Michele smiled and wiped the forming tears from her eyes.

"Come on now ladies, this is supposed to be a very happy time, Thanksgiving. Here I am burdening your ears with my problems and ... ," and Terri squeezed her tight. Michele continued, "Thank you so much for listening and for being my friends."

"You know we love you, girl," Justine said.

"Amen to that!" Rhonda said. "Now let's eat. Somebody *please* get Michele a drink!" she laughed.

"I'll get the champagne," said Terri, "and I would like to make a toast."

"Let's make a toast when Gigi gets here!" said Justine.

"Okay, that sounds good," Terri replied, and sure enough Gigi came through the front door within a few seconds.

"Hello Ladies! I am so sorry, my driver was caught in traffic and my phone died."

"That's all right Gigi, we're glad to see you," said Terri. "Come on over we're about to make a toast. You can charge your phone afterwards."

The Toast:

Michele: This Thanksgiving, I am grateful for all the love from all of you guys. Your support really means the world to me. Thank you. I love you.

Shante: I am very happy this Thanksgiving to know each of you. You all have such strength, and I hope I can become just as strong a woman one day.

Justine: I love you guys, and I love this knitting shop, and I love that it always feels like home, and I love that the people here love me! Happy Thanksgiving!

Rhonda: I'm grateful to Terri and Sherri for opening such a loving knitting shop. I am especially thankful for all you ladies for loving and caring for me. What would I do without you?

Terri: I am thankful for my family, for my twin Sherri, and of course, for all of you.

Gigi: I am grateful for the entire knitting community that has loved and embraced me beyond what I ever could have imagined. Sistah Knit is such a friendly and loving yarn shop!

Sherri: I feel so blessed and thankful for our shop and its community. I hope the love of friendship will *always* keep us together. Cheers!

The ladies sat around for the next two and a half hours enjoying good food and fun and laughter, each of them forgetting about their personal pains and sorrows, if only just for a little while.

Wednesday, November 27th, 2008

5:45 P.M.

Michele finished work at the office; she was looking forward to taking time off for the Thanksgiving holiday. She shut down her computer and said goodnight to her fellow co-workers as she walked toward the elevator. When she reached the lobby, she wished a Happy Thanksgiving to the security guy then exited out the front door.

Bradford was standing outside. Michele froze. He walked toward her, trying to kiss her. She quickly regained her strength and walked on past him, avoiding eye contact.

"Michele? What's wrong? I tried calling you. I miss you baby," he sped up, trying to keep up with her. Michele stopped and looked Bradford directly in his eyes. She kept her voice low.

"I am not your baby, Bradford. *Do not* call me baby." He raised his eyebrows.

"Girl, I just want to be with you. We have a lot to talk about."

"No. We don't have *anything* to talk about. We had one night. And that meant *nothing* to me."

"Michele, you must be lying. You wanted me." She wanted to scream.

"Bradford. I made the worst mistake of my life that night."

"What? What the hell are you saying?" Michele was trying not to make a scene in public.

Through clenched teeth she said, "Bradford ... don't act like a damn fool. *Hear me clearly*. I love my husband. Charles is the man I plan to have a future with. Not you. *Never* you." Bradford took

240

a step back. He could not understand why she was acting so cold. He felt vindictive. He hated Charles.

"Well suppose I tell Charles where you spent your wedding anniversary? Better yet, Michele, how about I tell Charles that I spent *his* anniversary between his wife's legs." Michele's eyes grew fiery; she took one step closer toward Bradford and looked at him with rage in her eyes.

She smirked, "Did you forget that I am a reporter for the biggest news network in the country?"

Bradford was confused, "And?"

"*And* ... as a reporter, I investigate stories. I have a hot mess of a story about you, Bradford."

"Me?"

"Yes, you! You got an eighteen-year-old girl pregnant two years ago, and then you paid off her family to keep quiet about the baby girl she gave birth to." Bradford lost all expression in his face. She continued, "That could make headline news on every social media platform by tomorrow, one of the biggest days in football, if you push me." Bradford was stunned. Michele smiled, "I can see it now! *All-Star NFL quarterback Bradford Wilson has a secret love child.* Or, how about I report about how a gay NFL player was seen on his knees with his head in your crotch in the locker room?" Bradford grabbed her arms and lowered his voice to a mere whisper.

"Michele, baby. Please ... you can't do that. I have a career." She broke away from his grasp.

"Exactly, and I have a husband. You think well and hard before threatening me, because your ugly mess will tarnish your clean NFL good boy image." She whispered, "Now let me say this one more time, and you hear me good Mr. NFL Superstar. I regret with every fiber of my soul what happened between us. It's a nightmare worse than any horror movie I have ever seen in my life." Bradford pressed his lips tightly together, trying to manage his anger. Michele continued, "Now I am going home to my husband and daughter. I suggest that you go wherever the hell you might be wanted." She turned and began to walk away, only turning her head back once to say, "And by the way, Happy Thanksgiving! I hope I never see your black ass again." She looked him up and down. With a quick flip of her hair she turned back around to straighten the collar on her shearling mink coat and walked away. He watched the red bottoms of her black leather boots fade away in the distance.

6:00 P.M.

Shante sat next to Cherise on the sofa. Mrs. Brown and Phillip were asleep. The house was quiet except for the ticking of the cat-shaped clock that hung on the kitchen wall. The wooden tail moved with every tick-tock. Shante put her arm around Cherise and kissed her on top of her head. Shante could smell the scent of sulfur on her hair.

"You know I am going to find a new place of our own for us to live," she whispered to her little sister.

Cherise looked up at Shante, "You really mean it?" she asked.

"Yes. I've been speaking with some counselors at school. They can help me with finding a job."

"I wish I was old enough to work," Cherise's eyes were wide and bright. Shante giggled.

"Don't rush it, girl. One day you'll be able to work."

"But I want to help you, Shante."

"I know, but look, all you have to do is keep your mind on your school work. That's how you can help. Okay?"

"Okay, Shante," Cherise sighed.

"I want you to promise me that you'll stay in school and get good grades."

"I promise," said Cherise. "I will stay in school and get *excellent* grades." Shante smiled.

"You know I want only the best for you."

"I want the best for you too, Shante."

"What are you girls chatting about in here?" asked Mrs. Brown as she came into the living room. She had sponge rollers in her hair and her bunny-eared slippers were on the wrong feet. Cherise starting laughing. Mrs. Brown looked down at her slippers.

"Oh, my Lord!" they laughed together. "Come on you two. Help me season the turkey for dinner tomorrow." Mrs. Brown took the apron off the back of her kitchen chair and tied it around her chubby waist. Cherise and Shante followed her into the kitchen, still laughing at her slippers.

7:30 P.M.

Justine was excited about her brother coming home for Thanksgiving. She grated sharp cheddar cheese while her mother mixed cake batter.

"Red velvet is your brother's favorite," she smiled.

"Mother, you know chocolate is *my* favorite cake?"

"Yes, I do sweetie, and I will make a chocolate cake for you." Justine laughed.

"Thanks Mommy Dearest." Justine's father was fast asleep in his old recliner. He had a newspaper on his lap and the television turned on to an old western. His snoring muffled the sounds of horses and gunfire.

"Justine, will Ronald will here for dinner tomorrow?"

November 28th, 2008

12:00 P.M.

Thanksgiving Day

Michele snuggled close to Charles as she kissed him all over his face, "What's up sleepy head?" He pulled her closer and buried his face in her warm breasts. He whispered in his raspy sleepy voice.

"I just want to stay right here, Michele." His right hand was rubbing on her smooth left thigh. Michele giggled.

"Charles our parents will be here soon."

"I know ... but they're not for a few hours. Let's just stay in bed a little longer."

"Baby I wish I could, but I have to help Ashley pick out something nice to wear. She has some friends joining us for dinner," she moved away from him. "And the caterers will be here at two and I need to set the table and pick out a dress to wear and – "

"Michele!" Charles interrupted her, "Relax, baby. You and Ashley will look beautiful. You both have more nice clothes than any department store." Michele laughed and wiggled her way out of the bed and into the bathroom. She turned on the water to take a shower. Charles watched her with one eye barely open.

"Come on Charles, join me! The water feels good!"

1:00 P.M.

Justine was on a video chat call with her brother Stanley. She could hardly contain her excitement. She missed him.

"So, Stanley ... what time are you guys getting here?"

"In time for dinner," he laughed. Justine made a face. "Just kidding, Sis. I'll be nice and early. Probably around two."

"Great. Now. Who is this young lady you're bringing?" Justine batted her long eyelashes at the screen.

"Her name is Tammy."

"And?"

"And, she is very special to me."

"How special, Stanley? I noticed how you smiled when you said her name."

"Well ... she is the one."

"AH! Are you serious?" Justine sat up in her chair.

"Yes. I am serious."

"Mom and Daddy are going to be surprised. You know Mom is always ready to plan a wedding."

"Well ... what about you and Ronald, Sis?" Justine said nothing. She looked down at her ring-less left hand. "Everything okay with you guys?"

"Yeah, we're okay ... he wants to get married next month."

"What? Next month? So you're getting married?"

"No. I am not," Justine was firm.

"Have you set a date?"

"No."

"So you aren't getting married?"

"NO! Not yet at least. I don't know!"

"Justine, what is going on with you?" he tried to laugh.

She sighed, "Ugh. I really don't know, Stanley."

"You love Ronald, don't you?"

"Yes. I do."

"Well Sis, all you have to say is *I do*, and you're married!"

"You got jokes brother," she giggled, "I'll talk to you later." Stanley loved to see his sister smile.

"All right Sis. See you and family soon."

2:00 P.M.

Rhonda was basting the turkey when her mother arrived.

"Chile, it sure smells *good* up in here!"

"Sure does Mama!" Rhonda replied. "You taught me well."

"Yes, I did Rhonda." Barbara gave her daughter a warm loving hug. Rhonda still had oven mittens on her hands.

"Mama, put the cornbread on the counter and pour yourself a drink."

"Yes, in a minute chile. Where my grandkids at?"

"In their rooms."

"Tyree!" she yelled, smiling. "Twinkle! Get over here and give your grandmother a hug!" Tyree opened his bedroom door and shouted,

"What did you say, Ma?"

"Boy get out here and greet your grandmother," Rhonda said.

"Hello Grandma." Tyree gave his grandma a hug and kissed her on the cheek.

"Boy look at you! So tall and handsome. You play basketball?"

"No Grandma, I play football." She shook her head.

"Boy you wasting all that good height on football." Tyree and Rhonda laughed.

"Tyree, you know your grandmother is serious?"

"That's right boy. Your grandmama knows all about basketball. Now that Kobe Bryant, he – "

"Hi Grandma!" Twinkle had her arms stretched out wide to hug her grandmother. She had a big smile on her face.

"Hello Twinkle. How is my favorite granddaughter doing? Girl you are prettier than pretty!" She hugged her Twinkle tightly, "You is prettier than that Halle Berry girl." Twinkle laughed. "Hollywood needs to see you! Rhonda, send this child's picture to Hollywood. She'll become a star in five minutes." Rhonda shook her head laughing. "Yes Lord. *My* granddaughter in *the movies.*"

Tyree frowned, "She can't be no movie star. She can't act."

"Yes, she can! Twinkle, don't waste all your beauty on just looking in the mirror. Grandmama will get you an agent." Rhonda laughed.

"Mama, why you filling these kids' heads with all that silly talk?"

"It's not silly talk, Rhonda. They got talent." Rhonda rolled her eyes.

"Mama *I know* I have talented children."

"Yeah, well, we need to talk about getting these kids some sports and acting contracts." Tyree smiled and put his hand under his chin.

"Grandma, I think you're really on to something!"

"Oh, stop it," Rhonda laughed. "Mother, will you please help me make the mac and cheese?"

"All right now. Come on Rhonda. Let's get started."

"Twinkle do you want to help us?" asked Rhonda.

"Sure."

"I guess I'll just chill out and watch some football," said Tyree. He dipped his finger in the icing of the red velvet cake his mother was frosting.

Rhonda slapped his hand. "Boy stop that!"

3:00 P.M.

Shante could hear Mrs. Brown singing as she hustled around the kitchen.

"Amazing Grace, how sweet the sound that saved a wretch like me. I once was lost, but now am found, was blind but now I see." The aroma of collard greens and smoked turkey filled the entire apartment. Phillip and Cherise and sat in the living room watching *March of the Wooden Soldiers*. Shante thought to herself, "I wonder what's going on upstairs at mama's house." She walked into the kitchen with a bright smile on her face.

"Happy Thanksgiving, Mrs. Brown."

"Happy Thanksgiving to you," she paused and looked up from her cooking, "How you doing Shante? You were very quiet back there in the room."

"I'm fine Mrs. Brown. Just thinking about my family upstairs."

"Well why don't you and Cherise go see them?"

Shante sighed, "Maybe later. I'll think about it. I just want to have a nice Thanksgiving right here with you."

"Well chile, I am happy you and Cherise and Phillip are here with me. You know old folks don't get as much company when they

248

get old. Seems like everybody forget all about the elderly sometimes."

"Mrs. Brown, you always have people calling you and stopping by to say hello."

"Yes, that is true, but holidays are when everybody wants to be 'round family."

"I understand what you mean, Mrs. Brown. I promise you when I get on my feet, I'll come visit you all the time." Mrs. Brown smiled. She was grateful for Shante's kind words.

"Like I told you before Shante, my home is your home. If you do go upstairs to see your mama, take her one of these sweet potato pies. I remember how much she always enjoyed my pies."

"Thanks Mrs. Brown."

"And look, no matter what, child, she is your mama. Love her and pray for her."

"I know, Mrs. Brown."

4:00 P.M.

Michele and Charles enjoyed their holiday dinner with friends and family. Charles was extremely happy. He gazed at Michele from across the dining table, smiling at her. She looked lovely. Her face seemed to glow with happiness. Thanksgiving was her favorite time of the year. As she smiled and chatted with guests, she could feel Charles looking at her. She smiled back at him. The silent "*I love you*" floated from his lips. She returned the same words with her eyes. Charles looked at his daughter Ashley. She was a joy. She laughed with her cousins Tracy and Linda as they talked about tough teachers and silly boys at school.

Charles' mother was seated at the table alongside his father. They had traveled from Charleston, South Carolina, and would stay in New York until the new year. Charles felt grateful this Thanksgiving Day. He tapped on his water glass with a spoon to get everyone's attention. He stood, "Thank you all for your attention. I know we have already said the blessings for today; however, I just want to take a few minutes to express how happy I am today." He looked at Michele, "Honey, you are truly the love and soul of my life. I could not imagine my life with anyone else except you." He turned to Ashley. "Ashley, baby girl, I want you to know that your father loves you with every heartbeat in my chest. I would move heaven and earth for you." And to his parents, "Mom and Dad, I love you both very much," finally, gesturing to everyone at the table, "To all my family and friends, I want you all to know that I cherish each and every one you." Michele felt tears forming. She took a dinner napkin to wipe her eyes. Charles continued, "My heart is filled with so much joy today. I am grateful to be in your presence and for the love I get from each of you. I hope we will spend many more days like this together."

"We will," Michele replied, "We will."

The minute Shante heard police cars pull up in front of the building, she knew it meant trouble at her mother's apartment.

"Come sit down and enjoy your dinner," Mrs. Brown said.

"Mrs. Brown, there's something going on upstairs. I just know something is wrong."

"What's wrong?" asked Cherise, looking at her sister with wide eyes.

"Nothing is wrong, chile. Eat your dinner," replied Mrs. Brown. "Shante come away from the window, girl."

Shante took one last glance and said, "Yes Mrs. Brown." She made her way back to the table and sat next to Phillip, who was enjoying his sweet candied yams. Most of it was around his mouth.

"Shante, it's Thanksgiving. Relax your mind girl," Mrs. Brown put food on her plate.

"Yeah Shante, it's Thanksgiving! Eat up," Cherise joined in.

"I didn't mean to leave the table like that, Mrs. Brown. I'm sorry. I know better than that."

"I know you know better. I am glad you're here with me this Thanksgiving Day."

"Mrs. Brown ... I would hate to think where we might be if it were not for your kindness."

"Well I am glad you don't have to think about being any other place but *right here*." Mrs. Brown smiled, looking around the table. "You know Shante, life is beautiful all the time."

"What do you mean? Shante asked.

"Well we're all here together, like a family should be. If there's trouble upstairs, you're not there to be mixed up in any wrong doings."

"I suppose you're right, Mrs. Brown."

"You made some nice friends at the yarn shop. You said yourself how much you like them, and how they like you ... You're doing well in school, I just know you will get a good-paying job," she paused and looked down, "and possibly a husband in the future ... " Shante grinned.

"A husband? Really Mrs. Brown?"

"Yes Shante! A husband. You're beautiful and you deserve someone to love you." Shante shrugged.

"I never thought of a husband before. Not really."

"Think of your future, girl. The right man will come along for you. Stop worrying about your mother and the situation upstairs. Your life is this boy of yours and your little sister." Shante thought her chances of marriage were little to none, but she felt good at the thought of one day being a bride.

4:30 P.M.

All Ronald talked about was how he could not wait to become Justine's husband. Justine wanted to throw the sweet potato pie at him so he would shut up.

"Yes sir, Mr. Whitaker, I love your daughter very much." Justine's father was always grilling Ronald every chance he got about the importance of being able to provide for his daughter.

"When *is* the wedding, exactly?" asked Mr. Whitaker, skeptically.

"Honey, leave the boy alone. You're embarrassing him," said Mrs. Whitaker. "You can see he loves Justine." Justine quickly got up from the table,

"Hey! Let's put some music on!" She hoped some tunes would get her parents off the subject. She plugged her iPod into the port.

"Justine *please* not hip-hop music today," her mother pleaded.

"I know Mother. How about O'Jays "Family Reunion?" Daddy's favorite Thanksgiving song."

"Sounds good to me," her father said. Justine returned to the table.

"Never mind me and Ronald, Daddy. Let's talk about *Stanley and Tammy's* upcoming wedding," Justine smiled, looking at her brother.

"What wedding?" asked Mrs. Whitaker.

"Stanley, you're getting married?" asked Mr. Whitaker.

"Well Mom, Dad, we *were going to* tell you on my own time ..." Stanley took Tammy's left hand and lifted it onto the table to display her five-carat diamond engagement ring. It sparkled brightly, displaying it rich fire and clarity.

"Oh my gosh! What a beautiful ring," smiled Mrs. Whitaker. Stanley continued, staring at Tammy,

"Family, I love this woman. Tammy is beautiful and sweet, and everything a man could ask for. She knows how I feel about her." He looked into her eyes, smiling. "Mom you know I've never brought any girl home before."

"Yes, Stanley that is true. I was beginning to wonder if something was up with you!" The table giggled.

"Well, I never found the right woman ... until now." He kissed his Tammy on the cheek.

Ronald look at Justine and smiled. Justine smiled back and quickly returned her attention back to Stanley and Tammy.

"Tammy, welcome to the family!" said Mr. Whitaker.

"Thank you, Mr. Whitaker ... Your son is a wonderful man."

"Please, call me Dad."

"And please, call *me* Mom!" Mrs. Whitaker was beyond excited that both of her children were getting married.

"Thanks Mom and Dad," Stanley smiled. He put his arm around Tammy.

"Have you set a date?" Ronald asked.

"We're thinking of a spring wedding next year," replied Tammy.

"Son, your mother and I are very happy for you. Can she cook, boy?" Stanley laughed.

"Yes Dad, Tammy is an excellent cook." Justine was happy to have the attention of the marriage topic off her and Ronald. The only thought she had was, *How can I get out of marrying Ronald, the man I love?*

6:30 P.M.

Rhonda was enjoying the evening with her mother and children. Two neighbors stopped by with warm wishes and dessert. She sat at the table listening to her mother chat away with Tyree and Twinkle about being superstars. Rhonda could not help but think of Joe; deep in her heart, she did still love him.

Later on that evening, Barbara went into the spare room to rest. The kids had plans for after dinner to hang out with friends. Rhonda sat at the table alone. She tucked away any thoughts of love in her heart. She wanted to love someone and someone to return her love. *Is that too much for a woman to ask?* she thought, *My kids don't need me as much as they did before. My mother gets out more than I do. Even she has a few men interested in her ... from the AARP group ...* She quickly got out of that mindset. She sat up in her chair and thought once more, *I have to get my act together. I refuse to allow Joe to keep my heart buried in endless pain.*

10:00 P.M.

Terri and Sherri were happily spending Thanksgiving with their parents, aunts, uncles, and many cousins. Nonstop laughter could be heard throughout the house over the sound of '70s Motown classics. Mrs. Constable asked, "Sherri, how are things at the yarn shop?"

"Everything is going well, Mom. Terri and I are so happy with the success of Sistah Knit."

"Sweetheart, that's wonderful, your father and I are so proud you and Terri. The shop really took off fast ... But more importantly, when are you girls going to make us grandparents?"

"Oh Mom, not that again," sighed Sherri.

"Yes, that again! You girls have enjoyed a fabulous modeling career in Paris for years. Your shop is going well. It's time for you and your sister to think about settling down. Look at all this family here just waiting on the arrival of new little boy or girl!"

"Hey, what you two talking about?" Terri smiled at her mother.

"Sis, Mom and Dad want to be grandparents."

"Well Mom, it will happen one day," laughed Terri.

"How soon, girls? You're not going to be twenty-eight forever."

Terri and Sherri kissed their mother and then mingled with the crowd of relatives, finally taking their seats at the dinner table.

Michele loved her family. She thought about how wonderful Charles as a husband and father really was. The day was over. Her in-laws had long retired to bed. Ashley and her cousins were quietly watching television. Charles was relaxing across the bed watching the football game. She looked at him and smiled softly. He glanced over at her and smiled back. She still could not believe that she had crossed the line of infidelity and cheated with Bradford. She thought, *I will never jeopardize my marriage and family for anyone, ever again.*

Funny how life can deal you a strange hand of cards. What's important is how you play them. People take too many wrong chances on purpose and come so close to losing everything for the thrill of a few moments of hot passion.

Justine was happy that Ronald had left hours before. He wanted to visit his family before the evening was over. Justine told him she was not up to accompanying him, but asked that he give his mother her regards. Ronald was not happy at this, but as always, he loved Justine and would do anything for her.

"Ronald is a nice young man. You should have gone with him."

"Mom. I just want to stay here with my family."

"Well Ronald's family will be part of your family soon."

"I have work to do upstairs. I'll be down later to help clean up."

"Justine, you work too much. It's a holiday, girl. Can't it wait?"

"No Mom, it can't wait." She went upstairs to her room. Her mother could hear the door shut.

"Shante, your mother and her boyfriend were fighting earlier. His kids were up there eating up the Thanksgiving cakes and pies!" A neighbor had come by Mrs. Brown's place to give Shante news. "Your mother yelled at his kids and then he got mad and hit your mom on her arm with a wooden spoon! They were throwing all kinds of stuff at each other. Cups and flower pots ... and then the other people in the house started fighting too."

Shante sighed; she didn't want to hear any more. "Thanks Tasha," she said, "I knew something was wrong when I saw the police cars in front of the building," she paused and looked at her sister and her baby boy. "That's why I'm staying with Mrs. Brown. It'll be a nice and peaceful Thanksgiving for us right here."

Rhonda felt she was dealt a lying hand of cards, or that she was "Stuck on Stupid in Love" with a man who has a wife. Lord have mercy, life is so unfair at times. She spent Thanksgiving night holding her pillow tight with tears rolling down her face.

Monday, December 22nd, 2008

3:00 P.M.

The Sistah Friends gathered around the table at Sistah Knit talking about their holiday plans and New Year's resolutions as they drank wine and knitted on their projects.

Michele had a huge smile. "Charles and I are planning a trip to Paris this coming spring!"

"OMIGOSH! Paris!" Shante shouted. "I could only dream of going to Paris," she said wistfully.

"I know ... Paris is such a beautiful place. We've always wanted to go," Michele replied.

"That's wonderful!" said Terri. "Sherri and I *loved* living in Paris."

"One day I'm gonna go to Paris," said Shante, smiling. "Phillip and I. And I also really want to take Phillip to Disney World one day."

Rhonda looked over at Shante, "I took my kids to Disney World when they were about Phillip's age. They had so much fun. I know Phillip will love it."

"Well, I have to get a job after I finish school first before I plan any future trips," Shante giggled.

"Don't worry Shante, you'll find a job," said Justine. She nudged Shante's shoulder, "Hey ... I'm sure I'll have an opening at my new record company once things get started up." Shante's eyes widened.

"Really Justine?"

Justine smiled, "Yes, really Shante!" Justine always got so happy whenever she spoke of her record company.

"Justine, how are your wedding plans going?" asked Sherri.

"Ugh. My mother has been giving me bridal dress magazines for *months*."

"What kind of dress do you think you would like?" Michele asked.

"None," replied Justine.

"What do you mean none?" Michele asked.

"I don't want a wedding dress," said Justine.

"Well you could always wear something like an elegant African style dress," said Shante.

"Oh yes, I like that idea," added Sherri.

"No-no-no ladies, I don't want to marry Ronald," Justine looked at them as she continued knitting.

"What are you talking about?" Michele asked. Everyone was stunned.

"You can't be serious?" asked Terri.

"Yes I am. I don't want to be married right now. I want to own my record company and build on it and pursue that."

"So, you haven't told Ronald?" asked Rhonda as she folded her arms in disagreement.

"No ... I haven't. I've just been stalling and delaying wedding plans for months."

"You don't love him, that's what it is. Right?" Michele asked.

"I do love him. I just don't want to marry him."

Michele shook her head in disbelief. "Are you crazy?"

Shante looked at Justine directly, "Girl, if Ronald was like Phillip's father Phil-Quan, I could understand you not wanting to get married, but Ronald sounds like a really good man. A working man who loves you, girl!"

"Look, I understand what you're all saying is right, it's just – "

"No, I don't think you do," said Michele. "A good man these days is a *rare species*. You are lucky to have found a great guy who wants to make you his WIFE and not his WIFEY!"

"That is the truth," said Rhonda. "It would be wonderful to be married to a good honest man. I would love to have a husband of my own ... Justine I hope you know what you're doing."

"Does Ronald know how you feel?" asked Terri.

"I know he's sensing some pushback from me every time he brings up the wedding. He actually wanted to get married on December thirty-first."

"New Year's Eve!" the others exclaimed at the same time.

"Wow!" said Rhonda, "He really wanted to marry you before this year is out!"

"Yeah, he does, but I'm not happy with a December ... or even a June wedding. I don't want *any* wedding."

"Damn Justine, you really serious?" asked Michelle.

"Yes, I am Michele. I want to run my record company and be my own boss and be married to *that*."

"We know you love and care for Ronald," said Sherri.

"If it's really meant to be, then we will get married, but right now, I just want to get my company up and running. That's *my* plan for the new year."

"I hear that Justine ... and Happy New Year to you!" said Shante. The others chuckled lightly. The doorbells jingled and a customer walked in. A spunky woman about thirty years old announced in a high-pitched squeaky voice:

"I would like to make a cowl for my future mother-in-law. Can someone please show me some cashmere or silk yarns?" Justine looked at the woman and rolled her eyes.

Wednesday June 1st, 2011

5:30 P.M.

Two Years Later

"Shante is doing a wonderful job as my executive assistant," announced Justine as she knitted the edge of a cashmere shawl for her mother. Shante flipped through the latest edition of *Vogue Knitting* as her smile grew from ear to ear.

"I knew she was the perfect person to hire," replied Michele.

"I really can't thank Justine enough," blushed Shante. "I've learned so much about the record business ..."

"And honestly," Justine added, smiling at Shante, "I couldn't run the company without her help."

"Sherri and I very happy for you, Shante," said Terri as she helped her sister place balls of Turkish wool yarn in woven baskets at the counter.

"So, Shante," giggled Michele, "tell the truth. Is Justine the boss from hell?" They all laughed. Shante blushed. "I'm just kidding, Shante," Michele assured her. The bells jingled as the front door opened; it was Rhonda and Gigi.

"Well hello ladies!" said Gigi as she turned to Rhonda, "Rhonda met me at the metro north station." Gigi and Rhonda were greeted with sisterly hugs and kisses.

"Rhonda, Gigi, would you like something to drink?" asked Sherri.

"Iced tea for me!" answered Gigi.

"Same for me," added Rhonda.

"So, Gigi, how did the meeting go this morning with Unlimited Yarn Designs?" Terri asked.

"Surprisingly ... everything went very well. I was shown several different colors of orange yarn. I chose my favorites and they said they'll mix and dye a special blend for me and call it *Gigi!*"

"That's awesome!" said Terri, "and when will it go on the market?

"The CEO told me it could be in all major craft and fabric stores in two months," Gigi beamed.

"Wow, that soon!" said Michele. "Girl, I have to do an interview with you soon."

"I can hardly believe this is really happing," said Gigi as she sat down.

"We are so happy for you Gigi. You know Sistah Knit will stock the shelves with your yarn!" smiled Terri.

"There's going to be a special mix of fiber blends to follow within six months, too," said Gigi.

"Well, look at you go Miss Gigi!" said Rhonda. "That's fabulous."

"Yes, it's wonderful news," said Justine.

"Wow," Shante said in awe, "Yarn blended and dyed to your satisfaction for sale ... that's awesome, Miss Gigi."

"Thank you. I'm so excited. In all there will be a wool blend, silk, cashmere, and a few others."

"Oh, now I *really* need to do an interview with you much sooner than later Gigi!" Michele said excitedly, "You've become such a positive force in the knitting community. Everyone loves you."

"Yes Gigi, Terri and I are also excited that you'll be speaking here at Sistah Knit in July. So many people have signed up. This place will be packed! Many of your New York followers have been calling. They want to meet you and give a hug," Sherri giggled.

"I'm just as excited to be a part of the Knitting for Kindness week in Harlem."

"Gigi, we are just thrilled to have you be part of a great event in the community," smiled Terri.

"Well, I cannot express how happy I am to do what I can to support Sistah Knit!" Gigi paused and stared at her glass. "However, I just have one question ..."

"What is it?" asked Sherri a little nervously.

"Can you make sure there's plenty of this iced tea on hand for the event? It's *delicious*." The twins laughed.

"No worries on that," said Terri. "Our grandmother's iced tea is always a big hit."

"Ladies, what's in it? I've never had iced tea this good."

"It's our grandmother's – and great grandmother's too – old country secret recipe ... and we promised never to tell," said Terri. Sherri smiled in agreement.

"We will never tell." Gigi gave out a little sigh then laughed,

"Okay, I understand how important it is to keep family recipes and traditions."

"On a knitting note Gigi," said Terri, "what orange project are you working on these days?" Gigi reached inside her large handwoven straw bag and pulled out a beautiful three-foot-long featherweight silk yarn wrap. It was held on a size three twenty-four-inch mahogany cable needle. Everyone's eyes locked onto the finely stitched design of tiny stars and moon shapes.

"Gigi," Michele gasped, "what a beautiful and delicate project! You surprise us all the time."

8:00 P.M.

The hot June weather was almost unbearable. Not even the breeze from the water of the Yonkers Pier provided any coolness. Shante enjoyed having central air conditioning inside her new apartment. Working for Justine, she was finally able to afford a lifestyle she had always dreamed of. She now lived on a 12th floor two-bedroom Hudson River View apartment. The best part – the entire apartment had ceiling-to-floor windows with a 360-degree view of the Hudson River and the twinkling lights of the Empire State and Chrysler buildings of New York City. She could look below from her kitchen window and see the Yonkers Library and Metro North Station. She took a deep breath in relief, considering how far she had come. She was so grateful for the love and care Mrs. Brown had shown to her. It was great to have a lovely place to call home. Phillip enjoyed having his own room full of toys, and Cherise liked sharing a bedroom with Shante. The room was large enough to fit two twin beds. There was plenty of closet space throughout the entire apartment. Shante was taking charge of her life and loving all she had accomplished.

She was grateful that, after graduation, Justine gave her the work opportunity she needed. She was glad to leave her old life behind. Phil-Quan had recently been sentenced to five years in prison for selling drugs to a cop with a prior armed robbery charge. Her mother had tried several rehab programs but was still drinking and having wild parties. Her sister Denise never did move in with her boyfriend but had actually gotten a job as a waitress and had found a small kitchenette in a house on South Broadway in Yonkers. She hadn't heard much from her other siblings.

Although she lived less than four miles away from them, Shante felt like she was millions of miles away from her old life. Mrs. Brown had moved to Raleigh, North Carolina, to live with her oldest son and his family. Shante had no reason to ever go back to the projects.

She looked at the monogrammed gold-plated pen Mrs. Smith from the library had given her for graduation. She smiled as she recalled the many encouraging words she had spoken to her. For the first time in her life, Shante could cry tears of joy because she was really genuinely happy with her life.

Saturday, June 4th, 2011

11:45 A.M.

Joe was sitting in the car waiting for Erika as she shopped for new yarn at Sistah Knit. Rhonda peeked out the window and watched him scroll through his cell phone. She could see a toddler strapped in a car seat in the back, playing with a toy rabbit. Rhonda asked herself, *Why do I still have his number in my phone?* She did her best to avoid making eye contact with Joe's Erika by keeping her back toward the counter and pretending to be interested in some skeins of yarn in a basket by the window.

"Thank you for your purchase, Erika. It was very nice to see you again."

"Thank you, Terri, I love shopping at Sistah Knit. Please say hello to Sherri for me."

"Yes, I will. Have a good day and stay cool. It's unusually hot for June."

"Oh yeah, it really is!" said Erika as she walked toward the door. "See you next time." Rhonda watched as Erika got in the passenger's seat next to Joe. Erika looked back at their son. Joe started the car and drove off slowly.

"What's wrong, Rhonda?" asked Terri.

"Terri, I hate him and yet ... I still love him after all this time. Am I crazy?"

"No Rhonda, you're not crazy. Your feelings are your feelings."

"He played me like a fool, Terri," Rhonda sighed and put a hand to her face. "I suppose I hate seeing him look so happy."

266

"Well, I can understand that Rhonda ... but you really have to get over him."

"I know. I just really thought Joe was the one for me."

"There *is* someone for you. He just hasn't *found* you yet."

"That's a kind thing to say, Terri. I don't know if I will ever find a man I can love and who loves me. The kids are getting older. My mother has a fabulous life. She travels with her friends. Even she has a boyfriend now. You know they're going to Martha's Vineyard next weekend? And what am I doing? I'm still hung up on Joe ..."

"Don't sweat it, Rhonda. Love will find you," Terri walked over to Rhonda and put her hands on her shoulders.

"Terri, I don't know. I feel like the doors to find love have closed for me."

"Rhonda, Joe was not for you. He is not worthy of you."

"My heart still loves a man who is married. This pain feels like it will never go away."

1:00 P.M.

Michele and Charles spent the hot Saturday afternoon lying in bed watching movies.

"Hey baby, here's cool glass of lemonade and some popcorn," said Charles as he crawled into bed next to his wife. Michele smiled.

"Thanks, honey. I love us spending cozy time together in our home away from all the daily distractions."

"I could be with you all the time, anywhere, Michele. I love you so much." She giggled.

"Maybe we should buy a small island. Go off the grid and just live our lives being minimalists."

"You a minimalist?" laughed Charles. "You wouldn't last a day without your laptop and cell phone."

"And you, my sweet husband, would not last a day without all your digital gadgets."

"My dear sweet wife ... you are so right." They laughed.

"Okay, my *dear sweet* husband, let's just pretend this king-sized bed is our island with all our digital stuff including lemonade, popcorn, and all."

"I like the sound of that," said Charles. He took his wife by the waist and cuddled her in his arms. "You are the love of my life Michele. You make me so very happy. I love our life. I love our home. I love our beautiful daughter. There is nothing else in this life I need or want."

"Charles, I am a blessed woman to have a husband like you. You are my life and soul."

They made love and fell asleep in each other's arms. When Michele awoke it was almost 9:00 P.M. Charles was still sleeping. She looked at his naked and muscular deep chocolate body. He was lying so peacefully. She kissed his lips gently so as not to wake him. She looked at the wedding band on his finger, then looked at her own. She touched the fiery diamond and thought back to her wedding day. They had traveled to Aruba a month earlier for seven days and had had a wonderful time together. In the back of her mind, Michele was constantly haunted by the fear of Charles ever finding out how she had cheated on him on their anniversary day. She carefully concealed her feelings of guilt. Bradford continued to spend time in the New York City area. Michele watched his every move like a hawk.

4:00 P.M.

Justine worked most Saturdays since opening her company. She had more than twenty new artists and even some who had switched over from other record labels. Her desk was piled with paperwork and her two work laptops: one for digital sound tracks and the other for contracts and other legal matters.

Working hard for almost twenty hours a day, seven days a week helped Justine to keep her mind off the fact that Ronald had moved on with his life. He could no longer wait for Justine to decide when she wanted to get married. Ronald wanted to tell Justine face to face, but she was always too busy working. After inviting her to meet with him eight times, he figured sending a letter to her was his only option. Justine received his letter at the office. It read:

Justine,

It's been a long time since we have been together. I wish things between us had turned out differently. Our lives have taken a turn onto two different roads and I've accepted that fact. You are a one of a kind beautiful woman who is full of life and exploring her new beginnings. It's great that your record company is doing well and is noted as a top business on the rise. I know that makes you very happy. You will always have a special place in my heart. I wish you all the happiness and love you can find.

I only ever wanted to write love letters to you. This will be the first and last letter you will receive from me. I showed you all the love and patience I had in me. You were my heart and dreams. You were my life Justine. I would move Heaven and Earth to make you happy, but I have realized I cannot make you love me enough to marry me.

Justine had to put the letter down as her eyes filled with tears. She took a deep breath and continued reading.

My life's road has brought me love once again. I fought it for a while in hopes that one day you might come back to me. But I've found that I can't fight the love I have been searching for just because the person is not you. I love the love that loves me. I am getting married in two weeks and moving to Atlanta by the end of the year. I wish you all the best of love and happiness in the world.

Love Ronald.

Saturday, June 11th, 2011

12:00 P.M.

The Sistah Knit Podcast

There was much excitement once again as the yarn shop launched its first podcast. Terri spoke into the mic about everything Sistah Knit, from the start of their yarn shop to where they found themselves now two years after opening.

"It's been an awesome journey so far. We've had many knitting and crochet classes for elders and youth in the community. We've partnered with The Harlem Knitting Circle to knit for the homeless. And we've donated to many shelters and hospitals."

"That's right!" replied Sherri, "And we've had several celebrities stop by since our grand opening. Let's see ... Patti Labelle, Alicia Keys, Oprah and Gayle King, Robin Roberts ... and big news for our Sistah Knit fans ... Tyler Perry would like to use our shop to shoot a scene for an upcoming TV series he is working on!" Terri giggled.

"Sherri, don't give too much away!" They laughed. Terri continued, "Another of our biggest supporters is Gigi of GGmadeit.com. She is the creator of *We Knit Too*. Sistah Knit was a part of the New York City Yarn Crawl last summer ... we're a welcome vendor at Vogue Live Knitting Event on both the East and West Coast ... we'll be supporting the Rhinebeck, New York Sheep and Wool Event in the fall ... and you already know we'll enjoy Knitting in The City at Bryant Park in the summer!"

Sherri picked up, "Hmm what else? We started the Annual Yarn Market Place in Marcus Garvey Park shortly after our grand opening. We have a beautiful Black History Month event during February where we knit in memory of our ancestors and the sacrifices they made hundreds of years ago. Lastly, for some upcoming events we have classes for all the men who love to knit. Yo Brother Yarn classes are becoming very popular in this community! Bronx Boy aka Billy Rivera, a knitter from the South Bronx, started the group, and we welcome them one Saturday a month. Sistah Knit also has Knit and Sip Nights every Thursday! All are welcome! Thank you for joining us for our Sistah Knit very first podcast. Please tune in next week when we'll discuss knitting for Social Change in America." Terri took over for the final sign-off.

"Our special guests will be Regina King, Tracee Ellis Ross, Niecy Nash, and our very own Michele Nelson of *Good Morning News* here in New York! Please be sure to check out our Facebook page for all upcoming news and events. Terri and Sherri, signing off for now." The twins ended their livestream and stared at their friends who were sitting silently in the shop.

"Well ... ?" asked Sherri nervously. The ladies cheered.

"Great job! Congratulations!" said Rhonda.

"Fantastic podcast, I loved it!" said Justine.

"Yes, it was awesome!" said Shante.

"And I am *so* looking forward to being next week's guest! Thanks ladies," smiled Michele.

A small crowd of yarn crafters whom the twins had invited for the release of the podcast shared their expressions of joy and hugs with Terri and Sherri as they slowly left the shop.

"How about some coffee, ladies?" asked Sherri.

"That sounds great," replied Terri, "I need to relax after an hour and a half of talking."

"Well get settled everyone. It'll be a few minutes." Sherri smiled as she walked back to the kitchen. They all made themselves comfortable by kicking off their shoes and flopping down on the couches around the mahogany table. Michele put on relaxing ocean sounds. Shante flipped the open sign to closed and locked the door.

"Thanks, Shante," laughed Terri. Sherri returned with the coffee and set a tray on the table as she looked at her sister and friends.

"Wow you all are chilling like *you* worked hard all day!" she giggled.

"I have a lot on my mind," said Justine.

"Me too," replied Shante.

"Join the club!" said Rhonda.

"I just did," sighed Michele.

"Sister girls, what's wrong?" asked Terri. The four of them started to speak all at once.

"Hey, hey, hey ladies! Slow down, just one at time, please," said Sherri. There were a few seconds of silence as they stirred and sipped their coffee. Justine spoke up first.

"I received a letter yesterday from Ronald. He's getting married."

"Ohmigod! Justine!" Shante gasped.

"Justine, I am so sorry," Michele frowned.

"We're sorry Justine," said Sherri.

"We wished things could have been different," said Terri.

"My heart goes out to you," said Rhonda.

"Thanks guys, you know the saying. All is fair in love and war!" replied Justine with a half smile, trying to cheer up.

"How are you taking the news?" asked Shante.

"Well ... I'm sad for myself. He wanted to tell me in person but I was too busy at the office signing new talent. He's moving to Atlanta by the end of the year." Justine wiped a tear from her eye.

"Did he say anything about the woman he's marrying?" asked Rhonda.

"No, he didn't. Ronald is so kind and loving. I know he wouldn't want me to doubt anything about myself. He really is a beautiful person. I hope whoever she is, she realizes what a good man he is."

Michele grabbed Justine's hand, "Everything will be okay now, Justine."

"I know. It just feels so strange to know that he's actually moved on."

"Well honestly ..." Teri began. "How long did you think he was going to wait?"

"Yeah, the man wanted a wife," added Sherri. Justine sighed.

"I know, you're right. He deserves to be happy in life and have the things he dreams of."

"Are you happy for him?" asked Shante.

"Yes, I am. I'm trying. I wish it could have been me ... but the road of life took us in different directions. I accept that he had to move on for his happiness." The ladies nodded and there was silence again. Shante spoke next.

"Phil-Quan got five years in prison and I haven't seen much of my family since I left Mrs. Brown's home."

"Do you plan to see Phil-Quan while he is away?" Justine asked with wide eyes.

"No, I don't. I have no feelings for him."

"Don't you want Phillip to see and know his father?" Michele asked. Shante sighed.

"I don't know ... I really don't want to take Phillip to a prison hundreds of miles away. I'm not trying to punish Phil-Quan but I mean ... he was always in and out of Phillip's life anyway. He never asks for his father ... He's four years old, and happy and healthy. I think that right now, I'm all he needs." Rhonda placed her hand on Shante's lap. She continued.

"I've managed with Phillip on my own since the day he was born. It wasn't easy for us but now, things are so much better." She paused and looked around the room, "I just ... I just wanted to say that I'm grateful to the many women that helped me along the way. Mrs. Whitaker at the library, Mrs. Brown, Justine and all of you for being the kind of loving friends I'd never had before. I see something in each of you that I hope to become. Sistah Knit has been more of a home to me than the home I grew up in. This shop is so full of love." Terri and Sherri dabbed tears from their eyes.

"Shante," Sherri said with a shaky voice, "Terri and I, as the rest of us, are always here for you and Phillip." Shante felt a sort of heartwarming joy like never before.

"I agree with Shante," said Rhonda. "This is home. You ladies are my sisters. I can share all my life's issues here." She paused, "And since that seems to be what we're doing right now ... I am still heartbroken over Joe. I watched him from the window sitting in his car with his little son just the other day." Sherri spoke up.

"But Rhonda, the man is married and he *lied* to you!"

"Oh, I know!" Rhonda said hopelessly. "I fell in love with his charm and the way he treated me."

"He is *not* the man for you Rhonda," said Terri.

"And you know that, Rhonda!" said Michele, "You have got to move on and forget all about him." Rhonda sighed.

"I know, I know. You're all right ... I've known this for a long time. I'm just dwelling on past memories of good times we had together. It has me stuck and crippled. But you know what ... seeing Joe in the car with his son made me realize that I am the lucky one."

"What do you mean?" Michele asked.

"Well, I could have been holding Joe's baby in my arms while I watched him from the window. I could have been fighting for child support at my age ... changing diapers and warming bottles in the middle of the night. I have two beautiful young adult children who are both wonderful." She paused again. "I've decided to move forward with my life and leave any memory of Joe totally in the past."

"Yes!" cheered Justine, "Good for you Rhonda!" The ladies nodded in approval.

"Good riddance," Michele added. She realized it was her turn to share what had been on her mind as the Sistah Friends stared at her. "Well ... as for me, I'm trying to move in my marriage with Charles. The fact that I slept with Bradford on my wedding anniversary continues to haunt me." She let out a deep breath. "I just feel so bad for betraying Charles like that. I pray every day he will never find out." She lowered her head in shame.

"Michele, don't punish yourself," said Rhonda.

"I admit, there was always something about Bradford that set off a curious spark with me ... but the guilt of crossing that line with him is still just eating me alive. I'm starting therapy next week. I need to deal with this. I am praying the therapist will not ask me to bring Charles in. Because he can *never* find out."

"That should be good for you," said Shante.

"Do you think he would leave you?" asked Justine.

"I don't know," frowned Michele. "But I do know that he is a very good husband and father, and that alone should have kept me out of meeting Bradford."

"We all make mistakes Michele, don't be so hard on yourself," said Sherri.

"Girl, well then this was a well-thought-out preplanned mistake!" Michele replied. There was silence and all eyes were on her. No one knew what to say. She continued, "I'm sorry, I just can't forgive myself because I knew exactly what I was doing. My husband had to work and promised to make up for being away on our anniversary date – and he did. And the crazy thing is that I was making love to Charles in the *exact hotel room* Bradford and I had shared just before! *What the hell are the chances* of something like that ever happening? But it did happen ... to me." She paused, "You ladies are my sisters, and you're the only people that I can tell ... I just feel like I am being judged."

"Judging is not what *any* of us are about," said Terri. "We're family."

Wednesday, June 15th, 2011

2:00 P.M.

"The pattern is easy to read once you understand the abbreviation codes and the chart symbols of knitting. K on RS means knit on the right side of the knitting and P on WS means purl on the wrong side," explained Sherri as she led a knitting class at Sistah Knit.

"Wow, look at all these young girls learning to knit!" marveled Shante. "I wish Cherise was interested."

"Don't worry about it Shante," Michele giggled, "Ashley isn't interested in learning to knit either."

"Maybe one day they'll both want to learn how!" said Justine cheerily. Michele and Shante looked at each other and laughed, knowing that Cherise and Ashley would probably never want to learn how to knit at any time in the near future. Terri brought out a tray of chocolate chip cookies for the little girls. Rhonda trailed behind, handing out small cups of fruit punch.

"Okay, break time, girls!" said Sherri. "We will pick up our needles again in a half hour."

"Wow, I counted sixteen girls," said Terri.

"That's great," smiled Michele, "They really seem willing and eager to learn."

"Yes!" replied Sherri. "Right now, they're learning to knit and purl. I have them making a six-by-six swatch as practice. I think most of them are doing pretty well at it!"

"It's wonderful to see these girls so eager to learn," said Rhonda.

"Are you working on anything new, Rhonda?" asked Justine.

278

"Actually, yes, I am." She picked up her large canvas bag from the floor and pulled out a large grey and lavender shawl.

"Wow, it's beautiful. Who's it for?" asked Michele.

"For my mother. Her birthday is coming up soon."

"I love the color choice," said Terri.

"Your mother will love it," said Justine.

"What a nice birthday gift for her," said Shante. Terri and Sherri agreed.

"What are you all working on?" Rhonda asked.

"I'm working on pair of socks for Phillip."

"I'm working on a silk scarf for Charles for when winter comes."

"Justine, do you have time to knit anymore? You're so busy signing new talent," Terri asked.

"I started working on some baby booties. The girl who does my nails is expecting her first baby. I don't have time to knit anything larger than booties!" They laughed. Justine continued, "What are you twins working on?"

"Well, I'm knitting a wrap with beaded yarn," said Terri.

"And I have nothing on my needles at the moment," said Sherri.

"That's odd for you Sherri. You always have a project going," said Michele with an eyebrow raised.

"Yes, I do ... but lately I've been thinking about writing a book ... about Sistah Knit." Terri turned to her sister in shock.

"Sherri, I had no idea you decided this!"

"Oh, that's a wonderful idea!" said Rhonda.

"Yes, it's awesome," agreed Shante and Justine.

"Great idea," smiled Michele.

"Well, I've had the idea for a while and had planned to talk to you about it Terri ..." Sherri began.

"It's a beautiful idea, Sherri," Terri replied. "What kind of book exactly?"

"I think a picture book or something that would be on a coffee table. It'll have our stories, photos of the shop and the community. Maybe some history on how we're the first yarn shop Harlem has ever had. It'll showcase pictures of our grand opening, our podcast, in which all of you ladies will be our special guests. The classes we teach ... there is so much we can do with the book. And I was thinking the profits would go to children's charities," smiled Sherri.

"You know I am *so* ready to have you sisters on *Good Morning News* for an interview!" said Michele excitedly.

"Slow down, miss news reporter, we have a long way to go on this," laughed Sherri. "Terri and I need to talk about this; in the meantime, I better get back to teaching these girls how to knit and purl."

6:00 P.M.

Bradford dated other women but still tried occasionally to contact Michele at the station. She refused to take his calls and asked for his number to be blocked from her office phone. Bradford watched her report the morning news every day. He stood outside the news building to watch her enter and leave from work. He was careful not to been seen.

Charles and Michele were enjoying a quiet dinner at home.

"So, I heard on ESPN that Bradford Wilson hasn't been showing up to team training."

Michele was a little unnerved by Charles' statement. "Oh yeah? I've heard some talk around the station about that."

"He's a weird dude," Charles replied, "He must be out of his mind. He's going to screw up his career." Michele quickly changed the subject.

"How was work today, honey? Anything exciting happening?"

"Well baby, my work projects are not half as exciting as you may think," chuckled Charles.

"So? Tell me about them anyway, Charles."

"Well my firm is thinking of expanding to Chicago."

"Wow! That's exciting, baby."

"It really is ... things are going along just fine." He poured more wine into their glasses. He sighed, "I really don't want to be away from home too much once this project gets going, Michele."

"Charles, let's cross that bridge when we get to it, okay?"

Friday, June 18th, 2011

7:00 P.M.

Rhonda had been secretly attending a singles ministry social twice a month. It was her mother who had suggested she go, in order to take the next steps to get over Joe.

Frank Sullivan was a handsome and robust man who stood six and half feet tall. He had beautiful neatly twisted salt and pepper dreadlocks that fell to his shoulders. His finely groomed beard complemented his lovely hazel eyes. He had noticed Rhonda from across the room and introduced himself. He shyly admitted that it was his first time attending a singles social.

"I've been coming here for about two months," said Rhonda.

"Is this your home church?" Frank asked.

"My mother is a faithful member. I drop in every now and again. Who invited you, Frank?'

"My sister Alice. She and her husband Colin met at a singles social here fourteen years ago, and they were married in this church ten years ago."

"That's really wonderful for them. Any children?"

"Yes, they have two beautiful daughters. Plum, the oldest, is twelve, and Candy is nine going on nineteen." Rhonda chuckled. "Do you have children, Rhonda?"

"I have twins in their third year in college. Twinkle and Tyree."

"That's great," smiled Frank.

"What about you?" Rhonda asked.

"I have one daughter. Her name is Bella and she's a fourth-year resident at Lenox Hill Hospital."

"Smart young lady," Rhonda smiled. "She must take after her father."

"Well, I don't know about all that," laughed Frank.

"I know you must be very proud of her."

"I am proud. Bella is a wonderful daughter to me and her mother."

"Are you divorced?"

"I am a widower. My wife Sarah passed away five years ago."

"Oh, I am very sorry," Rhonda frowned.

"Sarah was a wonderful woman, wife and mother. She had a long battle with a rare form of cancer. We had a good twenty-five-year marriage. Bella is like her mother in so many ways."

"I am touched by how passionately you speak of your late wife." They smiled.

"What about you, Rhonda?"

"I'm divorced. My husband was a good father when he was around ... but a not-so-good husband most of the time."

"Oh, Rhonda I'm sorry, I didn't mean to ..."

"No worries. It was a long time ago. I survived and I'm here now," she smiled.

"And I'm glad you're here, Rhonda," Frank replied. Rhonda smiled as she admired his eyes.

"Rhonda, would it be out of place if I asked you out to dinner tonight?"

"The church is serving dinner this evening."

"I know, but I would like to take you to dinner. A real dinner. We can go to Amy Ruth's or wherever you would like to go. Some place where we could just sit together in a quiet space and talk."

Rhonda had a good feeling about Frank's offer. He was soft-spoken and had a gentle way about him. He was casually dressed with the right amount of urban swag. She agreed to go to dinner.

They slowly walked to the restaurant laughing and talking along the way. Rhonda felt a kind of peace that was like the warmth of the sun on her face. She had not had that kind of peace in a very long time. She and Frank enjoyed a delicious meal of waffles with catfish. They lingered over peach cobbler and talked until the restaurant closed at midnight.

Friday, June 25th, 2011

2:00 P.M.

Shante was proud of Cherise for finding a summer job at a local flower shop on the Yonkers pier. Phillip enjoyed going to summer day camp and playing with his friends. Shante felt good about her accomplishments. At twenty-two years old, she was happy and believed her future would only continue to get better. She thought about her diploma hanging on the wall in a gold frame in her living room. She wanted to hang a bachelor's degree and a master's degree, too. No one in her family had ever gone to college. Mrs. Smith at the library had always talked to Shante about furthering her education.

"Maybe some online courses on the weekends would be a good place to start," she said out loud to herself.

"Shante, would you please scan these files and email these contracts to my lawyer?" Shante was so deep in her thoughts that she hadn't heard Justine approach her desk. "Sure Justine, right away."

"Shante, are you doing okay?" Justine asked.

"Yes, I'm well. I was thinking about something."

"Anything I can help you with?"

"Your advice would be appreciated if we could talk a minute."

"Shante, anything I can help you with." Justine glanced down at her watch. "You know what ... it's two o'clock and the office is very quiet. Let's call it a day." She smiled.

"Okay, I'll just email these contracts and shut down."

"Great, I was planning on going by Sistah Knit, you want to come? We can talk on the way."

"Thanks, Justine."

They walked down Saint Nicholas Avenue and through Marcus Garvey Park. Justine listened as Shante told her how grateful she was for the opportunity to work with her and how much she had learned from Justine, and her strong desire to advance her education. She told Justine how she used to dream of going to college. Spelman was the place she'd always wanted to attend. She dreamed of sitting a classroom with other students and learning all she could about everything. She dreamed of meeting a young man from Morehouse and falling in love.

"Justine, you and Michele and Rhonda are all educated women. Terri and Sherri are beautiful, educated, and smart – and they've traveled. They have their own business just like you! You've all encouraged me in so many different ways," she paused. "I know that I can't go to school after working hours because Phillip and Cherise need me ... I was thinking about online courses. What do you think, Justine?"

"Shante, I believe in you. And you can do anything you put your mind to."

"I really want to give it try."

"You got this, Shante. Let's go hear what Terri and Sherri have to say."

When they arrived at Sistah Knit they were happy to see that Michele and Rhonda were already there.

"Damn, do you ladies ever work?" Justine asked jokingly as she walked through the door smiling.

"Well, you and Shante are here, so I suppose you two don't really work either!" teased Michele as she hugged them.

"We joined the we-don't-work club," smiled Rhonda as she took a bite of an oatmeal raisin cookie and sipped some ginger tea. Terri and Sherri were assisting customers. They waved hello at Justine and Shante.

"So, what brings you ladies by so early in the afternoon?" asked Michele.

"Girl, you know none of us really need a reason we come here because that's what we do," answered Justine. They all laughed.

"You got that right," said Rhonda.

"I was telling Justine that I'm thinking about attending college online," Shante announced.

"Shante, that's awesome!" replied Rhonda.

"Yes, it is! That's great you want to get your degree," said Michele.

"What will you study?" asked Justine.

"I really want to study business administration and get my MBA."

"Well, all right now!" smiled Michele. "Anything we can do to help you, Shante?"

"Well ... I really don't know exactly how to start," replied Shante shyly.

"Don't worry yourself about all that, we will help you," said Justine.

"Shante, attending college online is great for people with very busy work and family schedules," said Rhonda. "You can work at your own pace and when you've completed your courses you can talk with other graduates from all across the country."

"I'm excited. It's something I've always wanted to do. I would be the first in my family to go to college."

"Shante, we are so proud of you!" said Michele. "You are our little sister."

The twins walked over as a customer walked happily out the door with her yarns.

"Hey what's going on ladies?" asked Sherri. Terri stood beside her smiling.

Michele replied, "Shante has decided to attend college and earn a degree in business."

"That's wonderful!" said Sherri.

"Yes, that's great, Shante!" said Terri.

"We're happy for you, Shante," said Rhonda.

"I'm excited," said Shante. "Justine will help me ... I am inspired by all of you. I want to do great things. I want to travel and see places all around the world. I want Phillip to see more and learn more." Shante spoke passionately. "I want to do things that my family has never done. I want everything to be different for Phillip and Cherise." The ladies were almost in tears as she continued, "My life has been one struggle after the other ... some of it my own fault. I often think how my life would have turned out if I was born into a different family or into one of your families. If my mother was the kind of woman who believed in education and teaching her children that they are smart and beautiful and can do and become anything they desire if they just work hard and focus on getting a good education. My entire family is a mess because our foundation was really a sinking ship from the start. In my heart I always knew that *somehow I had to get out to survive*. Mrs. Whitaker at the library, and Mrs. Smith ... and all of you have been the anchor and rock I so desperately needed. You all welcomed me and taught me through your honesty and truth." Shante turned to Justine and reached for her hand.

"Justine, you own your own business and gave me a great paying job which has allowed me and Phillip and Cherise to live in a safe, comfortable home. I could never afford it on minimum wage." Next, she looked up at the twins.

"Terri and Sherri, you sisters own this beautiful yarn shop after having a great modeling career in New York and Paris and all over the world. The Harlem community loves this shop and your podcast has over fifty thousand listeners in a little over a month!"

"And Michele, I am still in awe of you being a news anchor and reporter for GMN. You interviewed our first black president Barack Obama. *How damn cool is that?*"

"Rhonda, you are a head nurse at Columbia Hospital. You've worked with the neurosurgeon Dr. Ben Carson. You've attended to many celebrities and politicians. You've spoken at colleges and taught others about a career in the nursing field."

"You're all so well educated, you have great careers, and you're all financially stable. Justine has taught me how to invest money and even start a portfolio. A portfolio in my old neighborhood means you have some paintings or sketches inside a large black flat suitcase." The others cracked up, Shante grinned, and then she added, "I have a strong foundation here at Sistah Knit, and I am very grateful to all of you."

"I think we need a group hug here," said Michele, "in honor of our Shante."

July 2011

As the summer went on, Rhonda and Frank decided to see each other outside of the church singles ministry socials. She felt happy and free. Frank continued to be a perfect gentleman. He really enjoyed spending time with Rhonda. They went on weekend road trips to Martha's Vineyard, Virginia Beach, Charleston, and Savannah. They visited historical museums, plantations, and landmarks. On a trip to the Hamptons, they decided on a trip to Africa in the following autumn. Rhonda's mother smiled with a deep happiness as she listened to Rhonda talk about Frank as if she were a sixteen-year-old girl.

"Rhonda, he seems like a wonderful man. I am so very happy for you."

"Mom, he really is a great person. He's kind and gentle. He loves life and enjoys so many things. He has a wonderful book collection and he loves all kinds of music. He owns a lovely cottage home near Martha's Vineyard. He takes life easy and lets nothing bother him."

She grinned, and her mother did, too. "And Mom, what a beautiful baritone voice when he sings! He loves God and appreciates all the blessings he has been given. He knows where he is going in life, and most of all *he is at peace with himself.*"

She paused for a moment and then exclaimed, "Mom, I don't believe I've ever met anyone like Frank! He's an old-fashioned man, and with a beautiful heart and mind. Last week, he rented a log cabin in the woods of Richmond, and he built a fire and we roasted marshmallows together and even made s'mores. I know I love him, Mom. And please don't ask me how can I love him when we've only been seeing each other such a short time."

"Rhonda, I was not thinking that at all. If anything, I was thinking how you could possibly *not* love him."

Michele was no fool. The private investigator she'd hired to keep track of Bradford had paid off. She knew that he had been hanging around outside of the *Good Morning News* building. She knew he was not attending football training camp, way before Charles had mentioned it a few months before. Bradford soon turned to drinking and using drugs to cope with the fact that Michele did not want him. He had been kicked out of several bars and pubs around the city for uncivil behavior and drunkenness and disorderly conduct. He was kicked out of the Hilton, the Plaza, and the Grand Hyatt for noise complaints and rudeness to the staff and other guests. Michele's one fear was that Bradford would spill the secret of their time spent together on her wedding anniversary.

Regardless, Michele and Charles enjoyed a wonderful summer traveling with Ashley. In August they went to Raleigh for a family reunion. They took a five-day cruise to the Bahamas. They went to Washington DC for a visit with Barack and Michele Obama at the White House. They also met with the Williams sisters at the U.S. Open in Flushing.

Michele bought a handsome gold tie pin for Charles, and he bought her a pair of pink gold earrings. They made love and loved each other more with every passing day. They visited Rome, Greece, Germany, and Italy. They even renewed their vows while on vacation in Bermuda. Michele was committed that she would do anything to secure her marriage to Charles. They went sailing off Cape Charles and enjoyed each other's company with a wonderful seafood dinner. They took long walks as a family and listened to Ashley talk about her dreams and goals.

"Daddy, I am going to marry a man just like you." Michele smiled. Charles laughed.

"Well princess, you're off to a good start, if I do say so myself." Michele knew in her heart that Charles was right.

"Daddy, I want to live in the house where we live right now with my children *and* you and Mommy." Michele's eyes filled and she smiled through happy tears.

"Don't cry sweetheart," said Charles. "Ashley said we can live with her and her family."

"Charles, these are happy tears. It's a blessing to hear our daughter say such beautiful things."

"Yes, it is, honey. Ashley is a beautiful young lady just like her mother." He kissed them both on the cheek.

"Charles, we are so blessed. This has been the best summer of our lives. I love you and Ashley so much. Nothing would make me happier than for us to grow old together and be with our daughter, her husband, and our grandchildren."

Justine worked long hours every day. There were no summer vacations or weekend trips for her.

Her business had become her soul and her life. She was 37 years old with her own business and it had taken off with super-talented artists who had mega number one hits on the charts. She had everything she'd wanted, and yet she was sometimes lonely and full of heartbreak that Ronald had seriously moved on.

Her parents called to say they were enjoying their summer vacation in Switzerland.

Her brother Stanley and his lady had eloped and got married in Las Vegas. They were expecting their first child later in the year. Life seemed to be passing Justine by, she thought, and she didn't know what to do about it.

Her company kept her so busy that she really had no time for dating, much less a vacation.

She spoke out loud to herself, "This is no way to live."

She left the office every night around ten or eleven. Stay Paid Records had become her crutch. She needed the company to help her forget about Ronald. But it was also her excuse not to date. She admired Shante for leaving each evening to go home to Phillip and Cherise. Justine felt empty and alone with all her success. It was the saddest summer of her life.

Shante took Phillip and Cherise to the movies, to museums, and anywhere else she thought they could learn. They went to food street fairs around New York City. They took walks and bike rides around Central Park and enjoyed plays at Harlem's National Black Theatre. Phillip loved the Annual Black Comic Book Festival at the Schomburg Center. They enjoyed visiting the South Street Seaport, they hiked at Untermyer Park and Gardens in Yonkers. She learned to drive and even rented a car driving around Yonkers to get more practice. Cherise worked at the flower shop and spent time with her new friends. Shante enjoyed seeing Cherise and Phillip happy and doing well. Thinking of the rest of her family on the other side of town made her think about how far she had actually come in her own life. Her goal was to one day leave New York and purchase a home somewhere in the South. She dreamed of marrying and having a family – a family nothing like the one she was born into.

Saturday, August 27th, 2011

12:30 P.M.

The Sistah Knit podcast was listed as the number one podcast in the knitting community by *We Knit Too* magazine created by Gigi. *Simply Knitting, Vogue,* and *Crafters Today* magazines all gave the podcast five-star reviews.

★★★★★ *A podcast that invites listeners to call in live with comments and questions.*

★★★★★ *The best and only podcast that gives back to the community it serves.*

★★★★★ *The only knitting podcast to interview major film, television, and musical stars.*

"What awesome reviews about your podcast!" said Michele.

"Thank you, girl!" beamed Sherri.

"We're proud of the work we are doing. John Legend is our guest next week!" said Terri excitedly.

"Get out, shut the front door!" exclaimed Shante. "John Legend?!"

"Really?!" asked Justine.

"Well *all right now* ladies. Will Denzel be next?" asked Rhonda, laughing.

"If we get Denzel, Lord have mercy!" laughed Sherri. They could not help but laugh at the possibility of Denzel Washington visiting the shop to speak on their podcast.

Shante asked, "Why does every woman love Denzel so much?"

"Because he's Denzel!" said Justine.

"He's handsome and one hell of an actor," sighed Michele dreamily.

"Well dream on ladies, dream on," smiled Terri.

"All right calm down now, calm down," laughed Sherri.

"It's not easy to calm down when Denzel is the subject!" said Rhonda. Just then a Chinese food delivery guy interrupted their discussion. Terri paid him and set the hot bags on the coffee table. The ladies unwrapped egg rolls, wonton soup, veggie Lo Mein, shrimp fried rice, steamed broccoli, and dumplings. For a minute or two the only sound heard was the murmuring and eating.

"So how was everyone's summer?" asked Sherri

"It's been a hot minute since we've seen each other!" said Terri.

"I had a good summer exploring the city with Phillip and Cherise. I even got my driver's license," said Shante.

"Wow, Shante. That's really awesome. You got your license, will you buy a car now?" asked Justine.

"No, probably not. But I'll rent one if necessary." Shante smiled and felt happy for herself. She slurped her hot soup.

"Good for you, Shante. Knowing how to drive makes you much more independent," said Rhonda.

"I'm happy I learned. Phillip loves riding in a car."

Terri looked at Justine. "So Justine, how was your summer?"

"You know me. Busy working all summer. New talent always wanting to get signed. And I scored some fine ones."

"Well, how much fun is that?" asked Sherri. "You need to have some down time to relax, girl." Shante knew Justine was always working. She was always in the office before Shante arrived in the morning and still there when Shante left in the evenings. Justine had given Shante three weeks off with pay to enjoy her summer. She couldn't help but feel bad that she was enjoying her life while the person who'd helped change her life was sitting in her office all day working. Shante could tell that Justine was missing Ronald and pouring herself into running her business.

"Ladies, you know how it is when you run a business," said Justine. "There really is no time to do much of anything else."

"Oh, now Justine, Terri and I managed to get away for two weeks this summer. We closed the shop, put the podcast on hold, and vacationed with our parents down in Savannah. It was so good to relax in the hot South, sipping cool sweet tea while sitting on a porch swing in the summer. Or taking a cool dip in the lake."

"I would love to go to Savannah one day," said Shante. "I hope to move to the South in a few years."

"Well maybe next summer you can come with us! Our parents have a large family home there. It's been in our family for years," smiled Sherri.

"I would really like that," said Shante.

"Justine, you will have come with us too," said Terri.

"Sounds like a plan to me ... if I can get away."

"Michele, how was your summer?" asked Sherri.

"Charles and I took a lot of weekend trips with Ashley. Martha's Vineyard, Washington, Atlanta, Virginia Beach. We both needed to stay close to home because of work deadlines and projects."

"Michele, you sound like you're reading from a teleprompter," said Terri. "Is everything okay with you?"

"I'm good, my friends ... well, actually, to be truthful, I've had a private investigator keeping an eye on Bradford for some time now."

"WHAT? What the hell is going on?" asked Rhonda.

"Yes, Michele, what's going on?" asked Sherri. Justine and Shante stared wide-eyed.

"Why did you hire an investigator, did Bradford threaten you or your family? Or what?" demanded Sherri.

"No, no, he hasn't threatened us."

"Then why the investigator?" asked Justine.

"Because he's been hanging around outside my office building for weeks. He's always about a block away ... watching me when I get to work and when I leave for work. And he hasn't returned to training all summer."

"Oh Michele, that's terrible," said Terri. "Anything we can do?"

"No, it seems he is in a drug rehabilitation program in upstate New York. I suppose it was best that he was hanging outside of my workplace instead of Charles' business, right?"

"What do you mean by that?" asked Shante.

"Well, I wouldn't have to worry about him walking up to Charles telling him what happened between us. As you all know, I desperately don't *ever* want Charles to find out about me and Bradford."

Rhonda felt deeply sad for Michele, understanding maybe more than the others the bind Michele was in. "I am so sorry about your troubles, Michele."

"You're a sweetheart, thanks. It just keeps getting worse. Bradford was found drunk in the East Village a couple of weeks ago. He was thrown out of two different bars for fighting and destroying property."

"Michele ... honey, are you afraid?" asked Sherri.

"No, not at all. I just wish he'd go away. Far far away."

"Everything will be all right, Michele," assured Terri.

"Yes, I believe everything will be all right ... so although we had a nice summer, I had to stay on top of the updates on *Bradford Wilson sightings,* you know." Michele sighed and looked around at her friends. "Okay! Enough about me. Rhonda, how was your summer? You look happy and at peace. What's going on with you?"

"Well ladies ... I am happy," replied Rhonda, smiling. "I'm seeing someone."

"Who are you seeing – Joe?" asked Justine with wide eyes.

"No girl! I'm seeing someone new ..."

"Well don't just sit there grinning, girl! Who the hell is he?" asked Terri.

"His name is Frank."

"Well Rhonda! We don't just want to know his name! Spill the tea, girl!" laughed Michele excitedly.

"Yeah Rhonda, *talk girl!*" added Justine.

"Is he cute? And where and when did you meet him?" asked Sherri.

"Okay, slow down ladies, one question at a time please!" Rhonda could not stop smiling. All eyes on were on her as she began to speak. "I met Frank in June at a church singles social and – "

Justine shouted, "Girl! Wait! You have been seeing this man since June and you never said a word to us?"

"Shut up, Justine, let her finish," scolded Michele. "But she's right, Rhonda, you have told us sooner! Go on now, tell us more."

"Well, I like him very much. We went on a few weekend trips over the summer. He's a great guy."

"He's not married, is he?" asked Terri.

"No girl, no, he's a widower with one grown daughter. He's kind and gentle, he's soft-spoken and a man of God."

"Wow, so he's nothing like Joe at all," said Michele.

"You shut up Michele, let her finish," said Justine, giggling.

"I have a picture of us together at Martha's Vineyard. He owns a home there." Rhonda showed her friends the photo.

"Oh, he must be special Rhonda, the photo is your home screen on your phone. All right now!" laughed Michele. As the phone was passed around, Rhonda told them about her time with Frank.

"We are very happy for you Rhonda," said Sherri.

"You deserve all the happiness in the world, Rhonda," said Shante.

"Well, this calls for a drink of champagne!" announced Terri. Sherri went to the back of the shop to get champagne and glasses.

"You must feel wonderful," said Justine.

"I do Justine, it's been a long time since I've felt this good. He is nothing like Joe. I love that he was honest from the first day we met. My mother is happy for me. *And I am happy for me.*"

Sherri returned with a tray holding six glasses and a bottle of champagne. They each took a glass. Terri poured and offered a toast.

"Ladies, raise your glasses. To Rhonda, you deserve all the happiness and love that life can give you. We love you girl, and we are happy for you." They all took a sip in honor of Rhonda.

"Thank you, ladies. I'm very excited. It's been a great summer spending time with him ... and of course I told him about Sistah Knit and my wonderful friends here."

"Well, we look forward to meeting Frank," said Terri.

"I know he would love to meet you all."

"Well, we have our One Skein Wonder event next week; bring Frank by for a glass of wine!" said Sherri.

"Okay, I will do that. I hope he won't feel outnumbered in a room filled with women," laughed Rhonda.

"Didn't you meet him in a room filled with women?" Justine teased. Michele then jumped in,

"Rhonda, Frank will not be the only man here. Charles will be here too."

"Yes," said Terri, "it's Daddy Daughter knitting next week along with One Skein Wonder."

"That's great," said Rhonda. "I will be sure to let Frank know."

Saturday, January 7th, 2012

2:00 P.M.

"Knit on the purl side and purl on the knit side," said Michele as she showed Ashley how to knit and purl the stitches on a straight needle. The New Year Knit-Off event was enjoying a great turnout at the yarn shop.

"Michele, how did you manage to get her interested in learning to knit?" Shante asked.

"I did nothing, she just asked me to teach her." Ashley smiled at Shante.

"Ashley, you are doing a really wonderful job. That purple yarn is beautiful."

"Thank you, Shante. I think knitting is cool."

"Well, there might be hope for my little sister Cherise," Shante laughed.

"Maybe so," said Michele, smiling at Shante.

Terri presented a tray of warm snacks. "Hey, ladies, freshly baked chocolate chip cookies! I'll let them sit them right here for you."

Ashley took a cookie, "Thank you, Auntie Terri."

The shop was filled with customers who were sitting down knitting and walking around buying yarn. It was a mild winter day with just a few snowflakes in the air. Smooth jazz music and the aromas of baked desserts and muffins made the shop feel even warmer and cozier than usual.

"Knit two, yarn over, slip a stitch and then knit to the end of the row," said Sherri as she taught a customer how to follow a pattern for a lace shawl in silk blend yarn. Justine and her mother walked into the shop, dusting damp snowflakes from their faces.

"Hello Justine. Mrs. Whitaker, it's so nice to see you! Thank you for coming today," said Sherri.

"We brought a bottle of champagne. Happy New Year!" said Justine. She handed the bottle to Sherri.

"Hello Mrs. Whitaker," said Terri as she embraced her with a warm hug.

"It's nice to be here. This yarn shop is just so beautiful. I wish I had more time to visit you gals."

"Thank you, Mrs. Whitaker. Have a seat over here," Terri pointed to a soft leather chair. After she sat, Justine handed her mother a canvas bag.

"Here's your knitting, Mom." Mrs. Whitaker unraveled a forty-inch-long royal blue scarf made from a wool blend in Irish cable.

"Wow, what a beautiful scarf!" said Terri.

"Yes, it's beautiful," said Sherri. Michele joined the ladies to greet Justine's mother.

"Hello Mrs. Whitaker. It's great to see you. Happy New Year!"

"Happy New Year to you and your family, Michele. Where is Ashley?"

At this, Michele pointed. "She's over there, practicing knitting with her girlfriends. I'll have her come over."

"Oh no, let her be, I'll chat with her later on. It's nice to see her knitting."

Michele turned to Justine, "Hey, how are you doing Justine?"

"Doing well. Happy New Year." She hugged Michele and waved to Ashley and Shante.

"Mrs. Whitaker, would you like something warm to drink? asked Terri.

"Oh yes, coffee would be lovely," she paused and smiled, "and maybe we could pop that bottle of champagne later on?"

"Sure thing," giggled Terri.

"What a nice crowd you and your sister have here," said Mrs. Whitaker. Terri looked around the shop.

"Yes, we're so happy that people love visiting Sistah Knit. All our events have been filled and fun!" said Terri.

"Many continued blessings. Your parents must be so happy for you and your sister."

"Yes, they are. Actually, they'll be here in about an hour."

"It will good to see them. It's been a while since your mother and I talked."

Just then, Alicia Keys and her mother walked in. Behind them trailed Pam Grier and her sister. The yarn shop customers flocked toward them. Gigi and her daughter showed up soon after, followed by two of Michele's co-workers from *Good Morning News* who stopped in just to purchase some yarn and other knitting accessories. Michele was really happy to see them and introduce them to Terri and Sherri. Shante was pleased to meet Justine's mother, and being able to chat briefly with Alicia Keys was a moment she added to her list of wonderful things Sistah Knit had brought into her life.

As Shante wished a happy new year to Alicia Keys and her mother and then turned to make her way back to Ashley, she saw Mrs. Smith come through the front door with her bag of knitting in hand. Shante was happy to see her and hurried over. She gave her mentor Mrs. Smith a hug and thanked her for coming to the Knit Off event.

"Happy New Year, Mrs. Smith. I am so very happy to see you." Shante's eyes became teary.

"Oh Shante, don't cry, sweetie. I would not have missed this event for anything."

"Thank you for coming, Mrs. Smith."

"I am so glad to be here. How are Phillip and Cherise doing?"

"Phillip is doing well, enjoying playing with his new friends at the Harlem Saturday Day Care Center, and Cherise is doing just great in school and taking piano lessons on Saturdays."

"I am so happy they are doing well. Shante, you look wonderful. Are you enjoying your new job?"

"Yes, Mrs. Smith. Come here with me, I want to introduce you to my boss Justine and the owners of Sistah Knit."

Rhonda and her mother soon entered the shop. As the twins greeted them, Sherri could not help but notice the sparkling diamond engagement ring on Rhonda's finger.

"Hello Rhonda, Miss Barbara, it's so nice to see you! Please have a seat and make yourselves comfortable," said Sherri.

"Thank you, Sherri. What a big crowd. Is that Pam Grier over there knitting?" asked Miss Barbara in awe.

"Yes, Miss Barbara, it is," Terri giggled.

"Do you often have celebrities come in here?"

"They come by every now and then." Rhonda pointed to the door.

"Sherri, your mom and dad are here." The twins were extremely happy to see their parents. Terri put her arm around her sister.

"Sherri, I think 2012 is going to be a great year."

Michele checked her cell phone for messages. One from Charles:

I hope you and Ashley are having a good time. Love you.

Michele smiled and continued scrolling down; another message from her cousin Dina:

Hi cuz, on my way to Sistah Knit CU soon.

The last text was from Raymond, the sports producer at *Good Morning News*:

Bradford Wilson took his life early this morning in a Manhattan hotel.

6:00 P.M.

There was complete silence as the friends sat gathered around the coffee table. Terri softly spoke,

"Michele ... we're sorry about Bradford."

"It's awful," said Michele. "I wanted him out of my life, but really, *suicide?*"

"Michele, this is not your fault at all," said Rhonda.

"Rhonda is right," added Justine.

"The football world is turned upside down now. And of course I've been asked to comment on the situation. *Which I will not do.*"

"Every reporter is on this right now," said Sherri.

"Yes, I know ... I've just been trying to stay low-key here. It's only been a week." Michele let out a deep breath. "I'm still trying to wrap my head around the fact that he took his life in the same hotel room that we shared on ... well, we shared on *that night*. They found him on the bed." Michele got up and walked around the shop. "Bradford taking his life in the very place where we shared a night, where I betrayed my husband, is just unbelievable. This is brutal. *It's a direct message to me.*"

"No Michele, you can't think like that," said Rhonda.

"That's right, Michele," said Terri. His actions are just the result of his own demons," said Terri.

"This will all die down, Michele," said Shante.

"Yes, I know ... I know," said Michele dejectedly.

"We got you, Michele. You know that," said Justine.

"You guys are my true friends. You're the only ones who know about Bradford and me."

"We will all take your secret to our graves!" said Rhonda.

"I am so grateful to have you all in my life. I really love each of you," a tiny smile grew on Michele's face. "I'll be glad when this does die down ... so can we please not talk about it ever again?"

"Not unless you bring it up," said Terri.

"I promise you," said Michele, "after today, I will never ever talk about Bradford Wilson ever again."

Saturday, September 15th, 2012

11:00 A.M.

It was a warm and sunny morning, early in the autumn season. The ladies cheered and clinked their champagne glasses as they sat around their usual spot in Sistah Knit. Rhonda was getting married in Marcus Garvey Park that evening.

"Thank you, gals, for helping plan this wedding. Frank and I are grateful."

"Rhonda, we are so happy for you. Frank loves you so much," said Terri.

"I can hardly believe I am getting married. After Joe, really, I never thought this would ever happen."

"Come on now, no reason to bring up cheating, sneaky Joe – not today!" said Michele.

"It's your day Rhonda, enjoy every minute of it," said Sherri.

"I feel like a princess," smiled Rhonda. "At my age!"

"You are a princess, a very beautiful princess!" Justine told her. A tall slender woman with big curly hair walked into the shop.

"Hey there, I'm Penny, hair and makeup artist to see Rhonda?"

"That's me!" Rhonda waved her hands with a bright smile on her face. Penny giggled.

"I usually go to a studio or to a client's home. A yarn shop is a first for me." She looked around. "What an awesomely beautiful shop."

"Thanks very much," said Terri. "Would you like something to drink before you get started?"

"No, thank you. I have a bottle of water in my bag. Where can I set up?"

"Right here," said Sherri, pointing to a highboy table and chair set up near the window.

"Perfect spot. I can get good natural light. Come on over, Rhonda, and we'll get started." Rhonda hopped into the chair like an excited sixteen-year-old girl. She had a big smile on her face. Her friends were smiling at her and feeling happy for her. A young man entered soon after with a camera in hand.

"Hello, I'm Kenny, the photographer; can you show me to my set here?"

"Who ordered a photographer?" asked Rhonda, surprised. The twins giggled at her.

"Your soon-to-be husband, Frank," smiled Terri. "He called the shop yesterday and asked me and Sherri not to say anything. It's a surprise. He actually got a team of four photographers."

"Four? Wait, why?" asked Rhonda, looking very confused.

"Frank said he wanted you to have as many pictures as possible on this day. A photographer here at the shop. Two at the church and the reception, and another to travel with you on your honeymoon."

"*Yes, ma'am! That's right,*" said Kenny. "I'm here to take photos of you and your friends here at the shop and at the park." Rhonda's eyes filled with tears of joy. Someone handed her a tissue.

"Come on Rhonda. It's time to start with your makeup."

"Frank is a wonderful man, Rhonda. We are so happy for you," said Sherri.

"Well ladies, let's get this pre-wedding makeup party started!" said Rhonda. Shante quickly walked in. "Hi everyone! Sorry I'm a little late."

"No worries at all," said Rhonda.

"We're just glad you made it," said Justine. Michele helped Terri bring out more champagne trays with warm and cold seafood bites. Sherri turned on a playlist of love songs by Luther Vandross and current tunes by NE-YO ... photographers were taking pictures of Rhonda and her friends. It was a time, a moment that Rhonda would never ever forget ... she was in love with a wonderful man who loved her back ... and she was just overwhelmed. She felt great sisterly love from her friends at Sistah Knit.

"Flower delivery for Rhonda!" sang out a loud voice at the door. Michele signed for the beautiful flowers and then handed them off to Rhonda. The attached note card read:

> *With all our love to you on this day.*
> *Twinkle, Tyree, and Mom.*

Rhonda's tears of happiness just could not be contained.

The hours passed quickly as the ladies got ready. Rhonda needed to be at the park by four-thirty. A long white limousine pulled up at four. The friends huddled at the front door waiting on Rhonda. Sherri called out, "Come on out Rhonda, it's time to go!" Kenny's camera flashed several times as Rhonda walked from the twins' bedroom out to the front of the shop.

"Ohmigod! You look beautiful!" said Terri.

"She really looks like a princess," said Justine, wiping a tear from her eye.

"Rhonda, you look amazing," Michele blew a kiss at her.

"You look lovely," said Shante.

Rhonda's wedding dress was pastel pink with shimmer of white sparkling pearl beads. It had a wide boatneck collar with long sheer sleeves. She wore a set of pear-shaped diamond earrings and a bracelet given to her by Frank. They were the perfect accessories. She also wore matching pastel pink kitten heels. Penny had styled Rhonda's hair in a twisted French roll adorned with a touch of silver glitter and tiny baby's breath flowers. Her makeup was flawless; the highlight on her high cheekbones gave her the glow of an angel.

Justine stared at Rhonda and wondered if her wedding day would ever come. She thought about Ronald and how he had moved on with his life. She was starting to feel a little sad for herself, but the flashing from Kenny's camera brought her out of her thoughts and back into the moment. As they walked out of the shop, many people passing by had stopped to get a look at Rhonda.

Rhonda gently stepped into the limo. Justine carried a bouquet of pink roses, white calla lilies, asters, and lilacs. A beautiful fragrance filled the air as they all climbed in. The driver slowly closed the door making sure they were all seated comfortably before he drove off.

"I feel like I am dreaming," said Rhonda, looking down at her French manicured nails.

"This *is* a dream come true. We are so happy to share in this dream day of yours," said Michele, smiling.

"I'm so happy my heart is about to burst!" Rhonda announced.

"We are happy to be a part of your special day," said Terri.

"Yes, we are," chimed in Sherri.

Shante had never been to a wedding before and was happy to be able to enjoy Rhonda's. She knew she had truly turned the corner of ever going back to her old neighborhood. Most of the women she knew there were never married and had several kids. The excitement of seeing Rhonda about to get married only made Shante want to one day find a husband to settle down with, not just a baby daddy like Phil-Quan. Her whole outlook on life had changed since spending time with these women.

The driver pulled up slowly on the Fifth Avenue entrance to Marcus Garvey Park. There was a long white carpet trail with pink and lavender rose petals scattered on each side. The carpet from the sidewalk led into the center of the park near the cast iron tower and bell. A choir stood along the steps that circled inside the tower overlooking the park. There was a ten-string orchestra, and next to them, John Legend sitting at a baby grand piano playing a soft melody. The flute and saxophone players followed his tune. Michele whispered to the twins, "Wow, you and John Legend must have really hit it off at the podcast!"

Sherri winked and said, "You know it!" Terri giggled along.

The seated guests chattered lightly amongst themselves to the pleasant sounds of the music. The other photographers Frank had hired hurried up to the limo and began taking pictures alongside Kenny. Everyone stepped out of the limo to make way for Rhonda. The driver held her hand as she stepped out and positioned herself on the carpet. Her mother and children waved at her from their seats near the altar. Twinkle and Tyree smiled at Frank as he stood tall and proud in a light grey tuxedo. His best friend and best man were at his side. He smiled back at the kids, "Your mother looks so beautiful."

At the direction of the wedding coordinator, the bridesmaids each positioned themselves six feet apart, one behind the other, to walk in front of Rhonda. Terri, Sherri, Michele, Justine, and Shante all wore different style lavender dresses and they each held a pink rose. The lead singer of the choir started singing "He's Been Faithful."

312

The ladies walked down the aisle with a one, two, three step they had rehearsed. John Legend and the other musicians joined in. As the choir sang, Rhonda's mother cried in happiness and praised God for a blessed day. As the bridesmaids stood in their respective positions at the altar, the choir stopped singing. There were a few seconds of silence.

The guests stood. John Legend started singing all "All of Me." Rhonda then walked down the aisle. Frank had a tear in his eye as he watched her.

Michele smiled at Charles and Ashley. Charles blew a kiss to her and mouthed the words "*I love you.*" The warm summer breeze felt good as it brushed over Justine's face. She had noticed a handsome red-headed flute player glancing and smiling at her every few seconds. She liked his little flirtation. Terri and Sherri whispered to each about how happy they felt to see Rhonda have this beautiful day for her wedding. Shante looked around, admiring the beauty of everything. She began to cry; her tears were of a happiness that consumed her soul. Rhonda graced her way to the front of the altar. John finished the singing. Frank took Rhonda's right hand. His eyes focused on her. The guests were now seated.

Pastor A.R. Bernard of Christian Cultural Center in Brooklyn started to read scriptures from the bible about love being kind and patient. He then announced, "Today Frank and Rhonda come before our Lord with wedding vows they wrote to each other." He handed a microphone to Frank.

"Rhonda, my heart fell in love with you from the first day we met. I saw a woman who was easy to love and had so much love to share. I felt like I had known you all my life. I know I cannot live without your love. You make me better every day. I need you in my life for the rest of my life. I stand here before the Lord, family and friends to let them know how much I love you. You are my every heartbeat Rhonda. You are the woman Christ has sent to me to love and cherish forever. There is no place on this earth that I would want to be if you were not with me."

"You are the sunshine and joy in my life. I promise before God to love and keep you wrapped in love from this day until death do us part." Frank smiled and handed the microphone to Rhonda.

"Frank, my love. You are a beautiful man with a beautiful heart of kindness, tenderness and love. I didn't know I was alive until I met you. My heart found peace and unconditional love that has filled my soul every day. Your humble character and Godly leadership is gentle and your words of wisdom are music to my heart. I love you. You are the man Christ has sent me to love and cherish. My angel on earth. I never thought love could be this beautiful. You make me laugh, you warm my heart; the pureness of your love touched my soul beyond measure. I will always love you. Until death do us part."

Pastor Bernard said a short prayer over the couple, "... and what God has put together let no man separate." He instructed them to put their rings on each other's fingers. The string orchestra played softly as the choir hummed hallelujah in a heavenly tone. Pastor Bernard held Frank's and Rhonda's left hands in between his and then he spoke, "And with the power vested in me by God our father, I now pronounce you husband and wife!"

The choir released pink and white rose petals from the tower over the couple. Petals floated around with the breeze, making it appear like snow. Frank and Rhonda kissed as man and wife. John Legend began to sing "Conversations in the Dark." They stood in front of their guests as a married couple. As they began to walk down the aisle on the white carpet leading to the reception area in the park, Rhonda's and Frank's families surrounded them with hugs and kisses. The bridal party followed behind the newly married couple. The musicians and choir continued to play and sing. Champagne and other refreshments were served. Roosters, Melba's and Sylvia's restaurants all catered their finest hors d'oeuvres and dishes. Wynton Marsalis began playing trumpet, and Frank and Rhonda had their first dance. The guests smiled and cheered as they joined on the dance floor.

"Are you happy, Rhonda?" Frank asked.

"Yes, Frank. I am *very* happy."

"My only desire is to make you happy, Rhonda."

She looked into Frank's eyes, "Sweetheart, you are my desire."

"Don't they look beautiful together?" asked Michele.

"Yes, they do," replied Charles. "I hope they will be as happy as we are." Michele held her husband's hand and leaned her head on his shoulder.

"I believe they will be happy for the rest of their lives, just as we will, Charles."

Justine was enjoying a glass of champagne when she heard a deep baritone voice speaking to her from behind.

"Good afternoon. My name is Hilton." Justine turned around and was happy to see it was the handsome flute player.

"Hello Hilton, I'm Justine. Nice to meet you."

"I take it the bride is a friend or family member of yours?"

"Yes, Rhonda is family." Justine admired Hilton's red hair.

"Justine, would you like to dance with me?"

"I would love to." He escorted her to the dance area.

Shante, Terri, and Sherri enjoyed their champagne and food as they watched the crowd.

"Hey, look at Justine! Who's that she's dancing with?" asked Shante.

"Oh, that's Hilton. He's a cousin of Wynton Marsalis. I saw him looking at Justine earlier," said Terri.

315

"Well, you go Justine," said Sherri smiling at them. He's cute. Look at his beautiful red hair."

"They do seem to be enjoying themselves," said Shante.

"It's nice to see Justine smiling," replied Sherri. "Her breakup with Ronald was not as easy as she would have us think."

"Justine is a strong woman. She'll be all right," Shante said.

"Well she's doing all right with Hilton right now," said Terri, smiling and pointing at them on the dance floor.

"Today has been such a beautiful day. It's feels like a new beginning," said Shante.

"Yes, I agree," said Terri. "Today is a new beginning for all of us."

Made in the USA
Monee, IL
11 August 2020

6/4/24